LastRites

LastRites

John Humphries

First impression: 2016
© John Humphries & Y Lolfa Cyf., 2016

*This book is subject to copyright and may not be reproduced
by any means except for review purposes without the
prior written consent of the publishers.*

Cover design: Sion Ilar

ISBN: 978 1 78461 253 5

Published and printed in Wales
on paper from well-maintained forests by
Y Lolfa Cyf., Talybont, Ceredigion SY24 5HE
e-mail ylolfa@ylolfa.com
website www.ylolfa.com
tel 01970 832 304
fax 832 782

Chapter 1

JACK FLYNT EASED himself off the bed, hesitating before answering the phone after midnight. INS weren't about to send him off to cover another war, not since his demotion to raking through the ashes of almost forgotten ones. He was deadwood, the agency burying him under crap assignments, hoping he'd get the message and quit.

The call would be from the kid left watching the News Desk overnight and wanting help.

'Jack?' The voice was vaguely familiar, not the kid on the desk, much further back.

'Who wants to know?' Flynt asked cautiously.

'Jack, it's your brother Dafydd.'

'You know the time?' snapped Flynt, his mobile blinking 3 a.m. 'Couldn't it wait?'

'No, Jack. Mam's dead.'

Flynt picked pensively at the stubble on his chin, his emotions uncertain. The umbilical cord was severed long ago, Flynt never looking back except for funerals – the last, a younger sister who'd drunk herself to death. Having so far dodged that bullet, funerals reminded him of war zones, about wasted lives, a Press flak-jacket and tin hat no match for what warring sides threw at each other.

'When did she die?' he asked, retreating from his younger brother's grief.

'Last night... I've been trying to get you all day. The office said you were in Brittany... that it would pass on the message.'

'I will be later today... in Brittany... the anniversary of the sinking of the last U-boat. A cuttings job but they want me out of the office, permanently.' The News Desk hadn't mentioned Dafydd's call. It didn't do personal stuff, only news.

His mother must have been sixty-five – barely fifteen when he first saw the light of day in that dreary terrace clinging to the side of the mountain. Never a day passed without Mam complaining bitterly about 'not having a life', blaming everyone but herself for the six siblings who followed Flynt in quick succession. Mam eventually got sterilised, by which time it was too late for a life.

The world was forever knocking at Number 62 Quarry Hill, seven different fathers leading the charge, and never paying a penny for the pleasure. His mother was too kind and warm-hearted, laughing and singing under circumstances that would cause others to throw themselves off the mountain. She drank too much but so did most on Quarry Hill, Flynt tipsy for the first time when only eight after stealing sips from his mother's gin and tonic. But she was always loving and protective, not allowing any of her partners to lay into him. And so it was until he got the old bunk-up over the wall and was away.

Quarry Hill was a veritable traffic jam of single parent pushchairs, Mam's greatest asset leading their owners to the state handouts under every cradle. But it was always so – the grim inevitability of lives and aspirations never to be fulfilled, frustrated by a rusting, corrugated iron roof. The doyen of Quarry Hill, Mam's last 'partner' until he was deported was a bull-necked Estonian seaman called Boris.

'What happened?' asked Flynt, remembering how his mother had fed and watered Dafydd and the others after he cleared off.

'Massive heart attack they say. She was exhausted… never gave up, even after Boris left.'

'And when's the funeral?' asked Flynt, ignoring the snide reference to their mother's indiscretions.

'Friday next week… can you make it?'

'Don't see why not. The Brittany job won't take long. Can I help with expenses?'

'No need… the social will pay. If we don't get a grant Mam always said to wrap her body in clingfilm and dump it at the back door of the crematorium.'

'Where can I stay?'

'There's no room here. The place is awash. I don't know half of them. Mam's genes are all over Quarry Hill. How about yours? Still keeping the stopper in the bottle?'

His brother didn't need to spell it out. Too close to fifty and having spread himself around so far unsuccessfully, Flynt was tiring of the effort. 'Obsessional, that's what the quack told me.' By morning everyone on Quarry Hill would think the Fleet Street bigshot at Number 62 fired blanks.

'Obsessed with what?' Dafydd pounced on any chink in Flynt's armour to drag him back to street level. 'You're seeing a quack because you can't have kids? That's not like a Flynt.' Dafydd pressed the dagger home.

'I'm OK… OK,' said Flynt hurriedly. 'Stress… seems I've been working too hard.'

'And Emilie… nothing wrong there, surely… Better get cracking, Jack, before the ammo runs out.'

Flynt changed the subject. 'If I can't stay at Quarry Hill then fix me a hotel.'

'You got to be joking! I'll ask Irene to put you up.' A teacher, Irene never taught after Mam sat her down and explained about welfare dependency: how she was better off on the 'social' than prodding a bunch of dullards into life. Irene called it the Poverty Trap.

'OK, fix it… better ring-off, Dafydd… this is costing you a packet. Pick me up at the station midday Friday…'

'No car… just a bike. Get a taxi. See you soon.'

Taxi! Flynt choked on the chances of finding one. Hoofing it up that bloody mountain was no joke, Quarry Hill climbing out of the valley bottom like the index finger on an upraised hand, Number 62 the nail.

Flynt was dozing in an armchair, first light bleeding through a crack in the curtains, his subconscience struggling to square the rights with the wrongs when for the second time that night a ringing telephone crashed in upon his dreams. Flynt's eyes went straight to his collection of antique telephones in a glass display cabinet before crossing to the heavy, black Bakelite rotary-dial ringing on a small table beneath the window of his third floor Paris apartment. Not to answer was tantamount to a dereliction of duty for a hack whose life was ruled by ringing telephones. On the other hand, picking up the receiver was madness. The rotary-dial couldn't ring. Like all the others in Flynt's collection it wasn't connected, hadn't been for many years. Best ignore it until the hallucination faded. Callers, real or imaginary always hung up if kept waiting long enough. Didn't he? Christ, they'd inscribe it on his tombstone: 'Jack Rang Off!' The telephone was an extension to his body, a protuberance, not natural like fingers and toes but grafted later. It was hardly surprising he dreamed about the bloody things. But why didn't this one go away when he woke up?

Shaking himself, Flynt watched his hand move instinctively towards the heavy black receiver. 'Yes,' he snarled, 'what the fuck do you want?' Not getting a reply, Flynt lurched forward, pressing the receiver harder against his ear until a woman whispered through a burst of static, 'Help! He's trying to kill me.'

Banging the receiver angrily in the palm of his hand to shake out any bugs, he listened again. The line was dead, not even a dial tone. Why should there be? Flynt felt a little crazy staring angrily at the cable hanging lifelessly from the Bakelite's casing. Real fear he could handle – ducking bullets in Iraq, expecting to be dumped by INS – but this was different. Having traded too much moral fibre for headlines, Flynt had precious little to lean on when the inexplicable challenged reality. Nor was there anyone to turn to after jettisoning help and understanding when he parted from Emilie. If your mantra was 'nothing given only taken', Flynt should have expected something would start fucking with his mind.

He'd always rationalised his way out of tight corners. Was answering a phone that couldn't ring a sign of mental instability or a bad case of hallucination? That's how he'd write it. Flynt's instinct was to question everything. The bizarre he spiked, at most cut it to a paragraph on an inside page as a health warning for readers.

Like his other antique telephones, the Bakelite reminded Flynt of stories he'd covered, the most interesting in the collection one with an ornate ebony handle and mouthpiece. Flynt was in Israel covering another blow-up on the Gaza Strip and being bawled at down the line by a particularly objectionable news editor called Higgins for missing a deadline. Suddenly there was a clatter at the other end, Flynt assuming an Israeli shell had taken out the line. In fact, Higgins had dropped the receiver when he dropped dead. A large dollar note bought Flynt the phone from the Palestinian café owner, a must-have to delight his poker-playing pals who'd also suffered verbal lashings from Higgins.

With grim determination Flynt walked slowly around the apartment, examining everything from the faded blue-patterned wallpaper to the white liquor stains on the poker table. It was just the sort of shitty trick his poker pals would play… hide a mobile in the Bakelite.

Rifling through a kitchen drawer for a screwdriver, Flynt had the phone on the table and the base plate off. The mechanism, the bunch of coloured wires and the usual bits and bobs was no different from others in his collection. No matter what their age or appearance, his trophies had a common feature – none was connected. How could they be? There was no junction box, no landline to the apartment. A mobile was all he needed. Flynt shook his head several times. Ringing in the ear, he thought... a touch of tinnitus, or had his drinking finally shaken something loose?

Flynt closed his eyes wearily. 'I've done it now... I've blown it this time... must give up,' he muttered. Every morning, staring at the worn edges in the mirror, he promised himself a booze-free day. His Sunday school teacher had warned him: unless he signed the pledge the demon drink would get him. Oddly, he felt no pain, only weariness, the more desperate the hurt, the less he seemed to feel it.

Crossing the apartment and bolting the door against whatever he imagined was outside, Flynt went to the window and threw it open. The day was early but the air already heavy, the hum of traffic faint, the only sign of life a woman standing alone on the corner below. After watching her climb into a radio-cab and drive away, Flynt sank into his armchair to snatch an hour's sleep.

The Bakelite on the table beneath the window woke him a second time with 'Help! He's trying to kill me' struggling to break free from the static. It was like a cancer diagnosis, not for broadcasting, certainly not to anyone at the office. For them, the cranky telephone was Jack Flynt's pink elephant at the bottom of the bed. Jack had to be different; couldn't settle for what normal drunks wrestled with in the middle of the night. Lay off the booze, Jack, and the phantom caller will hang up.

A few hours later Flynt was lugging the Bakelite in a plastic Carrefour carrier bag along the platform at Paris Gare du Nord to the train for Brittany and Lorient, the phone not leaving his side until he had an explanation, or the caller stopped ringing.

Brittany was an anniversary story, an easy peg. The Paris desk of INS was no different to those the world over – the seventieth anniversary of the last U-boat a gift for the schedule, a cuttings job easily written off the desk. But INS couldn't claim to be an international news service unless its stories carried datelines and a few local quotes to freshen-up old facts. The train was packed and the roads traffic-clogged with Parisiens leaving for *les vacances*, the city abandoned to sweaty tourists and shuttered restaurants. Departing punctually, lemming-like on the first Saturday of August, they returned in one vast, tanned traffic jam on the last.

The chunky black Bakelite, circa Ericsson 1940, sat with Flynt in the restaurant car between a bottle of Beaujolais and his 'War in Lorient' cuttings file. Smiling with the uneasy resignation of a man for whom peace of mind was always just out of reach, Flynt closed his eyes, his fellow passengers intrigued by the balding Brit picking at his food and slurping red wine while waiting for a phone call.

'I'm a collector,' he explained to the puzzled young Frenchman sitting opposite after the TGV screeching to a halt shook him awake. The man half-smiled at the Bakelite before twisting his head against the window, searching for the reason for the hold-up. They'd hit a cow, according to the inspector, and would be delayed until an engineer inspected the damage. There was none, the express slicing and dicing the poor beast at 160mph. Squinting through the window at the mangled corpse, smoke pirouetting from a field of stubble beside the track, Flynt mused, 'Cow cooked by train'. Try that on INS and they'd bury him with the remains of the cow. To make the wire, bodies had to be human, and preferably piled high.

Flynt had counted lots of bodies, but no longer. Left with only memories of the news frontline, he waited for the chop which was sure to come once INS found how to avoid messy consequences. Denied column inches on nothing-stories, Flynt knew he'd probably go in the next round of cuts unless boredom drove him out sooner. No wife, no kids, no house, most assumed he had a cushion stashed away off-shore.

Did it really matter if his adrenalin rush of death and disaster was choked off? If he was honest, it did. What else did he have apart from collecting bloody telephones? News was all he'd ever known, the absence of domestic baggage propelling him into the top league. When other correspondents were agonising over missing junior's debut in the school play, Flynt was packing a bag for the airport and the latest trouble-spot with crumby hotels and pox-ridden women. He told himself availability was not the reason – that he was the best man for the job, although by the time his copy reached the wire the by-line was the only bit he recognised after it had been hacked around by the desk.

Flynt blamed no-one for his broken life, certainly not a broken home. How could he blame a mother too loving for this world, or a father he'd never known? Selfish and indifferent, he was the archetypal cynic with nothing to show but a drink problem, his only future the next story, only reward a by-line. Once there was the congratulatory telex, then email: 'Well done. You made the lead on the evening schedule.' Now correspondents were forgotten once the story was fired into the ether. With 24/7 news and the internet, few stories stayed in one place long enough for the hack on the ground to get any credit.

Flynt always claimed he recalled the very moment the tide turned against the resident correspondent. Liverpool were playing the Italian football club Juventus at the Heysel Stadium on a warm spring evening in Brussels when a wall collapsed and dozens were buried by the rubble. Flynt and other hacks were door-stepping the match from a local bar a few hundred yards from the stadium when the ambulance sirens started wailing. 'Nothing, it's just the Belgians. Can't go anywhere without making noise,' said the man from Reuters taking another swallow of Stella Artois. But the sirens kept coming until, as one, they charged for the door and across the road to the stadium. Bodies were stacked like logs alongside piles of broken masonry, hacks climbing over each other to get the story on the wire. No mobiles then, nor public telephone kiosks in sight, only row upon row of anonymous apartment blocks, the queue for the telephone in the bar stretching through the door. Flynt looked to the heavens for salvation, an overhead cable connecting to an apartment. He struck lucky, finding not only a telephone but a jumbo-size television switched to the match commentator describing what was happening inside the stadium – and watched by an emaciated woman stretched on a chaise longue from which two black bull terriers had taken generous mouthfuls of upholstery. Picking his way across a filthy, threadbare carpet sprinkled with small heaps of disgusting dog food, Flynt snatched the phone and ad-libbed the story, not once hesitating. INS had it on the wire first but minutes later the story moved to the UK, leaving Flynt to fight for the reimbursement of the ten dollars he'd pressed into the hand of the poor anorexic woman for the privilege of commandeering her home. Now, no-one went anywhere without at least two mobiles, better still a satellite phone for servicing the inexhaustible appetite of the electronic media and 24-hour news channels. The only correspondents to hold a big story for a full turn of the clock were the TV supermen who got to win wars single-handed with satellite communications. Flynt felt a dying breed but was still good at what he did, sharper after a drink than most hacks were stone-cold sober, although the bloody Bakelite was seriously distracting.

Flynt was fishing through his cuttings file when the Frenchman sitting opposite on the train leaned across the table and asked, 'Is that a picture of Lorient after the bombing?'

'Yes, they say a good black and white is better than a movie. Look at the detail.' The picture captured the drama of the morning after the RAF left Lorient in ruins having missed its target, the German U-boat pens on the Keroman Peninsula. The white gritty dust from dissolved masonry, naked walls lifting ragged smouldering arms towards the heavens after incendiaries had floated down like deadly sycamore seeds. The picture had everything. Flynt imagined the harsh, raw stench of burning, the footsteps echoing through the ruins.

'See the black cat picking its way amongst the masonry, paw poised to avoid glass splinters. It's a classic.' Flynt had seen lots of collateral damage and broken bodies but never a dead cat.

'They've got nine lives, cats,' he said.

The Frenchman said proudly, 'My grandfather took the picture with a glass plate camera. If you want a copy the office still has the original.'

Surprised, Flynt asked, 'What office… you work for a newspaper?' The young Frenchman was a reporter with *Ouest-France* returning from a job interview in Paris. Flynt knew *Ouest-France* as the most important regional in western France, covering everything that moved in southern Normandy, Brittany, and the Loire Valley.

'Did you get it, the job?' he asked.

'I think so, with *Agence France-Presse* in its London Bureau.'

'You should,' said Flynt. 'Your English is as good as a native, better than most.' From Flynt's experience that was almost always the case. The British were either too lazy or too arrogant to learn another lingo.

'Are you writing a piece about Lorient?' the Frenchman asked.

'Not Lorient… the U-boat pens… 70th anniversary of The Last U-boat.'

'Oh, yes… another excuse to dig up *Kapitan* Scheer. You must have something about him on file.'

Flynt shuffled through the bundle of newspaper cuttings…

plenty about the impregnability of the U-boat complex, not a word on Scheer.

'Tell me,' said Flynt.

'OK, you can have what I know for free… but not when I'm with AFP. Then we're rivals.' Flynt was reminded of himself when he was full of up-and-at-'em.

'Karl Scheer, at 23, the *Kreigsmarine*'s youngest and second most decorated U-boat Commander, with Iron Cross and Oak Leaves. His last command was the proto-type of a new U-boat – the Walter class. Hitler believed the super-sub could win the war. But only one was ever launched and this was sunk in May 1945 by a British destroyer while trying to cross the Valley of Death… what U-boat captains called the stretch of sea between the coast of Brittany and the North Atlantic. That's about all, except that after the war he became something of a cult figure among certain Fascist groups who claimed Scheer had taken a bunch of German staff officers to South America, including Hitler's deputy Martin Bormann.'

Flynt said, 'Where can I get more on Scheer?'

'If you call at the *Ouest-France* archive it's bound to have a packet. But that's in Rennes. There's a museum in the Keroman complex and a very good Press Officer. I'm sure he'll help.' The young reporter was preparing to leave the train. 'The next stop's mine… shall I leave this?' he said, offering Flynt his copy of *Le Soir*.

Searching subscriber newspapers for his by-line still gave Flynt a kick, even after his story was handed to a staffer to spin. But that was the deal. INS subscribers bought the right to represent the agency's news output as being freshly-hewn from the coalface by their own people. Once bright-eyed and bushy-tailed, weighed down by virtue and perspicacity, caring for every word, Flynt no longer agonised over whether some hack in Paris, London or New York hacked his stuff to pieces. Rubbing a finger across wine soaked lips, he knew that if the Bakelite ever woke up in public he'd kiss even that good-bye.

The train had arrived at the French reporter's station. Before leaving he turned to Flynt and asked, 'I'm intrigued… why the telephone in the Carrefour bag?'

Flynt had his answer ready. 'To remind me I've got a deadline to catch.' Adding with a broad smile, 'You won't beat me to the phone when you join AFP.' He forgot to ask the Frenchman his name.

Chapter 2

THE U-BOAT PENS straddling the Keroman Peninsula were a monstrous echo-chamber of memories, too well-built and massive to dismantle after the war. At first the French Navy adopted the complex as a base before opening it up to the public with a museum and gift shop.

Flynt wasn't much interested in any of this, other than as background. He'd eyed his angle – Hitler's Secret Weapon – and now needed to dress it with facts, especially about Scheer. Otherwise, all he had was a piss-poor story of a concrete bunker the French had failed to demolish.

K1 was the pen where the Walter prototype *U-1405* spent its last days before escaping into the North Atlantic to be sunk by HMS *Cornwall* shortly after Germany surrendered.

The museum yielded nothing about Scheer, but Flynt's guide Lieutenant Jean Louis was a rare person, an enthusiastic and helpful French Navy Press officer.

Leading the way into the dark interior, Lieutenant Louis switched on the floodlights, the burst of white light revealing a towering concrete cavern of cathedral proportions. 'I know... a monstrosity... impossible to destroy with conventional explosives. The Government at one point thought of using a small nuclear device but, as you might expect, that caused an uproar.' The thirty-foot reinforced concrete roof, with walls equally thick, contained sufficient concrete, said Louis, to build a four-lane highway from Paris to Rennes. Press officers were fed such lines to satisfy the media's need for something readers could grasp.

'And what about that?' Flynt pointed to the jagged hole

above their heads. 'Just the one,' explained the young officer. 'Of the 4,000 tons of high explosives dropped by the Allies, a British Tallboy was the only bomb to penetrate K1 and the U-boat wasn't scratched. You can't see from here... *frangost* the Germans called it... a 'bomb trap' directing the blast into a void between the layers of concrete... ingenious.'

'And that?' asked Flynt, pointing above his head again.

'The last line of defence... a steel net to catch the debris if the roof was breached.' Glancing again at his brief, Lieutenant Louis added, 'Contains enough metal to build a hundred Citroëns. The *U-1405* was the only Walter-class boat launched. The propulsion system was the next best thing to nuclear.'

'What was the propellant?'

'HTP – High Test Peroxide... gave it air-independent propulsion at fast submerged speeds, 29mph in your money with a range of over 3,000 miles. South America was reachable. It didn't need a snorkel to access atmospheric oxygen. The Walter boat could stay submerged that much longer. It's all in the hand-out.'

'The Allies never adopted the technology?'

'The hydrogen peroxide was too volatile. The British tried. Remember the *Sidon*? She sank in Portland Harbour in 1955 after a line burst and leaking HTP detonated a torpedo. Thirteen of the crew died.'

Flynt could have written much of this from cuttings back in Paris. His feigned interest in the dross was intended to sweet-talk the lieutenant into answering questions that really mattered, about Scheer.

'What do you know about the guy who made a run for it?' he asked Louis.

'*Kapitan* Karl Scheer,' said the Press officer, respectfully.

'You sound as if you admire him?'

'I suppose I do… an enemy yes… but very successful… Iron Cross with Oak Leaves…'

Scheer, he said, was stuck in K1 for three months for modifications to the propulsion system. 'You can imagine it… Scheer waiting to have another go at the Allies and the British destroyer HMS *Cornwall* patrolling the mouth of the estuary daring him to try.'

Louis led the way out of K1 to the slipway down which *U-1405* eventually escaped into the River Scorff. 'From here on a good day,' he said, pointing towards the river's mouth, 'Scheer could have seen the *Cornwall.*'

'I suppose he knew the risks,' said Flynt, 'when he got the order to sail.'

Louis shook his head. 'The only order Scheer received was after Admiral Donitz signed the German surrender – and that was to scuttle the Walter boat.' The Naval Officer produced a photo-copy from his briefcase. 'And this is it!'

'ALL U-BOATS… ATTENTION ALL U-BOATS… CEASE FIRE AT ONCE… STOP ALL HOSTILE ACTION AGAINST ALLIED SHIPPING… SCUTTLE.'

U-1405 was to be scuttled before Festung Lorient fell to the Americans laying siege to the port. 'Reputedly,' Louis continued, 'Scheer gathered his crew on the hull of the U-boat and announced he had different orders. They were to launch that night. According to those who did surrender to the Americans the next day, about half went with Scheer. *U-1405* sat on the bed of the estuary until Scheer was able to slip past the *Cornwall* when the destroyer made a turn. But she didn't get far.'

'How do you know that?' asked Flynt.

'From the accounts of survivors… not everyone drowned when *U-1405* was sunk by the *Cornwall*… and there's also this…'

Louis dipped into his briefcase again, pulling out a coloured brochure, the official guide to the Keroman complex. 'Have you read it?' Flynt hadn't. 'It's all here... in French and English... and German. You'd be surprised how many German visitors we get. The U-boat war is something they can be proud of... nothing to do with concentration camps.'

'Yes... yes,' mumbled Flynt, turning to a page headed 'The Sinking of *U-1405*'. 'This is sourced from British National Archives. How did you manage that?'

'I suppose there's still some life in the Entente Cordiale.'

'Can I use it?'

'Don't see why not... only costs a euro. Hardly a secret... we've sold thousands.'

If only more Press officers were as co-operative. Louis was new, not yet received a kicking for giving too much away. The time would come, thought Flynt, scanning an extract from *Cornwall*'s log:

1220 hours: Lookouts sight U-boat on surface in heavy weather at mouth of River Scorff, fires several rounds from its bow gun, then lost it... must have dived... preparing depth charge attack if Asdic contact made.

1315 hours: Searched for nearly an hour... nothing. Shut down search at position of the last known contact.

1340 hours: Contact regained at a range of 2,500 yards. Position closed. U-boat dived deeper; must have heard us. Full pattern, six charges set to 250, 350 and 500ft. Fired at 1350.

1410 hours: U-boat contact at 200 feet steaming 'full ahead' on both motors, stern down. A large bubble of air and oil on surface; target slowing, bubbling noises indicate tanks being blown.

1441 hours: Surface contact lost in fog... submarine dived again. New contact made at 300 feet... *Cornwall* attacked but only three charges with deep settings ready. Submarine is making oil track. Large bubbles breaking surface… probably from forward torpedo tube.

1500 hours: U-boat surfaced right astern of *Cornwall*. Aft group opened fire. Crew abandoning ship, submarine's motors running ahead with port wheel on, speed about 4 knots. *Cornwall's* whaler tried to board, but speed too great. Not clear whether all crew off. Another 23 rounds fired but no hits owing to the large swell. *Cornwall* tried to lay alongside for boarding but U-boat turned sharply to port ramming as we went full speed astern. Then she disappeared… survivors taken aboard *Cornwall*. Submarine's conning tower was open. The captain and others were still believed on board. *Cornwall* made several sweeps of the area without seeing any wreckage or making fresh contact.

'Wouldn't you agree this is not entirely conclusive? Scheer's body, I take it, was never found,' said Flynt.

'I wouldn't know,' replied Louis. 'Why don't you ask a survivor?'

'You mean someone's still alive?'

'He was last year when he visited Keroman… lives in Strasbourg.'

'You have a name and address?'

'And telephone number,' replied Louis. 'I'll ask him… not so sure he'll agree. The British tried to kill him. Might not want to be reminded of what he did. Some might think it a war crime – firing on a British destroyer during an armistice.'

Flynt didn't push it. He had his story and the office wouldn't pay for a side trip to Strasbourg without a name and address for the survivor of the Walter boat. He could always get back to Louis for a follow-up after the Press Officer had cleared it with the German in Strasbourg.

Lieutenant Louis's final stop before leaving K1 was the mess hall, walls plastered with the graffiti of dead *Wolfpack* crews

21

celebrating their latest kill in the North Atlantic. Sipping the best quality French wine and enjoying French women, Flynt imagined them huddled around a piano, belting out 'Lili Marlene', milking the last drop of comfort from shore leave knowing the next mission could be the last. Most would die before they were twenty-five. So who cared if they never washed away the stench of diesel oil, a badge of honour no bottle of cologne could disguise?

Flynt was already writing the story in his head, fancying the strains of a long-forgotten U-boat refrain drifting down the darkened corridors deep inside the bunker:

Pull on your leathers
Comrade, we're going to sea
Already the diesels spring reeking to life
Comrade, there's no going back.
Now we want to hunt them,
Strike the British
There out on the sea.
We are the U-boat men
The grey wolves
On the grey sea.

He'd use that although now the only sound was the rustle of fallen leaves blowing through the entrance – like the tiny curled-up corpses of grey wolves. Despite the cringe factor, that made the perfect last par.

Chapter 3

A FTER FILING HIS story Flynt e-mailed the INS desk: 'Mother's funeral... back in a couple of days.' Then he switched his mobile off. Compassionate leave was the only excuse for a no-show at INS. But given half a chance Yates, the City Editor, would be on Flynt's back before he'd finished sprinkling his mother's ashes in the memorial garden at the crematorium.

There was no quarry on Quarry Hill, a scarred mountainside, a classic piece of industrial dereliction. The grey stone terrace wound around the rim of what was easily mistaken for an abandoned quarry, a deep gash in the mountain plunging two hundred feet into a void filled with coal-rich colliery waste until it disappeared on the back of a fleet of lorries. In winter, the void flooded, draining dry in summer except for a large, stagnant, pestilential pool. Promises to fill in the hole and build a playground for the kids ran out once the coal was exhausted and the freebooters ran off, leaving a pool festering around islands of green wheelie bins pitched by Saturday night revellers over a security fence festooned with plastic bags. Although Flynt rarely returned, the tug was strong despite his efforts to turn the page.

The jazz band blasting out 'When the Saints Go Marching In' meant Number 62 Quarry Hill was almost in sight. The Carrefour bag with the heavy Bakelite didn't make the climb any easier, Flynt cursing every gut-wrenching foot of the way before turning a kink in the road and seeing the house, a shiny black hearse parked outside, and a very small jazz band, a trumpet, trombone and tuba punching way above its weight. By the time he was on the doorstep the band was murdering Mam's favourite hymn, 'There is a Green Hill Far Away'. Mam was never a great chapelgoer, the hymn chosen for the funeral more a metaphor for a wasted life.

The young nephews and nieces dancing around the jazz players wanted to know about the stranger arriving for *Mam-gu*'s funeral. That's what they called their grandmother. The only bit of Welsh she ever learned, she insisted they used it, a sort of totem that marked her as different from the neighbours who leaned the other way, acknowledging the English paid the bills. If the truth was told the Flynts were more Irish than Welsh, their ancestors fleeing the potato famine as ballast on colliers returning to the south Wales coalfield where they were left to crawl ashore across the mudflats of the Severn estuary.

The crush around the coffin inside the two-up two-down regulation Valleys terrace was exhausting the oxygen supply. 'Jack… here! Have a drink,' shouted Dafydd above the hubbub, one hand on the Welsh flag draped across the coffin. Dafydd sat his scotch down on the lid, thrusting a glass at Flynt. 'How are you keeping, broth? Mam would have loved it… got started about seven.'

The wake was a binge, a Valleys bidding, a hangover from the nineteenth century when funerals, weddings, in fact any event, was an excuse for lengthy drinking sessions. The place was bedlam, kids everywhere, under feet, sneaking drinks from half-empty glasses.

'How are we getting to the crematorium?' Flynt shouted.

'We've got a bus. In a bit we'll march down the hill behind the band… the bus is waiting at the bottom. Mam would have loved it…'

'The flag's a nice touch,' observed Flynt sardonically. Having discovered Welsh, converts like his brother damned the English for denying them their heritage when, in fact, they should be grateful for the handouts. Flynt's disdain must have showed. Smiling weakly and clenching his teeth, he waited for a verbal smack in the face. That was always the way when they met, fifteen bruising rounds of England versus Wales, he accused of betraying his birthright by ridiculing the notion of the Welsh going it alone, Dafydd blaming Wales's troubles on English exploitation.

'She was a good Welsh woman… and don't forget it!' growled his brother, drumming his fingers angrily on the side of the coffin.

Was he in touch with their mother's spirit? Flynt's cutting riposte died on his tongue. 'I know she was,' he acknowledged. 'A toast to our Mam.' But that was throwing liquor on a fire not easily doused when it came to things Welsh.

'So you're still taking their money,' Dafydd smirked, ready for a set-to.

'Not really… the Yanks pay me… offshore. No tax,' Flynt replied, contemptuous of his brother's petty politics.

'I don't hassle you about your drinking… don't hassle me about my politics unless you want to contribute to the fighting fund.'

'What fighting fund?'

'Semtex is expensive,' replied Dafydd, preferring to rile his elder brother than explain the fund was for elections, not to blow up bridges. 'No more easy-pickings for the English, no more the last colony of England,' railed Dafydd.

'You're more likely to blow yourself up.'

'Why not, Muslims do. Martyrs, that's what Wales needs.'

'You can't force independence down their throats… look at Scotland… a no.'

'A few bombs would change that.'

'It didn't fifty years ago… remember your hero. Bomber John Jenkins blew water pipelines and got twelve years for his trouble.'

'Get more today, I bet. Freedom fighters carry a premium.'

'Christ, you do talk rubbish. Wales has been part of England for eight hundred years. There's no way back to princes and bards. What will you live on, brother... the view! Wales doesn't have anything. Ah, I tell a lie – welfare, a growth industry.'

'And most of those are fucking English! They can't get the dole in England so they come to Wales... a softer touch. And there's White Flight.'

Flynt agreed about those flooding across the border to escape the immigrant invasion. Outside Wales Flynt was in denial of everything Welsh, language, history, culture, most of all the aspirations of the people. But cross the Severn Bridge and see the mountains in the distance, the tug of *hiraeth* was hard to resist. Perhaps what he really needed was a terraced house and a wife with a soft Valleys accent.

'I hope you haven't got yourself in too deep, Dafydd.' Flynt was concerned. Rather than capitulate, his brother grew more extreme the more often the ballot box disappointed.

Before teaching made him half-respectable, Dafydd had a public house confrontation with a Brummie holidaying in Wales, breathing beer fumes over him and demanding to know what he had for breakfast. 'Bacon and egg,' replied the man fearfully. 'And where,' demanded Dafydd, 'did you buy your bacon and egg?' Backing away, the man stuttered, 'Waitrose.' Dafydd glared. 'But we don't have a bloody Waitrose... brought the stuff with you... stuffed in the back of the caravan... don't contribute anything locally...' At which point the poor man jumped into his caravan and fled across the border convinced that the extremist genie was well and truly out of the bottle.

Glaring across their mother's coffin, Dafydd said, 'Mam would have been a suicide bomber.' At first, Flynt had dismissed his brother's nationalism as measles, something you grow out of along with scrawling slogans on a wall. But since becoming a Welsh learner he'd grown to support violent direct action.

Picking up the bad vibes between the brothers, their sister Megan moved in. 'No politics... not at Mam's funeral,' she pleaded. 'And how's Emilie?' she asked.

The family had met Emilie Quatrevents only once but took to her immediately, jet-black hair bouncing seductively at the nape of her pale, slim neck and with a figure to die for. Like most French women she had the knack of converting a penny into a silver dollar; take the plainest dress, pinch it in at the waist and tits, and with a red, silky scarf slung wantonly around her shoulders become an instant fashion icon.

Emilie was a junior reporter with a French commodities agency, her good looks and tender age an entrée to the inner circle of seasoned hacks eager to offer a supporting arm whenever she tripped over a story. Everything worked for Emilie, the smile, and the 'Merci, monsieur' with which she charmed admirers. Flynt met her at a World Trade Organisation conference in Marrakech, where, after five days locked in a concrete bunker called the Press Centre, even the women in black burkas were sexy.

Emilie was staying at the same hotel. La Maison Sahara was perfectly located for the conference at the Palais des Congrès, except for the five o'clock wake-up from the muezzin calling the faithful to worship from the minaret of the mosque around the corner.

Twitching hacks in various stages of inebriation and undress, accustomed only to see the sun rise at the fag-end of the night before, had taken refuge in the hotel bar, among them Emilie, head bent over a large whisky tumbler. 'Impossible,' she mumbled as Flynt approached. 'How does anyone sleep in this place... can't do much for tourism.'

'Unless you're the muezzin,' replied Flynt, his own eyes like piss-holes in the sand, 'and he's probably back in bed.'

'Asleep?'

'Yeah... switches on the tape, then rolls over.' Emilie's eyes opened wider, not wholly persuaded the Muslim world woke up to a recording. She knew of Flynt by reputation, his sometimes outrageous cynicism expressed with Anglo-Saxon candour; at times a cantankerous hack, unable to make allowances for failure and without the grace to keep his fault-finding to the wall. He knew Emilie from press briefings, those smouldering, compelling eyes undimmed by the most boring line of questioning, her breath so faint she seemed not to breathe at all.

Pale with tiredness tinged by anger, Emilie asked, 'Do they go to the mosque... the faithful?'

'Some, yes. Not all. I suppose they get accustomed to it... like living near a railway line. You don't notice the trains until they stop running.' She laughed. No-one kept Emilie from her bed, not even Flynt's strange melancholic appeal. Dissipated, yes, and old enough to be her father, Flynt still had a physique deserving of respect. Having fought his way from nothing, no-one would grind him to powder.

Throwing back her head, Emilie drained the glass. 'You want the other half,' he offered.

'I've had two already... large ones.'

'What you drinking?'

'Bells, I think,' she replied studying the last drop of amber liquid.

Flynt looked over his shoulder, caught the waiter's eye then lost him, the waiter evidently convinced all infidels were alcoholics.

'I guarantee one more and you'll only hear pearly bells. But there is another way.'

'What way... for what?'

'For a good night's sleep... silence the guy in the minaret,' said Flynt, smiling.

'But you can't... it's their religion.'

'Don't you want to sleep? How about we try? The conference will last another couple of days, agreed?' Emilie nodded. 'Not much longer, I hope. World trade bores me, like jogging.'

'So,' continued Flynt, 'we pay the mosque a visit when the muezzin is tucked up in bed. While you keep watch, I replace the tape with one of my own.'

'And that's?'

'*GOOD MORNING VIETNAM.*' Emilie gasped at the thought of actor Robin Williams screaming his wake-up call across the rooftops of Marrakech. 'They'd shoot us... or the other thing.'

'What's that?'

'Cut off our heads,' she whispered, leaning close enough for her breath to brush his lips. Flynt couldn't remember the last time he'd pursued a woman with enthusiasm. The women he knew played the game, eyes wide-open and with every intention of being caught. Never ill at ease in female company, his smile was always charming, his respect and courtesy beyond reproach unless the story gave him cause for a more direct approach. For once Flynt was shy, an old world clod lost in Emilie's young dark face. She was pretty, a young thoroughbred, distinguished from glossy black hair to the tips of her toes. He stammered, he blushed, conscious he was making a spectacle of himself. 'I'm not much good at this,' he mumbled, hand trembling as he topped up her scotch with water. Like a flash, Emilie was on to him. 'But you're still interested in women, or are we too tiring, a terrible waste of energy?' She laughed mischievously.

'Not at all. You can bring my slippers anytime.'

Behind Emilie's smile Flynt thought he detected a wish for companionship. The selfishness he always took along for ballast didn't mean he was opposed to some shared solace in noisy Marrakech.

The third whisky did the trick, Emilie's head falling against his shoulder. 'What's your room number?' She shook her head drowsily. 'You've nothing to worry about. A helping hand, that's all. I need sleep, too.'

There was no sign of Emilie when the conference resumed a few hours later, only a message in the Press Centre from her agency's Paris office. Guessing she'd overslept, Flynt took the call. The agency had heard a communiqué was imminent and wanted an update. 'She's at the French Trade Minister's press conference,' he lied. 'I'll tell her.' Not long afterwards the conference adjourned for delegates to consider the latest proposal for cutting European Union import duties on sugar. For Flynt, it was worth a paragraph, INS not having many sugar producers in the Mid-West where many of their subscribers were located. For Emilie, the communiqué was the main reason she was sent to Marrakech, her agency wanting every word, and what it meant. Flynt had done it before, cover for colleagues who'd gone AWOL or left early to catch the kids before they went to bed. With no wife and no kids Flynt was a soft touch for those needing a favour.

Crossing to a screen and logging on as Emilie he was sending the story when she appeared white-faced, hair hanging untidily around her shoulders. 'What's happened… what's happened? Where is everyone,' she mumbled fearfully.

The Press Centre was emptying, Flynt one of the last. 'What happened…?' she pleaded, face ashen, convinced that third whisky had washed her job down the pan.

'They've adjourned for the weekend.'

Emilie wasn't listening, busy logging on to her emails. 'How…?' she muttered, reading a 'thank you' from the agency.

'They wanted something fast… so I sent them the communiqué… I've done it before… and others for me when I've been… well… indisposed.'

'But can't they tell… I mean the desk?'

'Your desk is only interested in getting it… not the hand on the tiller. This was the first time I've had a thank-you email in years.'

'This is very good,' said Emilie reading the story. 'You must know a lot about sugar.' It hadn't been difficult after a colleague slipped Flynt a copy of his story. That happened between hacks.

'So we're stuck here for the weekend… and the call to prayers… five times a day. Did you know that?' he asked.

'That means drinking lots of whisky,' Emilie smiled, re-arranging her hair.

'I've hired a car to drive up to the Atlas Mountains tomorrow. Not far away. How about joining me?'

'Sounds good. No mosques in the mountains.'

'There are, but fewer and further apart.'

'You drive? I'll share the cost but not the driving. They're crazy here. I suppose there are rules.'

'I've known worse,' said Flynt. 'We could stop off at a local market and then Richard Branson's place for a meal. He's got a *kasbah* in the foothills. Seems he flew over it on one of his ballooning expeditions… now a hotel. After that, try to reach the snowline.' The High Atlas was a jagged white wall rising sharply just beyond the city limits.

Flynt's approach to driving was to dare the locals to a game of chicken. Since the hire car was loaded with insurance, his rivals, most of whom had none, were persuaded to steer clear of the crazy foreigner. 'No bottle,' Flynt told Emilie, avoiding another close encounter.

'What about the donkeys?' mumbled Emilie shifting uncomfortably as a cart carrying very large bales of hay brushed past.

'Now they are a problem. Berbers probably… can't read or write… or speak Arabic, not properly.'

'I thought the Berbers were the majority in Morocco.'

'Depends who you speak to… somewhere between forty and seventy per cent of the population.'

'And they teach Berber in the schools?'

Flynt gave Emilie a sorry look. Clearly she hadn't done her homework. A hack on a foreign assignment should know about the patch just in case the office asked for something off-piste. 'They started teaching Berber in the schools only this year. Wait until we reach the market… you'll see for yourself.'

The market at Tnine Ourika was prehistoric, unchanged in centuries, the makeshift stalls spilling out of the small town in the foothills across a rocky riverbed filling with creamy blue melt water. After promising to pay a local with a beaten leather face to watch the car, Flynt led the way into a warren of mud-brick and canvas stalls where donkeys were shod and sheep slaughtered while their owners waited. 'They treat their animals better than their wives,' he said. 'Without a donkey you're poor, very poor… only a couple of paved roads through the mountains.'

'What about the chickens?' Emilie pointed to a man in a black *jalaba* muttering '*La, la*' as he searched through a pen of fluffy white chickens feeling their crops and, after a withering sneer at the stallholder, tossing them aside.

'They blow maize into the crop to add weight. That's what the guy is looking for… "*La, la*" means "No, don't want it".'

At last he found a chicken not pumped up with maize, handed it to the stallholder who promptly rung its neck. Emilie was transfixed, then mortified when the executioner ripped open the belly and dragged out the intestines.

'Let's move on,' Flynt suggested, guiding her between mountains of vegetables, fruit and herbs.

'You're quite right… like the Middle Ages,' she said, watching a man shaving with a glass splinter before Flynt dragged her out of the path of a motorcycle weaving between the stalls, the pillion seat piled high with trays of eggs.

'You seem to know your way around. You've been here before?' she asked.

'Not here, further south.'

'Isn't there a war down there?'

'That's why I went... the Western Sahara. The Moroccans claim it, the locals – the Polisario – want their independence and the Algerians stir up trouble. That's why the border is closed.'

The crush was like a soccer crowd minus aggro until Emilie pointed her camera at an ancient Singer sewing machine. 'Must have a picture,' she said, meaning of the machinist whose wrinkled face was more ancient than the Singer. The old Arab did not agree, following them through the market demanding payment until Flynt threw him ten dirham.

'I'll buy you something,' said Flynt.

'Thank you, but why?'

'Because I can't resist a bargain.' Flynt meant from a stallholder offering local crafts, his selling line, 'Asda prices... buy one get one free.' Flynt laughed, slipping a ring with a glass stone on Emilie's finger, 'a small mememto.'

Flynt always sucked boiled sweets when he drove. It helped him concentrate on the twists and turns, the road following the grain of the mountains, through the austere drama of mud-brick villages and Berber shepherds grazing their sheep along the verge. 'I've missed the turning for Branson's hotel,' he announced eventually. 'Best if we carry on to the end of the road.'

'Where's that?'

'Imlil... there's a *riad* there... somewhere to eat. Another ten clicks and we'll be there... I promise... great views of Jebel Toubkal, the highest mountain.' Flynt failed to mention the view was up a long flight of stone steps – or by donkey. The fleas hopping on the animal's saddle blanket persuaded them to take the steps until their way was blocked by four smiling Berber children begging, not with their hands, but their eyes. Digging into his pocket Flynt handed around his last three boiled sweets, the smallest youngster missing out, eyes filling with tears behind a wrinkled frown.

'You shouldn't have,' said Emilie as they moved on.

'You heard me tell them to share with the little one.'

'They didn't understand.' Flynt looked over his shoulder at the little one still sitting on the step, his bleak Berber face flooded by a dark cloud. Flynt knew the feeling. Rejection had haunted him too, always the outsider no matter how hard he pushed, his determination having a chilling effect on others who thought him something of a curiosity.

After leaving the Berber kid without a sweet, nothing more was said until they reached the hotel. At almost 6,000 feet, the altitude tugged at their chests, the air crisp and clean, the snow along the flanks of Jebel Toubkal close enough to touch a group of climbers returning to the *riad* for the night.

Flynt couldn't forget the kid he'd left without a sweet.

'There's something I must do,' he said, heading for the shop across the hotel lobby. 'I won't be long.'

Emilie shook her head. 'There's really no need. The child has probably found another tourist with sweets.'

Flynt expected the climb back to the *riad* to be even more demanding but with a bag of boiled sweets in one hand, the other holding tightly to the handrail, he set off to find the Berber. The kid was still there, sitting on the step, waiting for tourists to pass, his face flooding with smiles and muttering, 'Buy one get one free.'

'I gather you found him. It's getting late,' said Emilie.

'There's still time to get back to Marrakech.'

'Not in the dark.' The sun dipping behind the mountains sent a deep shadow racing towards the *riad*. 'I'll check if they have rooms,' he said. They did, only one, a twin. Emilie hesitated about sharing.

'No need to worry... I'm too old for you.' But that wouldn't stop him taking a peep. Women were disappointed if you didn't try.

'I take it you're still interested... in women?' Emilie asked again.

'I am... but not at 6,000 feet.'

Emilie laughed a lot, sometimes defensively, still hoping for a man on a white horse to come riding by.

For dinner, the *riad* offered anything so long as it was a tagine, a brown earthenware cook pot filled with Moroccan stew. The conversation was mostly about Emilie, who answered with a long pause and soft 'huh' when Flynt got too close. Her parents had died in a road accident when she was young. Her early years were spent with her an uncle, Jean Kaudren on Île d'Iroise, a small island off the Brittany coast where it was wall-to-wall Breton.

'Like *Y fro Gymraeg*,' said Flynt, 'the Welsh-speaking heartland.'

Île d'Iroise, she explained, was one of the few remaining refuges for Bretons from the corrosive effects of French. Not until old Kaudren sent her to Paris to escape the influence of the island's fanaticism did she learn French, then English.

After pulling their beds further apart, they slept late, returning to Marrakech and the La Maison Sahara the next morning. 'Perhaps a meal back in Paris – get to know each other better,' Flynt suggested.

'And then what?' She flushed. That was a 'yes,' Flynt decided.

Why she took a shine to him he never really knew. Thinning hair, the jaded appearance of someone bent on abusing himself on rich expense-account lunches, Flynt was no catch. That he was middle aged and disintegrating didn't seem to concern Emilie. Evidently there were enough good bits left to interest her. Nor did she object to his petty chauvinism when, infuriated by a

Press officer who delivered the final briefing at the World Trade Conference in French, he rolled the press release into a paper ball and, flinging it across the Press Room shouted, 'It's not a story until it's in English.' Flynt struggled with French, distrusting it, otherwise he found France and Paris a delight, the heady mix of Gauloise and fresh coffee intoxicating until smoking was banned and public places became no more interesting than bus stops.

Flynt left Marrakech without filing a line, only a service message, 'Nothing in it for us.' The INS News Desk went berserk. Its man for all occasions was expected to squeeze blood from a stone. 'What about cotton... there must have been something about cotton... always is,' screamed Yates, wanting to please INS subscribers in the Bible Belt.

'They never got that far down the agenda... the whole thing ended in the usual deadlock.' Flynt had gone to Marrakech expecting to top the news file. That he didn't no longer seemed important.

Chapter 4

DAFYDD THOUGHT EMILIE wasted on his older brother. She was 'of the faith,' a Breton-speaking Celt, devoted to her cultural heritage. Flynt had sold out. That wasn't strictly fair. Flynt was a pragmatist. The illegitimate son of a single mother from the Valleys never expected to make much headway in a world where the Welsh were no more deserving of attention than trimming their toenails, occasionally. Having spent too long swimming with one arm tied behind his back, Flynt didn't have the balls to cheerlead. Unable to escape his environment, nor settle outside it, he kept moving, determined not to be cast down by calamity, his instinct for self-preservation strong, a large square jaw suggesting a man armed and engineered for combat. 'You got it from your father,' his mother said without saying who that was.

'How's Emilie?' said his sister Megan, believing Flynt had not heard her ask above the racket of those singing the praises of their dear departed Mam.

Without answering, he turned away, squeezing through the crush of mourners to the kitchen door opening on to a scruffy lawn with skimpy borders, a bunch of yellow chrysanthemums struggling to survive between the spokes of an abandoned bicycle wheel. Opening the gate in the pig-wire fence, he headed up the gravel track separating the back-to-backs until the terraces ran out and the ragged sheep took over.

The large grey, flat sandstone slab still guarded the entrance to the brooding loneliness, where sheep leapt from one ledge to the next, climbing the rocky steps like mountain goats. Flynt bent down searching for Emilie's farewell to Wales among the inscriptions scratched into the surface by those who went to kiss and cuddle. Behind him, a bunch of black crows flapped hoarsely from the shaggy branches of a solitary mountain ash, the crabbed terraces at his feet and the craggy slopes a canvass filled with memories.

'No you didn't!' Emilie had exclaimed when he'd told how as kids they'd chased the sheep off the ledges. 'The wily old buggers just moved higher up.' Emilie grieved for the animals grazing the sparse mountain turf, shaggy coats hanging from their backs.

'Mutton… tough as leather, only good for curry,' said Flynt. 'The Pakistanis come down from Birmingham every year.'

'And the wool… don't the farmers sell the wool?'

'Not enough to knit a pair of socks.'

Cupping her chin in her hands Emilie gazed across the wilderness, windswept and sublime, not unlike Île d'Iroise with a story behind every rock.

'You have fairies and hobgoblins… little people?' she'd asked.

'Of course… and they sing. All Welsh fairies sing and, if you're very, very good, you get a glass of milk but if you're not, the hobgoblins milk the cows and let the milk run to waste. Well, that's what my mother said. What about Brittany?'

'The same! At night hobgoblins eat the cream rising on the milk, and the cuckoo's call sets the date of your wedding or funeral whichever is nearest. Oh, yes! If a child gets its clothes wet in certain pools, it dies within a year. But Jack, tell me a Welsh fairy story, please.' Emilie slipped her arm around his waist. Flynt drew her close, kissing her hair, cheeks, mouth. Flynt hadn't felt this way since falling for the blonde in the front row of the chapel choir. Way back then he never had a chance. Emilie was different, not resisting, her mouth seeking his, her body shaking with a tiny tremor of delight.

'I only remember the one,' said Flynt drawing back.

'From your mother?'

'No, I read it in a book at the library. I never got a bedtime story. Well, here goes. It's long... I'll edit it...

'Near a lake dwelt a widow with a son, named Gwyn, who one day took his lunch of barley bread and cheese, and went to tend the cows. The most beautiful lady he'd ever seen rose up from the water, combing her long, luxuriant black hair with a golden comb.

'Gwyn fell for the lady in the lake, offering her his barley bread and cheese while inviting her to come ashore. She was tempted, but disappeared into the lake saying,

"O thou of the hard baked bread,

It is not easy to catch me"

'Gwyn's mother wondered whether this was because fairies didn't have teeth. Perhaps Gwyn should offer a softer loaf. Before sun up the next day, he was down by the lake again holding out his dough. After waiting all day she appeared, more beautiful than ever. But the lake lady shook her head, laughed and said,

"Thou of the soft bread

I will not have thee"

'Though she dived under the water and left him sad and lonely, she smiled so sweetly that he decided to try with a loaf half baked. That day it rained but when nearly dark the lady, lovelier than ever, rose up and came ashore. Gwyn rushed to meet her, holding the half-baked bread. This time, she took it and he said, "Lady I love you. Will you be my wife?"

'"I will be your bride," she replied, "but only on condition that, if you strike me three times without cause, I will leave your house forever."

'Eight long and happy years followed. They loved each other so dearly that Gwyn's vow passed entirely out of his mind, until one day he gave his wife a playful flick with his gloves.

"Remember your vow, Gwyn," she scolded him. "This is the first causeless blow. May there never be another."

'The years passed until one day he found his wife in tears. Tapping her on the shoulder Gwyn asked why she cried. Without explaining she replied, "Husband dear, you have once again struck me a causeless blow. Oh, do be on your guard."

'From that time on, Gwyn was on careful watch, like a sentinel with a death sentence hanging over his head should he fall asleep on duty, which he did when, for some unknown reason, his wife laughed out loud at a funeral and, mortified, he touched her gently saying, "Hush, wife!"

'Without a word, she rounded up their sheep and led them to the lake. There, they plunged in, vanishing without trace. Broken hearted and mad with grief, Gwyn rushed into the lake and was seen no more. Their three sons, grieving for their parents, spent many days wandering along the lakeside. They never saw their father again, but one day their mother suddenly appeared out of the water telling them their mission in life was to relieve pain and suffering with herbal medicines made from plants growing around the lake.

'All three became famous physicians – the Physicians of Myddfai. But that's another story,' said Flynt.

'Jack, is that a proposal…?' Emilie asked when he was finished.

'I always thought the story was about domestic violence.' Flynt's relationship with women was like his journalism, terse and to the point. 'I'm not Gwyn, the kid by the lake… more like his dad.'

'But you do care…?'

'You're very nice, especially today.' Emilie blushed. 'It's the simple truth – you're too nice for me.'

Emilie took his hand and held it to her lips. Flynt was too old to play but had wearied of poverty, the poverty of relationship.

She leaned closer, eyes tender. 'I know what you're thinking, Jack.' The kiss he'd not forget, the softness of her fingers on his cheek…

'Wouldn't you prefer a younger person… your own age? I would be taking advantage.'

'Taking advantage of what…? What does either of us know about the future only that we want to share it, Jack? We'll be starting out together. Does it matter what others think?' Her contented smile brushed aside his inhibitions, mostly that he wasn't worthy of her affection. 'Anyhow, how old are you?' she asked.

'Let's say,' said Flynt, 'if you're having trouble handling thirty, I've even more trouble with fifty. I lie to myself that I'm in the prime of life.'

'You don't look fifty. Have you been married before… got children?'

'No. I would quite like to have kids before it's too late… and you?'

'I'm thirty next week.'

'And you're panicking?'

'It's not a problem. I'm getting used to the idea.'

Flynt remembered the wind. It came from nowhere, whipping the bracken into a frenzy. Emilie's hands were cold, icy cold. He asked again, 'Are you sure you want to take the chance?'

'Three strikes and out… like the Lady of the Lake,' she'd replied.

Flynt closed his eyes in silent contemplation of that moment, the moment Emilie offered an escape from his own estimation of himself, from his enduring fear of cold reproach. A genuinely good person, she relieved the pressure Flynt exerted on himself but how long before he or she opted for a change of air?

On Quarry Hill they'd shared a room with Flynt's two youngest nieces – whose he wasn't sure. The five year old snored,

Emilie switching her off with a gentle nudge. Nor did Emilie object when the Flynt family dragged her down to the Athletic Club for an exercise in lifting pints, the dark green lavatory walls reeking of stale piss.

Flynt's reminiscences were interrupted by a tap on the shoulder. His sister Megan had come to find him. 'Are you ready, Jack? We're leaving for the crematorium.' Together they walked off the mountain back to Quarry Hill, his brother waiting with the still unanswered question. 'How's Emilie?' he demanded. Flynt couldn't hide it any longer.

'Emilie's dead,' he blurted. 'She fell off a cliff on Île d'Iroise.' Flynt told it the only way he knew, his words rippling around the room, noisy mourners chopped off at the knees, conversation reduced to hushed whispers, 'Who's dead… what did he say…?'

'I don't believe it,' said Dafydd. 'Why didn't you say… why leave it until today… isn't one death in the family enough?'

'I meant to.'

'Tell us later. We'd better go,' said Dafydd, glancing at his watch.

The band struck up 'The Saints' as the mourners poured through the front door, blinking in the bright sunshine before staggering down the hill to the waiting bus, the kids dancing ahead like motorcycle outriders. After the crematorium, the wake at the Athletic Club didn't last long, the family staring inquisitively at Flynt who would only say that Emilie slipped and fell; that her body had not been found. Anything more would give the local rag a headline, 'Local man in missing wife probe'.

Chapter 5

THE INS BUREAU in Paris was once the drawing room of a swish nineteenth-century family villa north of Place de Clichy in the eighteenth arrondissement. The radio antennae and satellite dishes sprouting from the roof of the elegant six-storey mansion were the only external clues to what it had become. Beneath the faded ambience of ornate ceilings and tired murals depicting pretty milkmaids skipping through the lush green water meadows of Arcadian France, whirring computers shovelled news and pictures around the world in a dozen languages. On the ground floor the International Press Bar was where Flynt did most of his drinking when in town, the bar far too convenient for the hacks upstairs. In the more distant Clichy-sous-Bois on the city's outer edge, estates of dreary high-rise blocks filled with jobless immigrants were engulfed by riots. 'Two dead, cars burned', screamed the headline Flynt read on his flight back to Paris from Heathrow. Place de Clichy in central Paris had fewer dark faces but the sullen apprehension of its well-heeled locals suggested racial conflict was just around the corner.

The bureau was divided into two. The City Editor, Yates, and the Picture Desk had one half, the other space shared by the agency's three Paris staffers. Paris was the European hub for INS, processing digital pictures and copy from correspondents which, after editing, were wired to subscribers around the world. They still said 'wired', a hangover from the days when a subscriber booked a dedicated phone line to INS, then waited anxiously for the picture to arrive for first edition. The internet and digital cameras had changed all that. A click on a keyboard in Paris and seconds later the picture was on screen at the *New York Times.*

Flynt had a corner with a desk, waste bin and shared a coat stand. Yates grabbed him the moment he walked in, demanding, 'Where is it... the story?'

'What story?'

'About the U-boat pens at Lorient. Remember – I sent you down to cover!'

'Christ... I filed it two days ago from Lorient. It's in your queue.'

A search for 'Hitler's secret weapon' found nothing. Moving closer, his nose twitching, Yates scented the reason. 'You've been hitting the bottle again... I've warned you... no more second chances.' Flynt stepped away, switching on his lap-top. 'Shit!' The story was still there, waiting for him to press the send button. Yates was smiling – the way a cobra did before it struck. Flynt didn't wait around, hurrying from the office, along the corridor to the men's room. Hanging his head over the pan he threw up. No chance now of getting his very own satellite phone. Soon he wouldn't have a nickel to make a call.

Yates was on the phone to human resources in New York when Flynt got back after dipping his head under a running tap. From what he gathered from the whispered conversation, the New York office didn't much care for instant dismissal. There was a procedure to follow and litigation to be avoided. No matter how much Yates shouted and screamed, Flynt had never missed a deadline until now, nor had he received a final written warning. INS would have to issue one before it got shot of him.

'Gardening leave,' Yates called out, plainly disappointed at being stuck with Flynt for a little longer. 'And take this with you... something to do while you're cutting the lawn. It's been waiting here a week.'

Someone at the London bureau had decided Flynt was the

agency's expert on Nazis after he went looking for 'Hitler's Secret Bunker' in the Austrian Alps. Like most stories of the genre, they were almost always rumours with long beards. He never found the bunker hidden beneath a farmhouse, only an owner extremely pissed off by people wanting to look in his cellar. But the search story was well received – and earned him a reputation as the in-house Nazi-hunter.

Stuffing the latest file under his arm, and with Yates screaming at him to stay away until his suspension was resolved, Flynt headed for the Press Bar where Helmut from BELGA, the Belgian news agency, was already hitting a tall, snub-nosed bottle of De Kuyper gin with his obituary probably written at the bottom.

'Hi... you've started early.' At four in the afternoon most hacks on the floors above were slaving over hot PCs, but not Helmut who was always ready to lend an ear to Flynt's personal troubles. A TV screen Belgian, short and round like Agatha Christie's Poirot, hair dyed jet-black, brushed flat across a pinkish scalp, Helmut spoke French and English, qualifications that helped him remain *in situ* at BELGA where, as far as Flynt could tell, he wrote very little. Some thought Helmut a plant – paid by someone's intelligence service to mingle with the media. Flynt wasn't worried by that. His secrets were splashed across page one for everyone to read. And Helmut was good company.

'I'm fired,' announced Flynt. 'Well, as good as... once Yates clears it with New York... on gardening leave until then.'

'But you don't have a garden... not even a window box.' Helmut's English was excellent, only occasionally thrown by the vernacular.

'I've got this... sort of farewell present, I suppose.' Flynt set the file on the bar while Helmut ordered him a large scotch. They poured big ones in the 'Last Drink Saloon', ten to a litre bottle. 'You've heard about Hans?' Helmut asked. Flynt shook his head. He knew Hans but not what happened while he was away. 'Fell off his stool… the one you're sitting on.' Flynt shifted uneasily. 'Never got up – dead drunk… too much De Kuyper.'

Helmut leaned across Flynt and tapped the file on the bar next to their drinks, 'DECLASSIFIED' stencilled across the cover in large black capitals.

'Never existed,' he said, asking Joe the barman for a refill.

'What didn't?'

'*Werwolf.*'

'Christ… is that what this is about?' Flynt flicked through the pages, some in German, most in French, too few in English. He'd read about *Werwolf,* the Nazi plan to create a resistance force to operate behind enemy lines and raise a Fourth Reich from the ashes of the old.

'My father was Editor of BELGA in the Sixties' – another reason Helmut had time to drink and hang on to his job. Patronage ran deep back home in Brussels.

'After the war there were scores of reports of arms caches,' continued Helmut, 'but no sign of Nazis hiding in holes.'

Flynt had his nose in the sheaf of photocopies from the Public Record Office at Kew, reading and drinking at the same time. 'According to this, MI5 suspected the SD had undertaken some post-war planning. What's SD… and *Uberseedienst…* what's that?'

'SD is *Sicherheitsdienst des Reichsführers,* the intelligence agency of the SS and the Nazi Party in the Second World War,' said Helmut. 'And *Uberseedienst,* the Trade Overseas Service-fronted Nazi cells in foreign countries… prepared the ground for war.'

'The Allies suspected an outfit called *Friedensnetz,*' said Flynt. 'What was that?'

'A German peacetime intelligence network… you should read my father's book… it's all there in French of course… how BELGA looked for evidence, found nothing. He took me with him when he did his research. I was only a kid – that's how old this story is!'

Flynt asked, 'Where did he take you?'

Helmut said, 'To the hotel in the Bavarian Alps on the Austrian border where the plan for *Werwolf* was hatched by Erich Stoltensberg, head of the Nazi Party's Intelligence Service and a bunch of staff officers. But they were shit scared of *Katastrophen politik* – the Führer's decree that "if we must die, then let the people die too." Hitler would have boiled them in oil had he known about the meeting. In the end Stoltensberg told the General Staff to discard their uniforms for civilian clothes, pass themselves off as priests, even monks, if Hitler fell.'

Helmut remembered the hotel, clinging to a rocky crag on the side of the Zugspitze, dark shadows moving slowly across the snow-covered slopes, a white, stone spire glistening in the distance on the shore of a melancholic alpine lake. The mountains and the cuckoo-clock houses clustered in the valley below were not touched by the war. The nearest they got to the chatter of machine guns was the rattle of a lonely tractor making its way along a green cleft in the pine forest clinging to the foot of the Zugspitze.

'Tell me more, Helmut… briefly. INS only wants a thousand words. I don't need reams of background.'

'Let's take a seat,' said the Belgian, picking up the *Werwolf* file and heading for a corner table. Flynt carried the drinks. The bar was already filling with hacks. He didn't want any looking over his shoulder, asking 'and what you got there, Jack?'

'It's indexed… that's good,' added Helmut running an eye down a list of names pasted inside the front cover. 'Radenac, Paul,' he muttered, turning to the page – a letter, in French from Deuxième Bureau, France's external intelligence service, to Guy Liddell, Deputy Head of Britain's MI5 after the war. The letter was annotated with the initials of a dozen or more top brass. Flynt guessed that 'GL' meant Guy Liddell, responsible for counter-espionage; 'JM' was almost certainly John Masterman who ran the Double-Cross operation; 'VR' could have been Lord Victor Rothschild, doyen of the banking dynasty and counter-sabotage chief; and 'JP' was probably Sir John Petrie, MI5's wartime Director-General.

'Oh, yes,' said Helmut, licking his lips. 'My father would like this... just as he wrote in his book.' Radenac, explained Helmut, was a leader of the Bezen Perrot, a group of Breton Nazi collaborators. During the war he also ran black-market operations in Paris.

'According to this the Nazis turned a blind eye to his activities in return for him informing on the Resistance. He sent hundreds to their deaths but got out of Paris just ahead of the Allies,' said Helmut. 'Radenac was a bloody gangster... got rid of rivals by having them and their families executed by the Nazis.'

Flynt read the copy of the Deuxième Bureau letter and asked, 'Why is this redacted?' One line was obliterated by a censor's black pen. 'I can't see the reason seventy years later.'

'Must be dead by now but Radenac was a war criminal.' Helmut took another look at the letter. 'From the context someone's redacted the name and address of the company that fronted his black-market rackets, perhaps to protect those still alive.'

The Deuxième Bureau's last sighting of Radenac was in the lobby of the Grand Hotel in Lisbon in October 1944, disguised as a priest and accompanied by five or six other 'priests'. 'The group were thought to be waiting to board a ship for South America,' said Helmut. 'A lot of Nazis escaped through Lisbon during the last days of the war.'

Flynt said, 'Thanks... but the office want a story about *Werwolf* not this guy Radenac.'

Helmut said, 'The file's pretty patchy about *Werwolf*.' Flynt waited for the Belgian to finish reading the correspondence between Deuxième Bureau and its agents. 'The general consensus was that while German Intelligence did some post-war planning, it was overtaken by the rapid deterioration in the military situation. Only three *Werwolf* cells – two in Bavaria – were ever found, and they surrendered, said Helmut. 'A directive was issued in the last days of the Reich ordering the formation of small, compact units to infiltrate Allied lines with explosives and sabotage equipment to be stored in camouflaged caches until the time came.'

'And?'

'We watched and waited – I mean the French and Belgians – but nothing apart from farmers ploughing up rusty rifles – most from the First World War. The occasional Bezen Perrot collaborator with nowhere left to hide surrendered. That's all.'

Emilie had told Flynt about the Bezen Perrot and Hitler's promise to reinstate the Breton language if they collaborated. Although only the extremists of Bezen Perrot believed this, France never forgot, cracking down on the Breton language after the war. For Emilie, saving the language was crucial. Flynt inclined to let it die, believing the process of one language and one culture replacing another as evolutionary. But this wasn't the cause of their break-up. He blamed himself for not making the time to grow into the marriage – too interested in chasing headlines.

Before ordering a last round, Flynt leaned across the bar and asked, 'Do you think I'm mad, Helmut?'

'How do you mean mad?'

'Out of mind – off my rocker.'

The Belgian was amused. 'Yes, you're mad, crazy to lose Emilie not once, twice.'

'Don't remind me... and I'm grateful for your support... that BELGA didn't make much of the story.'

'BELGA'S not interested unless it's about our own language divide. We leave Brittany to Agence France-Presse. I see it used a paragraph.'

Flynt paused. How far should he entrust his friend? 'What I meant to ask, do I act crazy?'

Helmut said, 'Look in the mirror... dissipated yes, but I'm hardly one to offer advice. But mad no, possibly eccentric.'

Flynt whispered, 'I've got a problem – as well as Emilie. You've seen my phone collection... one of them rings and there's a woman's voice.' Helmut choked back his drink, spreading gin and tonic over the table before pushing Flynt's scotch and water out of reach. 'Leave off the scotch, Jack, and it won't ring, I guarantee. It was bound to happen sooner or later. Christ, I hear my wife's voice ringing around the apartment when she's visiting her parents in Brussels.'

This was exactly the response Flynt could expect if the office got to know. 'You won't mention a word, Helmut, will you? Just what Yates wants – prove I'm nuts.'

When they left the Press Bar that evening Flynt was still looking for a peg for the *Werwolf* story. That's how it worked. The headline crystalised the story. 'Hitler's Secret Weapon' would press the right button if Yates consented to put it on the schedule now he finally got it, but '*Werwolf* – it never happened' was of interest only to The History Channel, not the INS news wire. The same could be said for 'Bezen Perrot, the Unforgiven'. Flynt was gathering up the file to leave when Helmut asked, 'Any more news... about Emilie?' He'd liked Emilie, was best man at their wedding, and later a shoulder for Flynt to lean on. 'Nothing... I'm still waiting to hear from the French police.'

Chapter 6

THE MESSAGE ON Flynt's mobile was from Lieutenant Jean Louis. The French Naval Press Officer had spoken to the survivor from *U-1405* – Bosun Heinz Hestler – who agreed to meet Flynt at a restaurant in Petite France in Strasbourg. 'Gardening leave' had one advantage. Flynt didn't need to ask the desk but would have to pay his own way.

In 1945 Heinz Hestler was one of the youngest to serve aboard a U-boat. By the end of the war, according to Lieutenant Louis, the *Kreigsmarine* was recruiting sixteen year olds.

Despite a scrawny neck perched on bent shoulders, Hestler's sunny disposition suggested a man in extraordinary good health for his age. After being rescued from *U-1405* and a short spell in a POW camp, he never went to sea again, spending the rest of his life planting trees in the Black Forest at the heart of Europe.

The restaurant in the centre of a tourist trap was expensive but the retired German forester ate little. All Flynt had to do was keep Hestler on track – not allow him to veer off into irrelevant reminiscences.

Flynt said, 'I'd like to know about that last day when Captain Scheer briefed the crew.'

Hestler said, 'Not everyone agreed to make a run for it. Most stayed behind and surrendered to the Americans. It wasn't that they were afraid to fight on. The Walter boat wasn't safe. There had already been a serious spillage… one of the crew badly burned by peroxide.'

'So why did you go with Scheer? The war was over… Doenitz said scuttle. Scheer was disobeying orders.'

'I've often asked myself the same question.' Hestler was staring over Flynt's right shoulder towards the canal flowing slowly past the restaurant window. 'It was the man, I suppose. What do they say about some people – he was a charismatic leader. I was with Scheer on my first boat, very briefly. Might have been even briefer had he not given me one extra minute to clear the bridge before crash-diving the ship.'

Flynt dragged Hestler back on course. 'That last day... you were saying...'

About half the crew volunteered, said Hestler, sufficient to sail the Walter boat to South America. 'That was to be our destination after picking up some staff officers waiting in Lisbon. Scheer said we had friends with money in Argentina.'

'Who were these friends?'

'*Werwolf!*'

Flynt didn't blink, not show any surprise – simply ordered another bottle of wine.

'Did Scheer have proof that *Werwolf* existed?'

Hestler shook his head. 'We believed in the man not what he was saying.'

That afternoon, several hours before high water and the departure of *U-1405* for South America, Scheer held a farewell party for the crew at the 'club' – 'the big house on the hill at Lorient... once Doenitz headquarters, now the garrison brothel,' explained Hestler.

'Could the U-boat have reached South America?'

'Yes! The ship had the range – and the *Kapitan* could perform miracles. I know... I saw Scheer do it.'

'Do what?'

'Perform a miracle... that afternoon at the club before we sailed. Scheer had a woman called Anna, a waitress, not one of the girls. No-one put it to the test. He spent all his time ashore with Anna. She wasn't much to look at, older than the *Kapitan*, a war widow, grey-haired with one of those faces, like corrugated sheeting. We called her "*feuer im loch*".'

'What's that mean?'

'Fire in the Hole... the only thing they had in common was between the sheets – Scheer was fanatical about that... and *Nationalsozialismus*. Anna was another fanatic... a Breton nationalist, one of those Bezen Perrot types. That's why she fucked him. Without the *Kapitan* the Resistance would have had her against the nearest wall.'

'How about the Scheer miracle?' Flynt asked.

Hestler said, 'I did try to get it published some years ago... but no-one was interested. Too close to the end of the war, I was told. *Deutschland* wanted to forget, not be reminded. But take a look.'

Flynt reached out a hand for the manuscript before dropping back into his seat. 'In German. I'll have to get it translated... really don't have the time.'

'No you won't,' said Hestler. 'I had a grandson translate it into French and another into English but I still couldn't find a publisher. In the end I stuffed it in a drawer.'

'That,' Flynt said, 'is the fate of all great works of fiction.' Not long enough for a book, Flynt thought, thumbing through a dozen typewritten pages.

'I know what you're thinking. It was only intended to be... what do you call an extract from a book?'

'A taster...'

'Yes... a taster for my war memories.'

Flynt took another swallow of wine before reading *Small Miracle*. Hestler bowed his head and with elbows planted firmly on the table and fingers pressed against both temples waited for the verdict:

'The club was quiet, the air filled with stale alcohol fumes. Behind closed shutters men and women sat smoking, their mission

to drink the place dry and fuck each other silly before the Americans arrived. The artillery bombardment had abated, replaced by the distant chatter of automatic weapons, the club emptying as the battle drew closer. Not everyone saw a POW camp as an escape, not the girls curled up in corners with their tortured thoughts. "Tell them I'm your wife," pleaded one, clawing at the chest of a young Wehrmacht officer. "But I have a wife... in Munich," he said, pushing her away roughly. The woman moaned quietly, fear flickering in her eyes like dying embers.

Anna, the Captain's woman, was standing at the bar when we arrived, at her side a woman cradling a newborn baby. "Dead... I told you the child was dead," said the woman, muttering a Hail Mary. After examining the child, Scheer slipped out of his jacket and rolled up his sleeves. Taking hold of the small limp body by the ankles he swung it to and fro like a plucked chicken on a butcher's hook. A woman screamed and reached out to stop him. "Get back woman, I know what I'm doing." Did he, I wondered?

"Get out of the way. I want all the room there is." Shrinking from his fierce gaze, the women standing around the bar were convinced he was mad. Scheer had done many mad things before but that was at sea in raids on the North Atlantic convoys. I thought he'd finally flipped.

"Scheer swung the naked body, faster and faster, sweat trickling down his face and neck, the room a blur before his throbbing eyes. Stunned by the spectacle, women screamed, when suddenly there was a sound distinct from Scheer's exertions.

"What was that?" someone croaked. The sound came again, like a drowning person fighting for breath.

"The child's alive," a woman said. Triumph glistened in Scheer's streaming face. The macabre dance ended slowly, the child's sounds more certain until it was screaming lustily, the women all crying and laughing at the same time. "It's a miracle!" one said.

"How?" I asked Scheer. The Third Reich didn't believe in miracles, only the Fatherland. "Not possible," I insisted.

"I've never seen a healthier child… now she only needs to survive the war," said Scheer, handing the baby to the nearest woman.

"The mother?" he asked. Anna stared at him grimly.

"Dead," she said, nodding towards the door leading from the bar to a row of cell-like cubicles separated by paper-thin walls. Scheer bent over, felt the child's pulse, then listened to the heart and nodded proudly.

"How?" I asked again. "I've never seen anything like that."

"Exercise," said Scheer. "The child was suffering hypoxia. Something was interfering with the flow of oxygen into the blood. Her respiratory system needed a kick-start. A gamble, I admit, but what was there to lose?"

"But how did you know what to do?" asked another.

"I was still-born… that's how my parents got me kick-started." Scheer smiled wickedly, then took Anna's hand and headed down the corridor of anonymous grey doors where they found the child's mother in a cubicle with a soiled bed sheet and faded grey flannel blanket, her body swinging gently in the breeze blowing through an open window.

By the time the party was over, I'd been promoted to Obersteuermann *because there was no-one else.* As the blast doors to K1 opened and the U-boat was winched into place I heard a pistol shot echo around the concrete cavern before dying.

"You'd better check the slipway," Scheer ordered. Debris washed in by the tide often got stuck in the mouth of the slipway. I took a boat hook and was pushing it back into the current when it snagged on a bundle of clothing bobbing amongst the debris. I saw her breasts first, snowy white but firm, dress wrapped around her head. The woman couldn't have been in the water long, grey hair still streaked red from the ragged hole in the back of her head. It was Anna, Scheer's Anna, from the club. The Resistance had sent him a message in a bottle.

"Bury her," said Scheer, seeing the corpse spread-eagled on the slipway.

"Where?" I pointed at the concrete.

"Then throw her back," Scheer ordered. "We mustn't miss the tide." The torpedoes were stowed and waiting to be primed, the U-boat a floating grocery store with crates of condensed milk, cans of butter, meat and chocolate filling every available space.'

Returning the manuscript, Flynt said, 'That's very good. Can I use it?'

'I see no reason why not,' replied Hestler. 'It would be nice to have it printed before I die.' Flynt would only pick the bones out of a story far too long for his needs.

Flynt asked again, 'And Scheer could have made it to Buenos Aires had the U-boat not sunk?'

'Who says she sank? Only the British.' Hestler was still fighting the war. Hardly a year passed without some former Nazi being hauled off the pampas on his zimmer frame to face retribution. That wasn't to say *Werwolf* didn't exist. But like flying saucers it hadn't landed yet.

'You were aboard the U-boat when the *Cornwall* dropped depth charges… correct?'

'I'll never forget. Scheer switched to batteries and dived after the conning tower was damaged. I can still see it… the fuel spewing from ruptured pipes… the batteries sucking out the air… my eardrums exploding. We tried to plug the leaks but the sea kept pouring in. The bow went down, maxing out at almost 300 metres, the hull creaking, rivets popping. Scheer screamed at me to get on the pumps. After more depth-charges he blew the tanks. Only one of the cells worked but we surfaced. When the hatch opened I climbed on to the bridge. Not everyone got out. The last I saw of Scheer before I jumped into the sea was in the control room trying to trim the boat.'

'And she went down?'

'That's what they said... that the conning tower was open and she filled with water. It was closed when I last looked. But no-one wanted to know, well, not until 1974.'

'Sorry... why 1974?'

'That's when the French Navy took a closer look. Remember, the Walter boats were state of the art, stuffed with lots of gear the Allies didn't know about. They couldn't find it... the U-boat, I mean. Spent a month looking but there was no trace of *U-1405*.'

'So she wasn't sunk?' Flynt's story was getting better.

'Not where the *Cornwall* said. Scheer probably moved her... and she went down somewhere else.'

Flynt closed his notebook. The desk would buy it as a follow-up. Yates might reimburse his expenses even though he was on 'gardening leave'. The hotel was cheap enough. Not that he got much sleep that night because of the taxi rank across the road and another call from the Bakelite lady, only this time he thought she had more to say than 'Help! He's trying to kill me.' But the call cut out before she could finish. Flynt shook his head vigorously. He had to stop imagining things. The phone couldn't possibly ring, let alone allow him have a conversation.

Chapter 7

THE GENDARME WAITING on the pavement outside Flynt's apartment told him to contact the *Poste de Police*. The news was not unexpected. A body had been recovered from the sea on Île d'Iroise and Flynt was asked to make a formal identification at the mortuary in Brest. The French judicial system was painfully slow but a magistrate had already been instructed to open an investigation into the circumstances. Someone must have had a shrewd idea it was Emilie.

The light was fading when the train arrived at Brest from Paris Gare du Nord. Flynt found the mortuary, a white-washed concrete blockhouse standing on the quayside, the morgue attendant anxious to lock-up. Mumbling unfelt sympathies he led Flynt into a small inner chamber, a cold, windowless final resting place. The corpse lay on a marble slab covered by a white sheet. 'Ready?' the attendant asked, one hand lifting the end of the sheet. Flynt had seen dead bodies in Iraq, and never gave them a second glance. This was different, someone who'd been close, with whom he'd been intimate.

Steadying himself, Flynt stifled a gasp when the sheet was lifted. The morgue attendant hadn't said there were bits missing. For three weeks after she fell, poor Emilie was swept by tides across razor-sharp, grey-black granite, twice a day every day until what remained got snagged on the rocks, the head missing, an arm, and most of a leg gone. What Flynt saw was indistinguishable from a badly butchered side of beef hanging in a slaughterhouse, except white and spongy, not bloody. The corpse was unidentifiable but for fragments of the red cotton dress Emilie wore the night she disappeared – and the wedding ring on the second finger of the left hand. Neither expensive nor unusual, it was identical to the one he'd slipped on her finger at the Register Office in Paris. That Emilie still wore it after their break-up was a sign she'd not given up on their marriage.

'Your wife, *monsieur*?' asked the attendant impatiently.

'I think so. It's difficult… but for the dress I couldn't say… and the wedding ring… if I could take another look at the ring, then…'

The mortuary attendant gestured to Flynt to step outside, emerging a few moments later, the ring wrapped in a tissue. 'It came off easier than I'd expected after being in the sea all that time,' he remarked.

'Yes,' said Flynt staring closely, afraid to touch. He didn't ask how she died. The police probably thought he pushed her.

The attendant handed Flynt a death certificate to sign. 'Injuries consistent with a fall,' was all it said.

'I'll inform the Investigating Magistrate you've identified the body. The name of your wife… Emilie Quatrevents… correct?' Flynt nodded. The man was in an indecent hurry to finish.

'And her age?' he asked, pen poised over the form.

Flynt thought for a moment. Thirty when they married, which meant she was thirty-eight. 'Too young to die,' he replied.

The attendant's smile was thin and fake. 'Her age?' he asked again.

Flynt told him but felt like punching his lights out. Instead he asked, 'The hearing is this Saturday, correct?'

'That's what I'm told. *Monsieur le Juge d'Instruction* will take the eight o'clock ferry tomorrow morning and hold the hearing the next day,' he replied while steering Flynt towards the exit.

A cold, penetrating drizzle swept the quay, the attendant casting a grotesque shadow on the morgue's white concrete wall as he fiddled with a heavy padlock. The security lights cut out, inky darkness hiding Flynt's grief – a lonely, pathetic figure, one hand holding an antique telephone in a plastic Carrefour bag, the other chasing strands of hair blowing across his scalp.

Leaving the dock and staggering along shadowy side streets searching for a hotel, Flynt's thoughts were all about Emilie and her red dress. She'd worn it on their wedding day when he ignored his mantra that hacks didn't marry hacks because every newsroom he'd known was strewn with the wrecks of such unions.

The banns had been posted at the Hôtel de Ville a few months after they returned from Marrakech. The wedding breakfast was small, at Bisclaverët, one of the finest Breton restaurants in Paris. Flynt knew it well – still passed it every day on his way to the office but had not set foot inside for eight years.

There weren't many guests, a handful from the International Press Centre, including Joe the barman who poured large drinks and Flynt's best man, Helmut from BELGA. Brother Dafydd flew over from Wales while Emilie's uncle, Jean Kaudren, crossed from Île d'Iroise accompanied by a large man with a full head of fair hair. Herve Brevilet was assumed to be the old man's 'carer', the pair whispering together in Breton. Whatever Brevilet was saying filled Kaudren's wrinkled face with deep apprehension until, suddenly, he leaned back in his chair and lit a cigarette while searching the table for a friendly face.

'No, Uncle,' Emilie called out in Breton. 'Smoking is not allowed in restaurants in France.' Kaudren sniffed defiantly, ground his teeth on the cigarette butt before letting it drop to the floor and stamping it dead with the heel of his boot. On Île d'Iroise, Kaudren did little else but smoke, whistle, and walk from room to room at Port Maria, the large fortress-like house the family had owned for generations. His swarthy face, beaten by wind and rain, resembled the rocky inlet of the same name Port Maria overlooked. Kaudren's faded blue fisherman's blouse might have been out of place in a swish Paris restaurant but it shimmered brilliantly in the splashes of sunlight bursting through an open window.

The old man's pained expression eventually exploded into a sharp exchange with Brevilet, sounding all the more serious for being in Breton. Emilie was struggling to pacify the pair when Helmut from BELGA muttered for no apparent reason, 'Bloody Bezen Perrot.' Kaudren and Brevilet rocked back in their chairs. Emilie's eyes opened wide and someone asked, 'What do you mean?'

'I was only thinking aloud… forget it,' replied the Belgian. Whatever the reason for the quarrel, it was immediately forgotten, the conversation reverting to type with questions for the newlyweds about their plans.

'Nothing planned,' said Flynt.

'Must have a honeymoon,' said Helmut. Flynt's shrug and Emilie's childish smile said they'd done that bit already.

'Come to Port Maria,' piped up old man Kaudren, surprising everyone by speaking English. 'The house is large enough… I'll not get in your way.'

Turning to Emilie, Flynt whispered, 'He speaks English?'

She frowned. 'I didn't know… never did, not on Île d'Iroise when I was there.'

'What about the other…?' Flynt nodded at Brevilet.

'Yes… very good… needs it for his business… and French, of course.'

Despite the old man's promises to confine his perambulations to the extremities of Port Maria, Emilie wasn't keen. She'd not been back since Kaudren packed her off to private school on the mainland. When, after graduating in English Studies, her uncle's monthly cheque stopped, Emilie assumed that this and her unanswered letters meant his commitment to her dead parents was over.

'You've seen Quarry Hill,' said Flynt. 'Don't you think I should take a look at your island… your language and culture… your home? We're both Celts. Let's see how the Breton branch of the family is faring against the wicked French. The wicked English have screwed us.' Flynt's uncharacteristic forthrightness was met by Brevilet's blue eyes flashing at him like bayonets across the table. The 'carer' didn't seem keen on Île d'Iroise hosting a pair of honeymooners.

From the moment they set foot on Île d'Iroise, Brevilet hung around like a bad smell, banging on in Breton to Emilie, leaving Flynt wondering whether there was more to their relationship than a common language. Not tall, yet broad-shouldered and strong, Brevilet's ruddy good looks would appeal to any woman, no matter what her age.

The day following their arrival was golden with shafts of sunlight bouncing off the surface of the water shimmering in the narrow inlet below Port Maria. Such days were rare, the light breeze barely ruffling the sea as Emilie and Flynt climbed on to the cliff path, wild flowers hugging the sides for protection from the gales that rolled in without warning from the Bay of Biscay.

'No-one swims there,' said Emilie, leading the way to Ar Poull-nevial Du, the Black Pool, a deep basin trapped between high cliffs by some ancient upheaval, leaving only a narrow entrance from the sea. 'Herve Brevilet always said it was too dangerous.'

'Tell me about him,' said Flynt frustrated, tossing his arms in the air. 'We've been here what…? Not much more than a day… and Brevilet's around every corner. I give up. If I could speak the bloody language I'd ask him what was up. I don't know what to make of him… or you.'

Emilie replied, 'I don't know what to make of myself sometimes.' It was their first spat.

'We shouldn't have secrets,' said Flynt. Emilie smiled. Was that a sign that whatever there was between her and Brevilet still smouldered?

'Remember, I didn't want to come. Now we're here we might as well make the best of it. Try to be kind to him.' That was it. Flynt couldn't be kind to someone Emilie refused to discuss. They walked on in silence, neither of them loosening up, Emilie's shoulders hunched and the small hairs on the back of Flynt's neck like antennae searching for a sign.

'What's that?' he asked suddenly. Just where the path divided, one track heading towards the Black Pool, the other turning inland, a sound bounced off the cliff below their feet like the pinging of a hammer against a metal plate. After several seconds it stopped. 'Did you hear that,' Flynt asked again.

Emilie shook her head. 'The weather is changing... we should turn back before it's dark... leave Ar Poull-nevial Du for another day,' she replied. Emilie held Flynt's arm tightly, her body trembling as they stepped off the coast path to cross a field of spiky green hillocks of bog grass towards a whitewashed farmhouse hugging the ground on the far side.

The Jalenes had always lived there, certainly for as long as Emilie remembered, following a way of life that served their ancestors for generations. Paris thought the islanders troublesome and backward when, in fact, they sought only sanctuary for their cultural identity.

Emilie's teeth chattered as Flynt banged on the Jalenes' solid-oak door. A light came on in the hall. Someone was at home but no-one answered. Flynt tried again, hammering until he heard faint whispers, then feet padding down the passageway towards the door. They waited expectantly, the porch light on, someone wrestling with a bolt. A few seconds later the light flicked off and the footsteps retreated. Silence descended like the grave.

Emilie called to the Jalenes through the door. 'I know you're there... I can hear you.' There was no reply, not a word, the elderly couple either totally disinterested, or afraid.

The storm broke. The rain was heavy, kicking up muddy

spouts. 'The barn,' shouted Emilie, dragging Flynt across the farmyard. The walls were thicker than a bullock's hind-quarter, the tiled roof plastered with cement, and no windows for the wind to penetrate. Bales of winter fodder filled one end, a large yellow tarpaulin sheet at the other covering what Flynt thought must be a piece of farm equipment.

'What's wrong with these people?' he growled.

'Afraid.'

'What have they to be afraid of?'

'Strangers perhaps…'

'At least it's dry,' said Flynt, lifting the yellow tarpaulin to peek at what it hid. 'My God… what's this?' he exclaimed, pulling the sheet to the ground. 'Where did this come from?' The Second World War German army staff car was in pristine condition. The open-topped Mercedes-Benz only needed Adolf Hitler sitting in the back. 'Must be worth a fortune… how has it survived? Did the Germans occupy the island during the war?' Emilie nodded.

'There was a road,' she replied. 'Not in my time… earlier. You can still see pieces of broken tarmacadam alongside the track.'

'Are you saying the Germans left the car behind… for the Jalenes to polish?'

'No idea, Jack. I've not seen it before.'

'Someone's kept it in pretty good nick. I'll buy it if we can coax the Jalenes from their dug-out… great investment… better than money in the bank.'

'The rain has stopped. We'd better go,' said Emilie. Flynt turned to take a look but couldn't because there he was again: Brevilet, a dark statue framed by the entrance, rain glistening on his yellow oilskin, his fisherman's sou'wester like a pointed Klu Klux Klan hat. He must have followed them. Not even the island's bush-telegraph worked that fast. The wind had dropped but still rustled the dark interior. Emilie's face was as pale as marble. Without a word, Brevilet removed the top half of his oilskin, and hung it round her shoulders. 'Incestuous' was the word that sprung into Flynt's mind. Islanders everywhere did it. The evil influence of *France 2* was out of reach. Those long, dark nights could be longer than most on Île d'Iroise.

Emilie was sixteen when she left, a romantic attachment to the older man not difficult to imagine. Flynt was angry, not with her but with Brevilet and the bloody Breton language for preventing him from having a verbal with the fisherman.

'Nice motor… yours?' Flynt patted the bonnet of the Nazi staff car. Brevilet was impassive, his only interest, Emilie.

'It's stopped raining, let's go,' she said. Brevilet stepped aside reluctantly, the two men exchanging cold, hard looks as they passed.

'What was that all about?' Flynt asked when out of range.

'Nothing… he was in the area and came to see if we needed help.'

Flynt didn't swallow that. He could spot a cover-up a mile away. Lies made him edgy, especially when from his new wife. He'd let it drop, at least for the present – see if Brevilet returned with his Breton whispers for Emilie's pretty ear.

That night it rained again. There was no mention of Brevilet over the mussels from the bay. Mussels, old man Kaudren claimed, were the reason for his great age. But he was not invited, the door locked against the whistler's perambulations and cigarette smoke.

Raising his glass, Flynt said, 'Why me… I'm still wondering? You can't say I'm the most comfortable person to be around… a grumpy almost old man, always inquisitive, never satisfied with an answer, restless…'

'But Jack Flynt will never be boring.'

'But how about our ground rules,' Flynt asked cautiously. The only rules he'd ever kept were professional. If he failed, his mistakes were splashed across page one for all to see. The problem was that his golden rule – never get involved, not personally – had just been broken. Emilie also had a rule: she wouldn't be a mere stop on the road for Jack Flynt.

'This means everything for me, Jack,' she said, 'new responsibilities, a family. Are you certain the old life is over – or will you return to the old ways, the old friends, the same bad habits? I'm not just a key in the door.'

Flynt's answer was the bedroom, the sound of surf draining through the shingle at the water's edge as she lay in his arms, quiet and close, specks of light bouncing on the ceiling above their heads. Emilie moved a hand beneath the sheets touching Flynt gently. 'Slowly,' he whispered. 'Remember, I'm old...'

Chapter 8

THE ONLY GOOD thing about the hotel Flynt checked into after leaving the morgue was that it was convenient for the ferry early the next morning. Otherwise it was his usual: clapped-out but cheap, the bathroom mirror dotted with black scratches where the silver backing had peeled away.

The night was only half through when Flynt woke suddenly, not because the hotel was noisy or the bed uncomfortable. For a busy harbour hospice the mattress felt in pretty good nick. It was the thought of that red dress, the fragments clinging to Emilie's body in the morgue: that she still wore it after all those years apart. Emilie didn't need a party dress to teach the kids on Île d'Iroise to read and write Breton, nor for the Saturday night hop at the village hall. There wasn't one. Islanders went to bed early. To survive, the language needed young blood.

The Investigating Magistrate was sure to ask about the dress, in which case he'd better get his story straight. France's legal system was inquisitorial – took no prisoners – unlike Britain's which was fairer to the accused.

Flynt was wide awake, his brain a runaway computer churning through the facts, before and after Emilie fell. More by habit than foresight he'd made a detailed note of what happened. What led up to that night would be forever engraved upon his memory.

Sliding off the bed Flynt rummaged through his Carrefour bag. Beneath the black Bakelite and the *Werwolf* file Yates had pressed on him before kicking him out of the office, Flynt found his private archive. He never left town without the pack of blue pocket-size reporter notebooks, all dated, each filled with neatly scribbled shorthand from his most recent assignments. This was Flynt's insurance against a comeback. The News Desk at INS could call at any time asking him to confirm a quote if someone complained. Whereas the majority of hacks used mini-recorders, Flynt stuck with shorthand for speedier access to what was material to a story without having to wade through all the inconsequential drivel digitals soaked up.

Thumbing through the pages, Flynt found the note he'd made after Emilie's fall: how Herve Brevilet's younger brother Lan, after witnessing what happened in the darkness, took him to their farm for his cuts and bruises to be dressed.

The brothers lived alone in a small farmhouse protected from the elements by a clump of wind-twisted pines. Herve knew something was wrong the moment he saw Flynt. After listening to Lan's account of what happened, he crumpled, shoulders sagging as he sank into a chair at the scrubbed pine kitchen table. Head bowed it took the older brother several minutes to recover. Then, without a word, he pulled a bottle of mercurochrome from a drawer to treat Flynt's cuts. From the appearance of the bottle of red liquid, Flynt guessed it was well passed its sell-by date. 'Probably left behind by the Nazis when they surrendered in 1945,' he noted later. 'I was coated with the stuff... like a bloody Red Indian. The fall didn't get me, the mercury might.'

Herve Brevilet hadn't much to say, only that Flynt should spend the night with them. The search for Emilie would start again at daybreak.

From the untouched appearance of the centuries-old panelled kitchen with large inglenook fireplace and smoke-stained ceiling, it was evident the brothers didn't spend their money on maintenance.

Île d'Iroise had been connected to the mainland grid some years previously but the Brevilets still used lamps fed by bottled gas. Furnishings were sparse, the only pieces of note a roll-top desk and a tall leaded glass-fronted bookcase. A brief glance across the titles suggested erratic and superficial minds veering towards the past but, surprisingly, not confined to Breton. There was even one in English, *Submarine Warfare in the 20th Century* and a DVD of the German U-boat epic *Das Boot*. Against another wall, an oval-shaped table was pushed beneath a window, the cigar stub dying in a saucer and the glossy travel brochure open at a cruise page, suggesting someone was planning an expensive trip.

But it was the framed photograph on a wall that truly caught Flynt's attention. Emilie was a pretty sixteen year old, one arm leaning on the kitchen window sill, her gaze mystical, reaching beyond the rugged cliffs of Île d'Iroise. Was this the reason old man Kaudren sent her to Paris to complete her education? Not that Flynt cared too much about what may have happened in the past. The image gnawing at his mind was of the sea tugging at Emilie's broken body trapped amongst the rocks.

A knock on the door seemed to lift Herve Brevilet's spirits, if only momentarily. 'A tall, lanky guy with shaggy beard, and wearing dirty-brown dungarees,' Flynt noted. What the visit was about was buried in a burst of Breton until Herve's angry stare stopped the visitor in mid-sentence.

'Wasted on me... didn't understand a word,' Flynt had written in his notebook, adding in the margin, 'Feels like I'm missing something.' When asked what was new Herve Brevilet said nothing, instead pointing to the narrow stone staircase winding around and over the inglenook up to first floor.

Flynt's room for the night was at the far end of a dark passageway, lit by a solitary light flickering above a niche in which sat the bronze bust of a smiling young man wearing a seafarer's flat peaked cap set at a rakish angle above piercing blue eyes. Flynt would take a closer look when daylight breeched the Stygian gloom but couldn't. The bust had disappeared.

And what a dreadful night, probably Flynt's worst. He barely slept, his mind racing ahead to what might happen next. Flynt knew way back then there was little hope of finding Emilie alive; that they'd be looking for him too if a clump of stunted gorse hadn't broken his fall.

'By dawn, the overnight rain had cleared, ragged patches of fluffy white clouds scudding across a deep-blue sky,' he'd written, noting the weather for reference later. Quotes were a matter of record, colour quickly faded from the memory.

The Brevilets had gathered a dozen or so men to search the cliffs, all wearing dirty-brown dungarees. 'All-weather gear or uniform,' Flynt had noted. 'No-one's very confident… Emilie's body probably washed out to sea. The currents are treacherous. The men have ropes and a stretcher just in case… and their wives… like camp-followers with food and drink… Brevilet's little army.'

Flynt's last entry read:

'Five o'clock – too dark to continue searching. We're all exhausted. Brevilet says it's usually ten to fourteen days before the sea gives up its dead. I knew that… but surprised to hear him say so in French.'

Flynt closed the notebook and listened to the binmen of Brest clattering around in the alleyway below his hotel window. By the time he'd finished transcribing his shorthand from a month ago, daylight was bleeding through the curtains. The Investigating Magistrate would expect the notebook handed in as evidence. Packing it away with the Bakelite, he shaved and dressed quickly, paid the bill and found a coffee and croissant at the ferry terminal.

The crossing to Île d'Iroise was uneventful until the sudden clatter of iron wheels across cobbles as the ferry moored just inside the harbour entrance at Tourmant, a cluster of white, bleached cottages hiding from the Atlantic rollers beating themselves to death against the island fortress. Like ants leaving their nest, a helter-skelter of grim-faced women buried in thick woollen coats buttoned tight under their chins emerged from the narrow alleyways, steering crude wooden boxes mounted on wheels in a rickety race to meet the ferry. This was the nearest they got to shopping, groceries and most essentials delivered once a month from Brest courtesy of a surrogate shopper. In no time at all the large brown paper bags lining the quay were packed into carts, the women disappearing behind locked doors and shuttered windows as quickly as they'd appeared. Not a word was exchanged with the disembarking passengers, none of whom spoke Breton, the language of the hearth on this cultural outpost in the Bay of Biscay.

Territorially part of France, the islanders paid French taxes, their children compelled to speak French if they ventured from the rocky shores of boiling surf and freezing spray. Few ever did, preferring the warm embrace of their ancient Celtic tongue and its rich cultural independence, older and more enduring than anything on the mainland. The community, sustained by fishing and farming, had resisted all attempts by France to subsume it, this conspicuous in every gesture, the message of the islanders defiant and unequivocal: 'Hands off.' To some critics, Île d'Iroise was the Island of the Dead, the mythical Brittia in the Bay of Biscay across which ghostly ferrymen transported the souls of the deceased. Unable to assert any cultural authority, the government in Paris whispered about pagan practices, how islanders worshipped the 'little people'.

Hostility towards outsiders was not the only reason there were so few visitors, even in summer on tranquil days when the heath was warmed by the sun. For much of the year the crossing from Brest was risked only by fanatical bird-watchers with strong stomachs. Ringed by reefs erupting from the surf like giant's teeth, the high cliffs of Île d'Iroise were a fearsome sight, the cemetery at Tourmant testifying to the coastline's brutal reputation. For good reason it was said that those who stared too closely at Île d'Iroise saw blood. But from a safe distance it looked as harmless as a raised game pie, a plateau seventy metres high, the only distinguishing features an automated lighthouse and the French military's transmitter array on the headland. Otherwise it was a flat, spongy carpet of pink heather in autumn between pockets of rough, marsh grass grazed by flocks of stunted sheep shaped by wind and rain to survive the cold Atlantic blasts.

Not surprisingly, the yachting fraternity descending on Brittany like locusts every summer gave the island a wide berth. So did any sensible tourist, thought Flynt, disembarking with bag and Bakelite, and heading for Hôtel du Port, just beyond the harbour wall beside a narrow strip of sand. Another day, another crap hotel, paint peeling from green shutters, the sand blown off the beach drifting up its walls and through open windows.

Hôtel du Port topped Flynt's league of doss houses, behind the neglect, profound hostility. The hotel had a death wish, the absence of anyone to check-in passengers arriving off the ferry part of the script. Shouting for attention, Flynt wandered aimlessly around the tiny lobby until eventually an elderly woman in a greasy apron appeared from behind a screen, her irritation at the sight of guests palpable, her grunts and groans entirely Breton. The rooms were bleakly furnished, iron bedsteads from an earlier age, the lumpy mattress coated in sand blown off the beach promising Flynt a sleepless night. Why should anyone stay at such a dreary place? But that day there was a queue at reception, Flynt claiming the only room with a view towards the harbour and the island's small fleet of trawlers bobbing at anchor. Next in line was a middle-aged Frenchman in a black leather jacket over a white T-shirt with a printed slogan across his chest. He wore tight maroon trousers, had a large Gucci man-bag slung across an effete shoulder, and two young women in tow to whom Flynt offered a tired smile. Next to register was an elderly, grey-haired gent accompanied by a younger woman, Flynt guessing from their whispers, the Investigating Magistrate and clerk. An Englishman followed, Eton-type, square chin, steel-grey hair swept back. His pin-striped suit had 'banker' stamped all over it, his muscular American companion of Mafia appearance. The last to stagger ashore was drunk, Flynt shuddering at his mirror image – the sunken eyes framed by dark rings, those of a man who slept when pissed, then only briefly. The drunk stepped into the lobby, crouching, not with the uncoordinated movements of delirium tremens but with the measured grace of the mime artist, each step, every small exertion choreographed. Later that evening at dinner, Flynt broke into a cold sweat at the sight of the sad old man sawing meticulously at a lamb chop, then aiming the loaded fork with measured determination in the direction of his mouth and missing. Not once did the fork reach its destination before the driver slumped asleep at the wheel.

Flynt was halfway through a bottle of Château Shit when the bloody Bakelite rang, screaming from inside the Carrefour bag between his feet. Clasping it to his chest like a mother with a sick child, he jumped to his feet, the banker and his gangster mate watching suspiciously as he stumbled past, the drunk stirring before relapsing after muttering incoherently. Ramming the key into the lock of his bedroom door, Flynt skidded across the linoleum onto the bed, ripping open the bag as he landed on the mattress. Inside, the black telephone was daring him to answer. When it rang at his apartment it pinged three, maybe four times then stopped, but not now. Flynt pressed his hands against his head to squeeze out the demons. How could a genuine 1940s Ericsson antique without a plug or jack, no connection of any kind, ring, he asked himself, knowing that the infernal noise wouldn't stop until he answered. Gently pulling the phone out of the carrier bag and laying it on the bed, he lifted the receiver cautiously as though expecting an electric shock. Through the crackling static came the voice again, the same woman, still indistinct: 'Help! He's trying to kill me.' Common sense told him there couldn't be static on an unconnected telephone. Not even cell-phones worked on Île d'Iroise. Slumped on the bed, Flynt cried out, 'Am I always pissed when it rings?' Another bad sign, he thought. That's what loonies did... talk to themselves. Much more and he'd take a dive off one of the island's rocky ramparts.

The knock on the bedroom door was faltering, inaudible had Flynt's senses not been sharpened by his latest brush with the Bakelite. The old man with the drink problem stood in the shadows of the hallway, his back bent, head cocked to one side listening intently – and holding a Carrefour carrier bag.

'You heard it then... the phone ringing... in the dining room?' said Flynt, appealing for a yes.

'Of course, I did.' The old man fell to his knees, and bending his ear to the floor said, 'Ah, it must be a fairy horn.' Flynt stared at him, eyes popping from their sockets. Christ, who was madder?

'Well, ask the fairy to get me a drink,' was the best he could offer. The old man bent closer to the floor, whispering, 'Drink, drink' before pulling a bottle of Beaujolais from his carrier bag with a crippled flourish and proclaiming, 'Fairy wine... excellent vintage not from the local grotto but Brest.'

Flynt managed a smile.

'But too many glasses will kill you. That's what they say about fairy wine.'

'Fuck the fairies... did you hear the phone?'

'No. I saw you rush from the table and thought you needed help.'

'Yes... how to get rid of the little people.'

'You boil a spoonful of milk inside an egg... that's how you get rid of fairies.'

'Let's do it then... better come in,' said Flynt suspecting he'd found a soulmate, an expert on pink elephants. Until now he'd only spoken of his nightmare to Helmut from BELGA, fearing the hoots of incredulity, the clenched fists lifted to lips in mocking adulation of his demon telephone if the office got to hear. Yates at INS would cheer a boozy hack heading for a psychiatric ward, possibly the newsroom in the sky.

'Can I sit down?' Flynt's visitor asked. The poor fellow shuffled across the bedroom to a chair which he drew slowly but with determination under his backside.

'I know you think I'm drunk,' he said, speaking slowly and deliberately, albeit slurred. 'I've had a stroke... lucky not to be dead. They found me on the office floor one morning... I'd lain there all night.'

'And you've swapped a hospital for this God forsaken island!'

'You're dead a long time... I wanted one last look. I know what people think about this place. My memories are different. I came with my wife... camping and walking. She's gone now. I've not got much longer. Sometimes I see her... think I do... hurrying along the cliff path ahead of me. Hallucinating they say but I want one last look.'

The old man said his name was Joseph Lebrun – that he was a retired civil servant. For someone searching for a ghost, his wife's, Lebrun was showing an unusual interest in the buff-coloured *Werwolf* file on Flynt's bedside table. '*Bisclaverët*,' he muttered. 'You're reading about werewolves. *Bisclaverët* is Breton for *Werewolf*. Fairies, werewolves, sorcerers, and druids, Brittany has the lot. But you must know this stuff. You're Welsh... accents hang on even during one's death throes. Aren't the Bretons your Celtic kith and kin?' Pulling himself up, Lebrun shuffled over for a closer look at the file. 'MI5 Declassified,' he said, reading the cover.

'I'm a journalist,' explained Flynt, 'supposed to be writing a story.'

'And the husband of Emilie Quatrevents, I believe.' That wasn't hard to guess. The whole island would know he was in town.

'Your poor wife – the teacher – had that dreadful fall...'

'That's right... I'm Jack Flynt. They found her body a week ago. I've come for the inquest. What do you call inquests in France? Are you sure you didn't hear the phone ring...?'

'Sorry... not a thing... I was cat-napping... you could have had a bomb in the bag. Why do you carry it around, the bag?'

'In case the phone rings.' Returning to his chair, his slightest movement a monumental effort, but blue eyes twinkling inquisitively, Lebrun settled himself before asking, 'How often does it ring?'

'I can't really say... probably rings when I'm not around. That's why I carry it... don't want to miss a call, do we?' Flynt knew what he'd just said sounded insane.

'Are you sure it rings?' the old man asked wearily.

'Yes... and there's a woman on the line.'

'What woman?'

'Christ, if I knew I wouldn't be asking you. The voice isn't clear... lots of static... the line keeps breaking up. When I ask who is calling she rings off. It's driving me fucking crazy.'

'Have you seen anyone about it?'

'You mean the man in the white coat? No way. No shrink. I'll find the woman first.'

'Sherlock Holmes! Didn't he say that when you've eliminated the impossible, whatever remains, however improbable must be the truth?'

'And truth is stranger than fiction,' retorted Flynt. 'Byron!'

Lebrun stroked his chin. 'When I said I imagine seeing my wife on the cliff path, it's quite true. When I say I hope for one last look, that's also true. But I'm told it's an optical illusion projected by my subconsciousness. I buried my wife six years ago. Isn't this the likely explanation... a hallucination brought on by your wife's death?'

Flynt didn't reply. How could the hard-nosed newsman who questioned everything from the crucifixion to the Big Bang admit his mind had blown a fuse? Flynt prided himself on being a one-man inquisition – an adversarial, querulous challenger, never allowing anything to shake him off course. He boasted of 'not doing emotion', deriding those who did as inadequate, although emptiness was the price he paid for being as cold as steel.

While others might cite 'mental stress' Flynt wanted a rational explanation – find someone who'd also heard it ring. Only if that failed would he see a shrink.

'Can I examine it?' asked Lebrun, indicating the Bakelite lying on the bed, his left hand shaking uncontrollably. 'Where did you get it?'

'Estonia... someone gave it to me... a souvenir from when the Soviets got kicked out.' Flynt sat the Bakelite gently in Lebrun's lap.

'I have no special talent,' said the Frenchman, 'just a passionate curiosity... but there's something missing?'

'Only the base plate... back at my apartment,' explained Flynt. 'Nothing special... took it off to poke around.'

'Quite old,' murmured Lebrun, examining the cable which in normal circumstances would be connected to the junction box. 'On later models the wires were twisted together to reduce interference… what you call static. Are you sure there wasn't another cable?'

'There could have been before I got it. What causes static?'

'An electrical charge, except that in this case there can't be static. Your phone's dead.'

'What about the bell? See anything unusual,' Flynt asked.

'Look, my friend, you don't need an expert to tell you the bell won't ring, in fact can't, without a connection. This isn't a cell-phone. Even if it were you'd never get a signal on Île d'Iroise. Check for yourself.'

Flynt switched on his mobile. 'No signal' was all he got.

'Why do the islanders need mobiles?' said Lebrun, staggering to his feet and beginning the long shuffle towards the door. 'It's odd really. The French have all those communications masts out on the headland and the islanders a manually-operated medieval telephone exchange.'

'Where's the exchange?' asked Flynt.

'Here, the hotel… in the kitchen I believe. No secrets on Île d'Iroise… the old woman operates the switchboard between courses. Don't imagine she's busy. Perhaps you've noticed how hospitable the islanders are? What do they want with telephones? They've got their language… need nothing from us.'

'You make it sound like jail,' replied Flynt. 'Emilie thought them friendly enough, although I can't say I have.'

Half-turning, Lebrun said, 'Here's my card. Call if you think I can help with your inquiries about *Bisclaverët*?'

'You mean *Werwolf*.'

'Same thing… human transformed into a wolf, then back again when it suited.' Brittany, said Lebrun, was full of such stories, a relic of cannibalism when the natives thought those who ate human flesh were no better than wild animals. 'To prevent werewolves from shape-changing they hid their clothes.

Hallucination most probably explains reported sightings… my wife's appearances and your telephone calls,' he smiled before closing the bedroom door.

Chapter 9

AFTER FINISHING LEBRUN'S Beaujolais, Flynt fell into a deep sleep broken by muffled explosions, first one and then another. A shower of silvery sparks fell from the night sky like the dying embers of a firework. More probably a distress flare, he thought, staring through the wisps of fog brushing the bedroom window. The trawlers had sailed that evening. One could be in difficulty.

Dawn was breaking when he was woken by nailed boots on cobbles, large boots, small boots, probably the fishermen returning after a hard night pulling on their nets. Again Flynt crossed to the window, the fog now a creamy-white wall just beyond the pane, hiding the village and harbour in misty folds. The boots on cobbles faded, then silence, apart from the pinging of a distant foghorn and the soft crackle of the chill damp leaning against the window.

By eight o'clock he was ducking his six-foot-something into a breakfast room of Spartan proportions, the dirty grey foam ceiling tiles and plastic tablecloths a reminder of those grim post-war years when Europe struggled to survive. But no-one could complain about the lack of intimacy, the tables so tightly packed it possible to dip a croissant in another's coffee if you thought it worth the effort. In one corner the Investigating Magistrate and female clerk were locked in conversation, preparing for the hearing at the Palais de Justice, a grand name for the stone schoolhouse commandeered by the French Justice Department for the occasion. Justice, thought Flynt, must rarely have disembarked on this tiny speck in the Bay of Biscay where the inhabitants counted on dying peacefully in their sleep.

Lebrun, having survived the night, was struggling to pin down a croissant jumping sideways each time he took a stab. Flynt, chin tucked in like a boxer, grinned at the 'banker' and his thuggish companion who, with binoculars and a copy of the *World Book of Birds,* were leaving on more important business. Flynt guessed the book was a prop to satisfy the inquisitive. As for the Gucci man and his companions – they were still doing whatever they came to do.

'I can't stand any more of this,' Flynt muttered, pushing aside a cup of muddy coffee. Unfolding his long legs he stepped outside, the morning dirty, the icy tentacles nipping at his face, focusing Flynt's mind on what to tell the magistrate about Emilie's death. Language would be a problem, Napoleon having decreed that French was the language of the Republic. Flynt survived in Paris by avoiding the natives which left him linguistically challenged when dealing with anything more demanding than a menu. On his only other visit to a French court, he was rescued by a colleague. But that's the way it worked. Hacks needed hacks, the relationship not unlike a marriage without the sex. Explaining about Emilie's death would be difficult enough in English, his schoolboy French certain to land him in the shit unless there was an interpreter. Could that be Lebrun? His English was certainly good enough. Flynt grimaced at the thought of the old man weighing every word with the same measured determination he used for pinning down his croissant! Christ, they'd be stuck on Île d'Iroise all winter!

Most harbours are agreeable, friendly places in which to idle, watch boats and boatmen, or dream, of the yacht Flynt would someday sail around the world. He didn't sail, had never tried, but the fantasy sustained him in his darkest hours.

Tourmant was not for dreaming, one slip on the green slime coating the stone footpath along the harbour wall pitching the unwary into the dock. Everything about the place was dreadful, Flynt's chest tightening as the drizzle weeping from the fog washed against his face. Through it he glimpsed the ghostly silhouettes of three fishermen repairing nets, their backs against the hull of an ancient trawler rotting on a slipway. Lobster from Île d'Iroise's rocky coastline fetched top prices at France's most exclusive restaurants. No-one would have guessed this from the demeanour of the islanders, the men darkly sullen and women dour and austere.

'*Devezh mat*' were two words Flynt had learned from Emilie. But the morose trio working on their nets were indifferent to his salutation, not because his 'Good day' was a poor attempt but, clinging to their language like crown jewels, they feared contamination by outsiders. The Bretons in Brest or Lorient would have replied cheerfully, even in English. It was not that the islanders were beyond a cheery '*Bonjour*'. They'd spoken French when Breton was banned in retaliation for Bezen Perrot collaboration with the Nazis. Pig-headed, that's what they were, Flynt decided, offering a defiant '*Kenavo ar c'hentan*' (see you again) before moving off along the harbour.

At least the walk cleared his head of the previous night's Château Shit. With help from the Brevilet brothers he'd be on the next ferry – provided it was running. The ferry was a totem signalling that French writ didn't extend to Île d'Iroise, its schedule for the convenience of delivering lobster to the mainland, not for visitors. The language was a running sore in Paris, a reminder that unless Paris drew the line, France might one day have to change its constitution to accommodate the Bretons.

Leaving the harbour to the taciturn fishermen, Flynt climbed the cobbles to the schoolhouse tucked on the brow of the hill – a bastion to the resolve of the islanders, the heather beaten into a frenzy against the whitewashed walls symbolising their struggle. The schoolhouse was both a cockpit and a bridge serving the generations who'd denied the edicts handed down by Paris. While the majority of mainland Bretons had acceded, the islanders were guided solely by their cultural prerogatives, education the most important and exposure to the perverting influence of France anathema. Emilie once tried to explain but Flynt wasn't buying it. He considered the assimilation of one culture by another a natural process which minorities resisted at their peril. Wickedly, to score a point, he'd drawn his wife's attention to the distinctly pointed ears and low foreheads of the islanders. His crack hurt, contributing to their final tragic bust-up.

The fog was retreating into a flat grey cloud hugging the horizon when Flynt reached the schoolhouse, the silky 'banker' from the night before and burly associate emerging off the heath, a most improbable pair of bird-watchers scrambling through the heather. 'Did you see much today?' Flynt shouted. 'I'm told a bunch of Arctic terns arrived on the south stack earlier this week.' It was all bunkum but got the anticipated response, a tactic Flynt often employed to squeeze quotes from unwilling subjects.

'Yes. Got some good shots,' said the Englishman with the public school chin, Flynt tempted to reply, 'With a camera or a rifle?'

Instead he asked, 'Were those the black or white ones with black tipped wings? Lucky if you got a shot of the black tips.'

Turning momentarily to his accomplice, the Englishman replied cautiously, 'White... weren't they, Charlie?'

Flynt's antenna was honed to spot phoneys whose cover he delighted in blowing. Peeping through the schoolroom's small window at the metal chairs and Formica-topped tables laid out for the hearing, Flynt continued his wind-up. 'Are those the remains of an Ethiopian elder's nest,' pointing the Englishman to a ball of mud clinging to the underside of a rafter, home to a pair of swallows.

'Do they get this far north?' queried the Englishman.

'Oh yes, by jumbo jet business class.' Flynt disliked men from the manor born treating the world as part of their estate and everyone a tenant. Like grit lodged between the teeth, he could never brush the bastards out. But whoever they were, and whatever they were doing on Île d'Iroise, the guy with metal-framed glasses and gunmetal-grey hair, and beefy companion did serious exercise. The padded green windbreakers zipped up to the throat framed muscles no-one got from playing croquet.

Not long afterwards they were back, having swapped fatigues for fawn Burberry jackets and awaiting the arrival of *le Juge d'Instruction*. So, too, were Lebrun and the Gucci man, all apparently interested in discovering whether Flynt did push poor Emilie off the cliff.

The Brevilet brothers had arrived to give evidence, not boycotting the hearing as Flynt feared they might, considering their rejection of all things French. Flynt wanted only that they told it straight but the fire burning in Herve Brevilet's eyes was strong enough to crack a pane of glass and a warning that they were planning something.

Gravitas was provided by the magistrate's black gown and the sharp whack he delivered with his gavel to the Formica-topped table serving as the magisterial bench. The business of the court, explained M Rouselle, was to determine for the public prosecutor whether the corpse recovered from the rocks not far from Port Maria was indeed Emilie Flynt (née Quatrevents) and also the circumstances of her death. A Breton-speaking gendarme sent from the mainland to investigate had provided written testimony and the pathologist in Brest had given probable cause of death, said the magistrate.

Rouselle was from Paris. A scrawny individual, with a bandit moustache and long shaggy hair, he sat bolt upright on the edge of his chair, black gown hanging like a shroud from narrow, pointed shoulders. Waspish, thought Flynt, easily riled if the inquiry didn't go to plan. Paris had sent someone who cared little for the Bretons. Just for a moment, he thought Rouselle and Lebrun exchanged polite smiles as Lebrun lowered himself slowly into a chair.

Nothing should go wrong, Flynt assured himself. Identification had been a formality. Now he must explain how Emilie slipped and fell when he tried to stop her headlong flight along the cliff. But would the Brevilets back him up – Lan say he'd seen what happened, caught it in the beam from his flashlight? Then there was the Bakelite stowed in the plastic bag at Flynt's feet. One peep out of that and they'd almost certainly lock him up.

'Monsieur John Flynt,' Rouselle's clerk said. Not even Flynt's mother called him John or Johnny, always Jack. Crossing to the witness table, Flynt raised his forearm to take the oath. '*Parlez-vous français?*' the clerk asked. Flynt shook his head, the magistrate grumbled to himself indignantly.

'I took the trouble to learn your language when I lived in London.' Flynt flinched at the jibe. 'My clerk will interpret when necessary,' Rouselle snapped.

'You are the husband of Emilie Quatrevents?'

'I was. She's dead.'

'That we know M Flynt, otherwise I wouldn't be here. When did you last see your wife?'

'Four weeks ago... that would be Sunday September 4, at Port Maria, her home.'

Rouselle lowered his head to read a file open on the table. My CV, thought Flynt, probably all bad.

'You were in Iraq – saw many people die?'

'Yes. I reported what happened, never got involved.'

'Huh, I see you don't like getting too involved. Please explain exactly what happened on September 4. Take your time… better to be sure than sorry.' Rouselle smiled at his familiarity with the vernacular.

'She'd written to me at the Bureau in Paris inviting me across for the weekend. We were separated… had been for eight years. Not divorced, just drifted apart. I had my job…'

'In Iraq?'

'The agency offered a posting to Baghdad not long after we married. That's why it never worked, Emilie and me. She wanted a family and a home… I could be anywhere, anytime. But why do you ask? People break up all the time…'

'Your wife is dead, *monsieur*. I have to investigate all the circumstances, including your relationship with her.'

'Are you suggesting I came back and pushed her off the cliff? I didn't even know she'd moved to Île d'Iroise to teach the kids until I got her letter.'

'But you did come back. Why was that after eight years? A long separation… why was that?'

'It just happened… we went our own ways.'

'Tell the court about that… why you parted.'

'Is this relevant?'

'Very! The court needs to establish if there was any residual animosity between you following the separation.'

'Not from my side. Emilie… it was her idea we got together… see whether reconciliation was possible.'

'Her letter… can I see it?'

'No reason why not, but I don't have it with me. It's back in Paris at my apartment,' he lied. Why should he share Emilie's letter with the world?

Flynt was surprised she'd written after all that time although, in darker, lonelier moments, he blamed his self-serving ambition for turning aside the opportunity to escape the dehumanising, demoralising grind of the twenty-four-hour news cycle. True and enduring love would have been nice but it was not to be. Flynt neglected Emilie's likes and dislikes, allowing the agency priority and excused himself for picking a woman who never wanted to pry into other people's affairs. A house, a husband with a steady job was the kind of stuff she had in mind, not someone chasing headlines for a living.

No-one was surprised when, like Emilie's surname, Quatrevents, the marriage was blown away. Their conversation dried up, reduced to 'Good morning' and 'Good night' – Emilie convinced Flynt believed God made women to grin and bear it.

After avoiding each other for a couple of weeks, he was about to suggest a trial separation when Emilie, anticipating this, opened her wide blue eyes and with a smile radiating kindness, dared him to pursue the subject further. With other women, he'd been brutally direct but Emilie's strange seductive something, which never seemed to fade, held him back.

'Marriage is forever,' she replied to his unspoken criticism.

'So is heaven.'

'And the other place,' retorted Emilie, leaning forward, her composure icy-cold. Did she really think he was the Devil? Their slow-burning quarrels were a recitation of woes followed by reproaches which left both sets of teeth on edge.

They were so different, impartiality Flynt's Holy Grail: his mantra to count the bodies, not waste time helping, Emilie wanting only to feed the world. It was not this, however, but Herve Brevilet who bugged Flynt most. He'd not gone away. On a visit to a Breton cultural *fest* at Lorient, Emilie devoted most of her attention to Brevilet who'd popped over from Île d'Iroise for the occasion. Fiercely proud of her Celtic heritage, it was hardly surprising she chose to immerse herself in Breton at a festival celebrating the language. But why devote the day to Brevilet, Flynt asked himself when the reason they were there was for

Emilie to walk him through Brittany's rich cultural heritage? Flynt knew little, only that Brittany was colonised by the Welsh driven out of Britain-proper by the Anglo-Saxons; that the standing stones – menhirs – dotted about the countryside were not unlike those scattered around Wales; and that Wales gave Brittany King Arthur.

On returning to Paris they quarrelled, Flynt refusing to share his marriage with an island, his euphemism for Brevilet. 'I'd sooner live in a cave than with you,' Emilie shouted before walking out, leaving Flynt wrestling with his conscience. When she hadn't returned by midnight, he undressed and rolled into bed only to jump out – there was someone in it, asleep. Entering through a back door Emilie had crept quietly between the sheets. That night they didn't make love but did have sex for the last time, Emilie lying on her back waiting for Flynt to finish. The next morning they went their separate ways, she quitting her job with the French news agency to teach at a school on Île d'Iroise. Flynt buried himself in his reporting, which didn't require much effort. And when he wasn't working he watched the French play happy families in the park until the kids were shepherded away, suspicion dancing in the eyes of their parents. Growing weary of this piteous procession, Flynt stopped going to the park. Alone once more, he patronised the Press Bar most evenings, crouching over a Stella in a tall, narrow glass, a whisky chaser and packet of Marlborough at its side, and twisting a cheap plastic lighter between his fingers. Flynt spent a lot of time studying lighter fuel before smoking was banned and he did his drinking at home, a very, very bad idea for the liver.

No acrimony, no divorce, no contact, not for eight years until, unexpectedly, the letter. Emilie had inherited Port Maria from Jean Kaudren. Was she still the woman who loved to laugh, their marriage worth salvaging? Flynt wanted to know.

'The letter… please hand it to your local *Poste de Police.*' Rouselle cut into Flynt's private recollections. 'I'd like to finish… sometime today,' he insisted, pushing himself taller, hands flat on the table. 'Yes today… still a way to go,' he repeated, his gaze settling on the Brevilets.

Rouselle shifted uneasily in his chair, about to say something but thought the better of it. Instead he smiled through puckered cheeks. The edge of authority was fading from his voice.

'Mr Flynt, please tell me about that last evening at Port Maria.'

'I hadn't heard from Emilie, not until she invited me for the weekend. Couldn't understand why she was bothering. Perhaps something was wrong. Anyhow, I went. She wasn't happy, disturbed. The island hasn't much to offer. But she loved teaching the Breton kids. I admired her for that.'

There was a murmur of approval from the islanders. Rouselle sniffed disdainfully gesturing to Flynt to move on.

'You see,' Flynt continued, 'Emilie was born at Lorient on the mainland. Her parents left Brittany when the Bretons were not exactly flavour of the month. She returned to Île d'Iroise to live with an uncle after they were killed in a road accident.'

'Flavour of the month?' asked the magistrate, his otherwise excellent English stumbling.

'I mean the Bretons collaborated with the Nazis, didn't they? The Bezen Perrot they called themselves… fought alongside the Nazis on the Russian front… were promised their language back if Hitler won the war.'

'Quite so…' Rouselle's enthusiastic nod was accompanied by an angry shuffling of Breton feet. Flynt moved on quickly, afraid of upsetting those he hoped to get him off the hook.

'Emilie wanted to try again… our marriage I mean. I was willing… can't go rushing around the world much longer…

time to settle down perhaps. And we were still married…
never got divorced.'

'Everything… you must tell me everything about that night,'
insisted Rouselle. Flynt hesitated. Poking into people's lives was
what he did.

Rouselle waited. 'We'd been talking and drinking and Emilie
was very affectionate,' said Flynt eventually. 'It was inevitable
we'd wind up in bed together.'

'So you went to the bedroom?'

'Not immediately…'

Only a few hours earlier Emilie had met Flynt off the ferry,
leaning against him sweetly, arm around his waist as they walked
to Port Maria along the potholed track, splashing through ruts
flooded by the previous night's heavy rain. She was as pretty as
Flynt remembered, except for the worry lines fanning from the
corners of her eyes. That she chose to wear her wedding-day red
dress for dinner that evening was a sign reconciliation was still
possible even after all that time.

The second bottle of wine into the meal, Flynt asked, 'Why
did you write?'

Emilie leaned across the table and kissed him, a burning
persuasive kiss, then took his hand and led him to the sofa.
Pressing her cheek against his face she drew him closer before
answering with a question. 'Why did you come back,' she asked.
'Not for the sex, I hope… that was never very good.'

'I thought from your letter you wanted to try again…'

She smiled, her face glowing in the candlelight, Flynt stroking
her hair gently until quite suddenly Emilie drew back. Something
was distressing her. A moment later she was on her feet, rocking
back and forth, not moving from the spot, wanting to say
something but afraid to before turning abruptly and hurrying
from the room. Flynt heard a bedroom door shut violently
and found her sitting on the bed, head in hands, mumbling

incoherently. When he asked what was wrong, Emilie trembled, pressed her head against the pillow. 'Make love to me, Jack, before it's too late,' she said slipping out of her red dress and whispering, 'Poor Jack.' One arm around his neck and kissing his forehead, she held her breasts against his chest, their thighs aching with desperation. After two, three convulsive heaves, Emilie and Flynt were overwhelmed in an agony of delight. When they were first married, she'd not moved a muscle, lying like a log, inviting him to be done. Now she lusted, abandoning herself to a pleasure it was not in her nature to enjoy.

'I mean afterwards… after you, huh, made love,' said Rouselle butting in on Flynt's memories.

'We talked about making a fresh start and all that stuff until I realised that meant living here. Emilie refused to leave the kids at the school. Why, I couldn't figure out. It was not as if they were hers. She was expecting me to move to Île d'Iroise… that cultural thing again.'

'Do you mean she was indoctrinated?' interrupted Rouselle.

'Perhaps. Something was hurting her but she didn't say what. I told her that if the Bretons wanted to keep their bloody language it wouldn't be at my expense. That did it. She leapt at me, pushed me aside, dressed quickly and raced down the stairs and out through the front door shouting that I didn't understand. I went after her.'

Stepping outside, Flynt was blinded by security lights before he saw Emilie heading off across the sandy inlet between the craggy purple rocks looming on either side. There were no rivers on Île d'Iroise, only ditches draining off the heath. One of these, stained and tainted by peat, tumbled into the back of the inlet at Port Maria. In winter it was a fierce little stream, in summer a trickle meandering across large white pebbles between deep ferns and croaking frogs. Emilie was skipping across the stream towards the path climbing up to the cliff, her red dress sticking to her body like clingfilm. Breathing heavily he closed the gap, the path rocky and slippery. 'Emilie... wait... wait. Let's talk.' She probably never heard, his shout snatched away by the wind.

'When I got closer I reached out to grab her shoulder,' he told the magistrate. 'I was only a yard away but she slipped and stumbled... so did I. We went over the edge together. I caught hold of a gorse bush, banging my head, scratching my arms and legs. Emilie fell on to the rocks below.'

'Did you push her, Mr Flynt?' Rouselle fired the question, as interested in Flynt's reaction as the answer.

'I never touched her,' Flynt snapped back. 'The cliff is eighty, hundred metres... she didn't stand a chance. All we found was a piece of red dress snagged on the gorse.'

'You reported the accident?' Rouselle asked.

'To whom? No police on the island. I spent the night with the Brevilet brothers who telephoned the mainland the next morning. Herve Brevilet got some men together and we searched all next day. The tide must have washed the body out to sea.'

Rouselle shuffled through the papers on the Formica-topped table. 'According to the *médecin légiste* – what you call a pathologist – the injuries your wife sustained are consistent with the fall on to the rocks and pummelling by the sea. But did you snatch at her shoulder, cause her to stumble? Easily done, wouldn't you agree?'

'No... I've already told you. Lan Brevilet will vouch for that.' The evidence of the younger brother was crucial. He'd told Flynt afterwards he was looking for some lost sheep by flashlight. Flynt found that hard to believe but didn't argue. Lan had pulled him to safety from the gorse and found that piece of fabric torn from Emilie's red dress.

'Thank you, M Flynt... I'd like to hear now from Lan Brevilet and then his brother.' Rouselle was shuffling through his papers again. 'Yes… according to what I have here the brothers recovered the body a month later after it washed ashore.'

Returning to his seat, Flynt was apprehensive when Lan Brevilet opted to take the oath in Breton in accordance with Article 407 of the French Penal Code, the same Article that allowed Flynt to give his evidence in English. The clerk stood up, waiting to interpret.

'No need,' snapped Rouselle. 'M Lan Brevilet is well able to speak French. The court provides interpreters but only for those not proficient in our language, and at my discretion. The purpose of these proceedings is to establish the circumstances surrounding the death of Emilie Quatrevents. Dialogue between witnesses and the magistrate should be, as far as possible, direct.' Smiling at his clerk, Rouselle added, 'The intervention of even the most experienced interpreter still involves the risk of statements being misconstrued. My discretion is reserved for those who do not understand or speak French well enough. M Flynt was such a witness. M Brevilet knows full well that the language of the Republic is French, a language in which he is perfectly competent. You are bilingual, so take the oath, M Brevilet.' Rouselle could have been reading from a script but was not prepared for what was coming.

Lan Brevilet turned towards his brother Herve standing at the back with a bunch of others in their muddy brown dungarees. They've planned something, thought Flynt. The bastards were about to let him fry just to make a cultural point. Without Brevilet's corroboration, Rouselle would almost certainly refer the case to the criminal investigation department.

'Come on feller, give me a break,' blurted Flynt.

'M Flynt, let me handle this,' said the magistrate. Then turning back to Brevilet, 'You will be in contempt if you do not give your evidence in…' at which point Brevilet started spouting Breton.

'I was looking for some sheep when I saw M Flynt chasing after a woman in a red dress…' the clerk translated.

'No, no, no,' Rouselle cut in. 'Tell him he must give his evidence in French otherwise he'll be reported to the *police judiciaire* and prosecuted for contempt.'

Brevilet's reply was to join his brother in a walk-out, leaving the question of Flynt's involvement in Emilie's death unresolved.

A hearing that should have ended by midday was adjourned, sabotaged by a bunch of cultural nationalists. Flynt was furious. His remonstrations with the departing Bretons having no effect, he turned his rant on the magistrate, railing against a French legal system that failed to recognise that quarter of a million spoke Breton. Flynt had never cared much about their situation, was dismissive of their plight. But that wouldn't stop him making a U-turn if it served his interests to be hypocritical. The French were a bunch of cultural barbarians he railed, until stopped by a restraining hand on his shoulder. 'I know how you feel,' said Lebrun, 'but there's history to our little drama.'

Flynt frowned at the man he'd written off as a drunk. 'Besides the stroke,' said Lebrun, 'I also suffer from narcolepsy. I can fall asleep anywhere, anytime. While I'm still awake perhaps you'd join me for coffee.'

Flynt and Lebrun were drinking the usual muddy coffee at the Hôtel du Port when Rouselle arrived, spitting blood. 'Cancelled… the ferry is cancelled… they say the weather's bad.' Angrily, he thrust a printed notice in Flynt's face as if somehow he was to blame before rushing away to find others to harangue. The sky was hidden behind a broad expanse of grey, splashes of blue breaking through the drabness at the edges. Sheets of foam and spray leaped above the stone piers at the harbour entrance. A pretty normal day for Île d'Iroise.

Lowering his voice, Lebrun said, 'You heard him. I know

Rouselle. He'll have the lot for contempt and, if he can, send a gunboat from the Seine to remind the rest about the constitution.'

'Would you, Lebrun? Send a gunboat?'

Lebrun stroked his chin but didn't answer instead asking, 'Your wife will be buried here, on the island?'

'Yes, that's what Emilie would have wanted. I'll ask the British Consul in Brest to make the arrangements when that bloody magistrate releases the body. Anyhow, why are you really here, Lebrun?'

'Just looking…'

'Not for the ghost of your wife, surely… and what possible interest can you have in Emilie?'

'I don't… only who pushed her.'

'She wasn't… she slipped and fell. You heard me tell the magistrate. You're not here for Emilie… nor are you hallucinating. Christ man, you can barely cross the road! The real reason, please. No bullshit.'

Lebrun grimaced, his face as black as hell. 'They're not all dead… the Bezen Perrot.' Flynt waited to see where Lebrun was heading.

'They murdered my father, you know.' Lebrun must have been a kid, only three or four during the Second World War when the Bezen Perrot became executioners for the Waffen-SS. But the French had revenge and with interest.

'He was in the Resistance, working in the fields, planting potatoes during the day and sabotaging the Nazis at night. But a Bezen Perrot traitor got him in the end and the Gestapo hanged him upside down from a telegraph pole. You've heard of Locminé?'

Flynt had. 'Didn't the Gestapo massacre the village?'

'No… the Bezen Perrot did. They left the bodies to rot, then swept the remains into a ditch after the buzzards had finished.

An old woman survived. After the war she told the tribunal the executioners were Bezen Perrot fanatics wearing Waffen-SS uniforms.' Seventy years later Lebrun was still consumed with hate.

He'd known nothing of this until returning to France from England where he and his English mother had spent the war years living with an aunt in the Cotswolds, his war the occasional thump-thump of distant ack-ack guns, a night sky chipped blood red and fiery orange around the edges. The nearest the young Joseph Lebrun got to the enemy was a Luftwaffe pilot sitting beside his crashed plane in a ploughed field nursing a broken leg and waving a white handkerchief. Otherwise, wartime summers in England were warm and gentle, cornfields ripening in the summer sun, the River Avon wandering lazily under sycamores, crackling across boulders and spilling into pools where Joseph tickled trout.

'And you learned to speak English, fluently... must have helped when you got home.'

'I was employed in the justice branch of Fonction Publique Française, the French Civil Service.'

The 'bird-watchers' were back, dumping their backpacks at the hotel entrance. 'So what do you make of 'em?' asked Flynt.

'To tell you the truth they're not bird-watchers.'

'I guessed that much,' said Flynt. Behind Lebrun's pain-filled eyes, the robot-like motions and sleeping sickness, Flynt saw someone to trust.

Hôtel du Port had heard about the ferry cancellation. Chicken frizzled on a spit and freshly-caught mackerel was grilling in an open fireplace. The meal that evening was quite excellent, Lebrun nodding off again but not before asking, 'Did you hear anything unusual last night?'

'Only what I thought were a couple of gunshots. When I looked out I saw the remains of a flare falling from the sky.'

'Anything else?'

'A fog-horn, but don't they moan? This pinged.'

'Some do ping. That's all... nothing else?

'Except my phone. It rang again.' Flynt didn't mention the footsteps in the night.

Chapter 10

THERE WAS NO mystery about the clatter of boots next morning – men's studded boots, women's light ones, and the clump, clump of children's all moving in the same direction. Overnight the harbour was transformed, the trawlers back, quay filling with boxes of lobsters for the mainland. That, thought Flynt, nibbling on a croissant and swallowing his coffee quickly, could only mean the ferry would be running – except it was Sunday and nothing moved in Brittany on Sunday.

Lebrun was already about, watching from the hotel entrance the islanders gathered on the quay below, the women in traditional red-and-black checked skirts hanging over the harbour's stone parapet smiling and joking with the fishermen. And there was the pig. Among the bustle, an old woman struggled to drag a pig off the quay and up the hill, the air filled with grunts and groans and blood-curdling squeals.

'Like another century,' purred Lebrun. 'You can feel the sense of community, the tug of their roots,' he whispered to Flynt. 'Nothing changes, no matter what we do. We banned their language and beat their children when they dared speak it. When that failed we said they worshipped their standing stones.'

Flynt's impression was of a film set, the pig woman an excerpt from the Hollywood musical *Seven Brides for Seven Brothers* which he saw as a kid. But was Lebrun right – that the islanders and their language survived purely because their remoteness defied corrupting influences?

The lyricism evaporated for Flynt when he spotted a small girl leading a mongrel on a rope amongst the crowd on the quay… begging. Every now and then she handed her tiny haul to a middle-aged woman, perhaps her mother, although she was fair, the child dark with long hair curling around a sickly, pasty face, red rims framing tired eyes. To Flynt, the child looked hungry. He'd seen something similar in Africa – her pencil-thin legs inside long black stockings barely able to carry the weight of her heavy boots. Again and again she was sent off into the crowd, pulling at coats to attract attention while the woman watched. There was something about that pale pathetic face. Not once did the woman reward her with a word or smile despite the child tugging at her skirt. At last the kid gave up trying and, squatting on the quayside, buried her head in the tangled coat of her old black mongrel.

'What do you make of that?' said Flynt, pointing to the girl. 'Not quite picture-perfect. Begging is the same in every culture.'

Lebrun shook his head. 'I've not seen that before. I wouldn't have thought they were short of money. Look at all that lobster.'

No matter what Lebrun said of the islanders, how they refused to bend to France, their way of life frozen in time, Île d'Iroise would, for Flynt, be synonymous with that child.

'The church…' Lebrun was on the move, albeit slowly. 'But I expect you'll want to visit the house at Port Maria. I imagine you own it now… or will when the court decides. Legally you're her next of kin.'

'No… not until this mess is sorted out,' said Flynt, 'and I can get on with my life.'

Flynt followed the Frenchman, he nattering on about how the islanders were devout Roman Catholics, a priest crossing from the mainland to say mass at the greyish-pink Gothic pile shielded from Atlantic storms by a circle of stiff green pines. A pair of skate-boarders were launching themselves into the square from the steps of St Anne's, its arched entrance framed by clumps of green fern sprouting from stone niches. A dog growled in the darkness beyond the weathered door.

'Wow! What's that?' Flynt exclaimed, stopping at the top of the steps.

'Rotting fish,' said Lebrun. A pile of evil-smelling fish boxes was stacked near the font just inside the entrance. Instead of holy water, the font was filled with human litter. If Lebrun was right about the Bretons clinging to their religion and icons, then why use their church for storing fish and dumping rubbish? That didn't fit with all that piety, the islanders crossing muddy fields and rushing torrents for Sunday mass. And where were the grave, sad, prayerful women in black, lighting candles and clinging to their memories?

The stained-glass window above the altar at the far end of the nave cast a solitary pool of light, the brilliant reds, purples and blues of St Anne, the Breton patron saint, smiling benignly upon her absent congregation. Elsewhere the gloom was all embracing, no white altar-cloth, no *lumino*, the ever-burning lamp.

'No candles either!' exclaimed Lebrun. 'And the pews have gone.' The church had been stripped, the stone floor bare but for the debris left behind by looters.

Lebrun ran his finger across the rough cold stone surface of the altar. 'Not neglected,' he said, holding up a thick layer of dust, 'abandoned!' The Frenchman's voice choked. 'I was last here with my wife. It was the saint's day, the church full… we knelt with the congregation, hands clasped, at peace with each other and the world. Alice died the following month. She was sick for only a few weeks. I cursed everyone and God for not diagnosing the cancer sooner. But this…' Lebrun held his arms out in dismay. 'I would not have wished this on the church, even then.'

Flynt had seen enough and was heading for the door when Lebrun called him over to a small side chapel. 'St Stanislaus,' he said, 'the statue… gone!' The saintly monk with cowl and shaven head was familiar to a long-lapsed Catholic like Flynt. 'Françoise d'Amboise.' Lebrun pointed to another empty alcove, the statue of the nun-saint, arms full of lilies, now broken off at the ankles. The Frenchman shook his head sadly. 'The islanders can't survive without their statues,' he said, 'need more than a vague Christ, a vague Virgin, vague saints interpreted by priests.'

The skateboarders had gone and taken their yapping dog. Stepping from the dark interior Flynt saw that the wind had dropped, the weather changing, the square flooding with sunlight. With luck the ferry would be running. Closing the church door on the scene of desecration, Lebrun shuddered at the graffiti scrawled across the wooden frame in thick black letters:

'*Bisclaverët!*'

'*Werwolf*... isn't that what you said it means?' Lebrun nodded. 'One moment devout Christians, now... what do you call animal worship?'

'Zoomorphism, deities depicted in animal form.'

'Weren't the Egyptians into that big time?'

'Yes, but not the Bretons. Some may once have believed in *Bisclaverët*... that they did leave food and drink for their shape-changing brothers. But worship them as gods, no!'

'Maybe they crossed the line?' Lebrun, intent on examining the graffiti, didn't answer. 'I don't think so,' he replied eventually. 'The umlauts – the two dots above the vowel...'

'I don't follow.'

'Umlauts are used in Breton and German to indicate a sound shift... draws two vowels closer together. Take a look,' said Lebrun nodding at the graffiti.

'Yes. I see dots... over an 'e'... so what?'

'The wrong 'e'... should be over the second.'

'So the graffiti artist made a mistake.'

'Or didn't know the difference. And strictly speaking the Breton spelling doesn't have a second 'e' at all – it's *Bisclavret.*'

They'd left the church and were crossing the square when Flynt sang out, 'Here they come.' The banker type and his associate barely acknowledged their existence as they hurried up the steps of St Anne's, stopping to photograph the graffiti.

'What would you say they're up to?' asked Flynt.

'Looking for wreckage, I suppose.'

'How would you know that?'

'Don't you read the newspapers?'

'Of course... every day... we get 'em in the office,' replied Flynt.

'Only the Paris newspapers, I imagine.'

'We're only interested in major French stories.'

'So you're unlikely to report bodies washing up on the Brittany coast?'

People were always getting drowned, hardly of interest to an international news agency. 'What are you trying to say?'

It was the Frenchman's turn to shake his head. 'That you can't have read *Ouest-France*. In the last month *Ouest-France* has reported bodies and wreckage washing up at different places along the Brittany coast, including Île d'Iroise. That's why our friends are here... looking.' Lebrun cocked his head towards the pair standing on the church steps taking photographs of the graffiti.

INS would want more than unexplained bodies on the seashore to put a story on the wire. 'Tell me more.'

'If you ask you'll find your agency already knows,' Lebrun continued, 'has received what you call a D-notice. We have something similar, a Government directive preventing publication of certain matters on the grounds of national security.'

'In which case you can tell me what you know about the bodies... since I can't use it.' Lebrun was right. There was no way around a D-notice even if Flynt tried. Yates wouldn't let him near the wire, while New York would shit bricks if it knew Flynt was sticking his nose into a security matter. The most he could do was tuck it away for another day, although some D-notices were never lifted.

'The bodies are the crew of one of our fisheries patrol vessels which sank not far from here.' Flynt was about to ask why that was a matter of national security when Lebrun added, 'OK, ships sink all the time. That's what the sea does, especially in the Bay of Biscay. But this went down on a quiet night, the sea dead calm. One moment it was there, the next a thousand pieces, torpedoed, some believe.'

Lebrun had no need to mention any of this, certainly not offer an explanation unless to lead Flynt in a particular direction. 'The Russians,' suggested Flynt. Lebrun shook his head. 'Don't get carried away... that's why the bird-watchers are here... looking for the evidence. There's nothing for you to report... remember we have the Bastille for those who do.' Flynt knew when he was being used, encouraged to take a closer look.

'You're asking me to write about this?'

'Not at all... not for publication... background only.'

'Background for what...?'

Lebrun didn't say. By now they were at the harbour, the quay deserted, the catch loaded, the ferry preparing to sail that evening. For a broken old man moving at a snail's pace and in the habit of nodding off in mid-conversation, Lebrun seemed exceptionally well-informed.

'And you know the bird-watchers?'

'Not personally, their type.'

'That must mean you're Renseignements Généraux, French intelligence.'

'I was once.'

'So you're not retired – no more the time-served Quai d'Orsay penpusher looking for the ghost of your wife,' said Flynt.

'I'm on gardening leave... just like you.'

'And that brings you to Île d'Iroise. Isn't Moscow a better place to look for an itchy Russian finger?'

Quai d'Orsay had not said one of its ships was missing, nor had Lebrun said why the pair posing as 'bird-watchers' were photographing *Werwolf* graffiti on the church door. On the ferry back to Brest, Flynt found a corner in the saloon and made a detailed note of what Lebrun had said, as well as he could remember.

Chapter 11

OPENING HIS LAPTOP and flicking the metal cap off a bottle of Stella with a practised thumb, Flynt sat at the window of his third-floor apartment, drinking and thinking. Paris was enjoying a burst of late autumn sunshine, humidity high, blinds motionless, the apartment's primeval air-conditioning noisy and ineffective.

The woman on the Bakelite was vaguely familiar to Flynt, not the voice, but the words. He'd seen 'Help! He's trying to kill me' splashed across the front page of a newspaper in large black type. Where? Not France. The Bureau took only a daily digest of the top French stories, and one copy of the *International Herald Tribune* which Yates usually snaffled to read at home. If the headline existed then Flynt would find it.

Turning over stones was what he did best, the Flynt by-line bomb-proof even if it meant his dogged research was a pain in the arse for news editors in a hurry. Only once was he slapped with a writ – and then because of a re-write man's incompetence, not his.

After trawling the Internet for five hours, Flynt had only dark spots swimming before his eyes, the room heaving like the deck of a ship. He'd give it another hour, focus on the red tops, 'Help! He's trying to kill me' more tabloid than broadsheet. But London's *Daily Gazette* and *Daily News* yielded only Page Three girls, their tits basking in fifteen minutes of fame stimulating Flynt's interest in female company. Then he got lucky. The *New York Post,* the *Gazette*'s stablemate, had published a few paragraphs on an inside page headlined 'Help! He's trying to kill me' – the last words, it said, spoken by a woman lying in a coma in a London hospital after a motor accident. No attribution, no source, nor was the headline the size Flynt recalled. Was it possible the London *Gazette* had published it first, that he'd missed it on his first trawl through the online archive? Newspapers in the same group often exchanged stories, and not always contemporaneously. Click, click, and he had it, not on the front page but splashed across the *Gazette*'s centrefold in 80-point Franklin Gothic Black two months before it crossed the Atlantic. That happened. News was not always as instant as newpapers pretended!

Helen Brenton had been in a coma for eighteen months at the west London Royal Hospital. Her car had hit a tree while driving home late one night. Not much there. Motorists were often killed by trees. The stand-out angle on the Brenton story was that a girlfriend, Julia Cross, was reported as having said she received a call from Brenton on her mobile just before the accident saying someone was trying to kill her. The police investigated but decided Brenton must have fallen asleep at the wheel; that no-one wanted to kill her. Anyhow, she was in a coma and, according to the story, unlikely to recover.

Flynt was trying to fathom how the message found its way on to his Bakelite when it rang – at least that's what he thought, scrambling to answer. No voice, nothing, not even the crackle of static.

Someone in the street below was leaning on the bell of his apartment.

'Yes,' he snapped into the intercom.

'Jack, it's me. Let me in.'

The woman spoke English with a sweet French accent.

'Who is it?'

'Help! He's trying to kill me.'

Flynt shuddered in the darkness, the only light the anglepoise above the laptop. Creeping across the room he pressed his nose against the window pane. The caller was hidden by the porch above the entrance to the apartment block. His street was not far from Boulevard de Clichy, leading down from the Moulin Rouge, hookers, and sex shops. Gullible tourists having been parted from their money occasionally drifted in Flynt's direction, as did hookers who on slack nights resorted to cold calling.

'Go away,' Flynt bellowed.

'Help! He's trying to kill me,' croaked the voice again.

A chill premonition sprang from the dark recesses of the room. Steadying himself, Flynt whispered, 'What do you want for Christ's sake?' Heavy breathing was seeping up the intercom, no longer disembodied but as real as the cold sweat on his brow. With a leaden finger Flynt pressed the entry buzzer, allowing the woman into the lobby and access to his third floor apartment. The elevator clunked past the first, then the second before shuddering to a halt. The door screeched open on rusty hinges.

The knock was hesitant, not a hammered threat. Flynt flung the apartment door wide open and barked, 'What the fuck do you want?' at the young woman propped against the door frame. She was dark, dishevelled and pissed, a lock of hair drifting across one blue eye, the mascara from the other wandering down a cheek bruised by whoever had slapped her around. Staggering into the apartment, she flung herself at Flynt sobbing, 'He's trying to kill me', repeating it until he sat her on the sofa and pressed a large Cognac into her hand.

The stray off the Paris streets wore the uniform of a Pigalle hooker – short, short pea-green skirt, see-through blouse and skyscraper heels, the ensemble screaming, 'If you wanna come in you'll have to pay!' The large black handbag swinging from a shoulder was not a fashion accessory. It packed the machine for swiping credit cards a dozen times a night perhaps.

She was in her twenties, sitting quite still, listening to Flynt's rant about invading his privacy. When he stopped for breath, she hurried across to the window and searched the road below, eyes filling with tears.

Of average height, thick, deep black hair, her lipstick was too red and flashy, complexion too white.

'Who's trying to kill you?' he asked. She answered with a sickly groan, Flynt pointing to the bathroom before an evening's carousing was ejected across the carpet. He heard the shower running and minutes later the door flew open, the woman wrapped in a bath towel looking for a bed and asleep on his before he could object. Climbing in beside her Flynt would throw her out the next morning.

The sound of violent retching woke him an hour later, a naked figure stumbling from the bathroom and collapsing on him like a sack of flour. Nothing that was sexually recognisable moved, no matter how hard he pressed for attention, until she mumbled, 'Go away old man, go away.' Passion extinguished, Flynt would get his name taken off the intercom panel the next morning.

Her name was Monique, her hangover of Everest proportions, and the person trying to kill her, Jean Luc.

'Husband... boyfriend?'

She hesitated, reluctant to say and then spat it out like a curse, 'My pimp!' Flynt was relieved his clumsy foreplay of the night before had ended only in heavy snoring. Monique had been busy – not sure how many men because of the numbing effect of champagne cocktails in some sleazy club. Exhausted and desperate for sleep, she fled after rowing with a dirty, dangerous client who was slapping her around because she refused to give him what he wanted. Monique didn't do blow jobs, she reminded Flynt sternly, which he thought odd, hookers usually offering a blow at half-price.

From Boulevard de Clichy Monique had staggered along some side streets, dark and deserted until, seeing a solitary light in an apartment window, gatecrashed Flynt's life.

'I think you had better leave. I'll call a taxi.'

'No, I stay. I'll pay.'

'I'm not buying… out,' at which Monique locked herself in the bathroom, screaming through the door, 'The Corsican will kill me.'

The poor wretch had taken one beating. Another could kill her, the pimp sure to hand out a hammering for going AWOL. That's what pimps did when girls stepped out of line. 'OK… you can stay… until you find somewhere else.' With that promise Monique opened the bathroom door.

Next morning, after several black coffees, Flynt reneged, picked her up bodily and dumped her in the elevator, pressing the button for the ground floor, and shouting, 'Go away'. The last he heard was the clip-clop of Monique's high heels as she hit the street, calling a taxi on her mobile from the corner. Minutes later a cab arrived and she was gone like a bad dream – but not Flynt's worst dream. The Bakelite was ringing again, not the loud, embarrassing chimes that reverberated around the dining room at the hotel on Île d'Iroise, but two, three barely audible rings. Snatching up the receiver, the now familiar voice delivered its message through the static before the line went dead.

Flynt had no time for the paranormal, the spike on his office desk the only place for stories about Christ's Second Coming in Fulham High Street. The subconscious was in much the same league. The idea that Helen Brenton's disembodied voice had escaped a deeply traumatised sleep to cry for help on his Bakelite was certain to end a beautiful career. 'Alcoholic hallucination' would expedite his dismissal if the office got to know.

That evening Monique was back, ringing the bell and pleading to be let in. No matter how much Flynt bellowed down the intercom, threatening and cajoling, the girl refused to leave. The next he knew she was at his apartment door having hung around the pavement the way hookers did before slipping into the lobby as another tenant left. Besides the previous night's bruises she'd acquired a large black, bloodshot eye and an injured right hand which she carried like a broken wing. Monique couldn't make a fist, her eyes feverish, shaking on her feet after taking a beating from the Corsican for not spending long enough on her back. Flynt imagined a scrawny individual in an ill-fitting double-breasted white lightweight summer suit with an earring in his dick and a passion for knocking chunks out of women. A specialist in his field, the pimp would target the stomach and thighs, the sight of damaged goods not good for business. Jean Luc was about to slam his bony elbow into Monique's midriff when she ducked and took it in the face. For ducking and damaging the window display, Luc held a finger in a doorjamb, closing it slowly until it almost snapped. After that Monique fled with only the clothes on her back and a fifty-euro note to cover that night's street expenses. Not even Flynt could throw her out again.

'OK… a few days, until you find somewhere, with your family perhaps. You have family?'

'*Oui, monsieur*… doesn't everyone?'

Flynt sniffed. 'What's your name then?'

'Monique.'

'I mean surname.'

The girl was suddenly so young and vulnerable. Smiling shyly through the assorted bruises and scratches, she replied, 'Monique Jones.'

'What?' Flynt roared, 'bloody Welsh get everywhere.'

After his first good laugh in months, Flynt discovered that

Monique's Breton mother met her Welsh father on holiday in Brest. 'So I suppose you speak Breton?' He was expecting a 'no' because the language was dying but got a 'yes' – learned at her mother's knee and English at her father's. After her mother died, Monique said her father changed, became austere, silent and reserved, leaving Monique to her own devices.

'Not easy for you,' said Flynt, a dab hand at commiserating when, what he really meant was how she wound up on the game. 'You must have been quite lonely,' he suggested.

Monique wiped away a tear. 'I cried myself to sleep,' she said, fishing for sympathy but not saying how she fell into the arms of the Corsican. She must have been a real catch, a prize asset, before the pimp became heavy-handed. Not even the scratches and bruises could hide the femme fatale, the jet-black hair tumbling in massive bands around her white neck, eyes deep blue, voluptuous, with long and silky eyelashes arched beneath finely-pencilled brows. Monique's gracefully rounded shoulders and faultless bust were contours some women would kill for, Flynt very tempted to fling caution aside, let her pay for board and lodging.

'You sleep on the sofa.' He pointed to a large, dirty brown monster with overwrought springs that screeched like an orchestra's string section tuning up. 'I'm in the bed… and you'd better see a doctor about that hand.' Returning from a pee a few minutes later, he found Monique sound asleep – in his bed. Recalling her drunken ramblings about being a no-go area for 'old men', Flynt settled for a noisy night, the words of the young hooker cutting deeper than the violins playing on his spine.

Sleep was elusive. After an hour trying, he left the sofa and switched on the laptop. The *Gazette* had published a number of follow-up stories about the Brenton woman, updates on her condition, the most recent three weeks ago reporting that her husband had successfully applied to the High Court to end artificial feeding so that his wife could 'die with dignity'. That was what she would have wished, David Brenton told the judge. They'd discussed the subject, albeit hypothetically, on several occasions before the accident.

Flynt gathered that in the majority of cases coma patients regained consciousness in about six weeks, those who didn't considered to be in a 'persistent vegetative state', not responding to stimuli even though they might still breathe without assistance. If there was no visible response after twelve months, the clinician's diagnosis was 'brain dead'. Helen Brenton had been insentient for longer and, although her husband agreed, her mother refused to let doctors withdraw artificial feeding. Recovery was still possible and Flynt found several accounts of patients who, unconscious and immobile for years, suddenly woke long enough to communicate with relatives, chat about current events, and watch television. But such recoveries were often short-lived and nearly always drug-induced, zolpidem, paradoxically a drug for treating insomnia, the one most commonly used. Researchers speculated that small doses of zolpidem reversed areas of the brain rendered dormant by injury. Not everyone agreed, suspecting that patients who recovered after treatment had been misdiagnosed.

The cessation of artificial feeding was a death sentence, most dying from starvation within two weeks. How could the husband agree to this – appoint himself executioner on the basis of a conversation over coffee and After Eights at some Kensington dinner party? Flynt had seen kids die in Africa, bellies bloated, tiny limbs as brittle as rotten branches, emaciated, tortured by flies, lips cracked and swollen, unable in their last days to swallow water offered by relief workers. Helen Brenton was being judicially murdered. Flynt had no difficulty imagining her slow death from starvation and thirst, suffering the same agonies as those African kids. Flynt shook his head, unable to escape the notion Brenton's subconscious had found a way into the real world. The thought that his Bakelite had become the conduit was too absurd.

Daylight was peeping between the blinds when Flynt felt a hand on his shoulder. 'Christ, don't do that,' he snapped, his hideous confusion not helped by the bleary-eyed hooker creeping up behind.

'Go away,' he said. 'I'm trying to work something out... I'd better...' Flynt's voice choked, exhausted by the inexplicable, his experience of real events no match for probing the nature of the unknown. 'I think I'm a bit loony,' he said in desperation, sharing his darkest fear with a hooker off the street.

'You look all right.'

'I have this hallucination... the phone... the black one on the table by the window... it rings.' Flynt knew this must sound absurd to someone who expected telephones to ring. Monique smiled and walked across, holding up the frayed cable falling from the back of the Bakelite.

'Oh, it rings all right. I've heard it,' insisted Flynt.

'A bad dream maybe. Leave the light on and it will go away.' Flynt shook his head incredulously. The hooker was talking as if he was a child afraid of the dark. What could this young kid know? It was pointless to have mentioned it. At least his madness might persuade her to leave sooner rather than later.

Monique looked at him squarely in the eyes. 'You should sleep... have the bed... and leave the light on.'

'There you go again... I'm not a bloody kid!' Flynt felt cold.

'When it rings... then what?' At that moment, the cuts and bruises of her trade meant Monique was closer to reality than Flynt.

'There's a woman on the line... sounds like a woman... lots

of static. That's why I let you in. She says exactly the same thing, "Help! He's trying to kill me".'

Monique didn't laugh. Instead, she picked up the heavy black receiver and listened. Nothing!

'I'm not stupid… can't afford to be in my job.' Monique hadn't said he was. 'I drink too much I agree, but only after the phone rings, not before.'

'Do you know anything about the woman?'

'Could be in a coma in a hospital in London… that's possible… but not what I think.' Flynt was sounding crazier by the second but needed to share his torment.

'Who else has heard the telephone?' How often had Flynt asked the same question!

'No-one… if only someone had!'

'You know this woman?'

'Only what I've read.' Clicking the keyboard, Flynt brought up the page from the *Gazette*. Monique stooped and kissed his forehead. Any second now she'd be tucking him into bed after he'd said his prayers. Instead she raised a hand and touched his cheek, the pale, beaten, tired-looking hooker not indifferent to his problem.

'Don't you think you should see someone?' Flynt knew this was coming. 'Probably stress.' He'd expected that as well. Everyone told him to slow down; that he lived entirely for his work, caring little for himself and appearance. But why invest in a sharp new suit when time was running downhill? Flynt had known a colleague who did, then dropped dead without anyone to hold his hand. When his apartment was emptied they found nothing personal, only twenty Aquascutum suits at £400 a throw, never worn, a new one added every year he was at the agency.

Flynt's obsession had almost killed him once before when, preoccupied with what he was writing, he failed to notice an office messenger slip lighter fluid into his coffee in retaliation for a reprimand. Flynt threw up across the newsroom floor but did finish the story. Afterwards he lay down to sleep and dream... of more stories.

Chapter 12

Yates was on the blower from INS next morning before Flynt was fully awake. '*Werwolf*, where is it?'

'It's coming… almost there. It's waited seventy years… another hour won't hurt.'

Yates said, 'In twenty minutes. I want it for the morning schedule. What you calling it?'

'"Hitler's stay-behinds" – but why the bloody hurry?'

'We've got company coming. I want it on the wire before he arrives. The *Chronicle* is sending someone over from London. A guy called Bill Dando. Know him?' Flynt did. They'd once worked together covering lowlife stories for the *Gazette*.

'You're to hold his hand. From what I gather he's never been beyond the M25.'

'I'm on gardening leave, remember. How long before I get paid off?' Yates guessed another couple of weeks before New York decided the package. 'In the meantime, pick-up Dando from the airport tomorrow and show him around. The *Chronicle*'s a valued subscriber. Don't screw up… and lay off the booze. I don't want them thinking INS employs piss artists!'

That was rich, thought Flynt. Yates was a drunk until INS paid to dry him out. New York was prevaricating because unless the package was spot-on it could all end in tears in a messy court case. Flynt's track record with INS was good, with a bunch of emails and letters to prove it. Dumping him because he forgot to hit the send button on his laptop would be difficult. A court might ask why Yates hadn't followed standard practice and chased Flynt for the story. 'Where's the story?' was carved on the forehead of every news editor, chasing recalcitrant reporters' part of the job description. Yates's aversion to the smell of liquor on a reporter's breath could be more about his own tussle with the demon drink than a sacking offence.

Dando was out of his depth the moment he heard a foreign language at Charles de Gaulle Airport. Only the *Chronicle* knew why it chose to send a novice. But it sometimes did that kind of thing, planting an acorn expecting a journalistic oak to grow.

'How can I help, Bill?' asked Flynt. The last he'd heard of Dando was that he was still doing 'kiss and tell' for the *Gazette.* 'The *Chronicle* must be a bit of a culture shock. How'd you manage the jump?'

Dando said, 'Tits, man!' Tits were all over the *Gazette* news schedule, mostly big ones waved in public. Dando struck lucky when he caught a cabinet minister playing with the wrong pair. Instead of phoning in the story to the *Gazette,* he emailed his resignation and swapped the story for a job on the *Chronicle* which grabbed at anything that undermined the government. Even Dando had reached the point where he couldn't face another story with cup size in the intro. But having not written anything much longer than six paragraphs for the *Gazette,* 'Mr Piggy' was about to be seriously challenged.

Mr Piggy was squat and square, Dando's jet-black hair curling over small piggy ears, a forelock wandering across a piggy eye set in a pink face, sweatier than usual after his brush with the language at French passport control. But why, Flynt wondered, had Dando chosen powder-blue for his first overseas sortie, the wings of his heavily-creased linen jacket pinned together by a single button at a bulging midriff? Perhaps he'd read that Frenchmen all wore powder-blue, were called Serge and had Riviera tans. After all, didn't they think the English were lager-swilling louts with their noses in bags of greasy chips?

Dando had started life as a newsagent phoning tip-offs until someone decided he might do even better on the pay-roll. 'Great stuff,' every story greater than the last, its news value always 'off the Richter Scale'. It never was until the politician's big tits scandal – and that got passed by the *Chronicle* desk to a real hack to polish.

Dando was affable enough, obliging so long as it served his interests. The resident hack was a natural port of call for a man on his first out-of-town job.

'Drink?' he asked as the cab pulled away from Charles de Gaulle.

Flynt said, 'Are you asking if it was the drink that got me suspended? Not really. Yates has been gunning for me... has a woman lined up to take my job.'

Dando said, 'No, I was suggesting we had a chat over a drink, Jack.' Flynt looked at his watch. Too early but what the hell! By the time they reached the Press Bar it would be happy hour somewhere in the world.

Once settled over their Stella, Flynt asked again, 'So what brings you to Paris?'

'This.' From a black Samsonite briefcase, Dando dug out a file stamped DECLASSIFIED.

'Snap,' said Flynt. 'I've got one too. Why is everyone suddenly interested in *Werwolf*? There's nothing in the story.'

Dando half-smiled, the way he did when suspecting someone was throwing a dummy pass. 'You filed this for INS.' Dipping again into his briefcase Dando produced a cutting headlined 'Hitler's stay-behinds' – Flynt's INS story about diehard Nazis who stayed behind to sabotage the Allies after Germany surrendered.

Flynt said, 'I never found any, only some rusty rifles belonging to the Resistance. *Werwolf* is just a name, nothing new.'

Dando said, 'I've been told to take a look at an office in 12 Byron Street? Do you know where that is, mate?'

'You mean Rue Lord Byron,' replied Flynt.

'Is it far?'

'Not really… a short cab ride. But what are you expecting to find?'

'I don't know. I'll have to take a look.'

Flynt said, 'So you're just doing the legwork, checking out the address?'

Dando replied, 'And I write the story.'

Flynt knew the drill. Rue Lord Byron was a loose end. Some smart arse on the *Chronicle* News Desk was working up a story. Flynt didn't want to wait until Yates rang after midnight and sent him to check out the *Chronicle*'s first edition lead. Better if he saw what Dando filed.

'Let's get a cab and take a look,' he said.

Dando scratched his ear. 'Suits me… we'll work together. You have the lingo and I the lead.'

Dando went to his briefcase again for a bottle of duty-free twelve-year-old double malt. 'That's for your co-operation.'

Weighing the bottle in his hand, Flynt smiled 'Have you done anything like this before… a feature?'

Dando shook his head. 'The *Chronicle* expects every man… I'll manage, always have… with a little bit of help from my friend.'

'And when does the desk expect delivery?'

'Tonight by six UK time. That's seven o'clock Paris, correct?'

Flynt smiled through clenched teeth. 'OK… I'll give you a hand… but nothing is sent until we agree the angle… OK?'

'You're the man, Jack… trust me.'

Flynt grinned. There was no answer to that.

Rue Lord Byron was set amongst some of the most expensive real estate in Paris behind the Champs-Élysées, a twenty-euro taxi ride from the Press Bar.

Number 12 was a stone-built neo-classical villa from the early nineteenth century, six floors, all with ornate wrought iron balconies painted glossy black. The poet Byron once lived thereabouts, hence the name. An apartment on Rue Lord Byron made a hefty dent in the wallet, although it was now mostly commercial, companies vying for an address in the prestigious Quartier Champs-Élysées, their names inscribed on iron plates set firmly on the wall. Number 12 carried a dozen nameplates, all highly-polished except for one. Flynt assumed the office was empty until scraping away the rust with a euro coin he read: 'Société Commerciale d'Affrètements et de Commission'. The name meant nothing to Flynt. Dando grinned.

'That's what the desk said I'd find. Someone got the name from… what do you call Companies House in France?'

'SARL – Société à responsabilité limitée – register for limited liability companies.'

Dando said, 'The search came up with this.' He pulled a slip of paper from his pocket.

Flynt read, 'Société Commerciale d'Affrètements et de Commission, 12 Lord Byron Street.'

'A front,' continued Dando, 'for a big shot French black-marketeer called Radenac during the last war.' Flynt's jaw sagged as he held up a finger to stop Dando in mid-sentence. 'It still exists, the company?'

'We've got some smart hacks at the *Chronicle*,' Dando replied.

Somehow they'd discovered the name and address redacted from the declassified correspondence between Deuxième Bureau and MI5 in the *Werwolf* file. How, Flynt had no idea, only that he'd walked right past, distracted by a ringing telephone and a bunch of bloody-minded Bretons.

Dando said, 'The office thought it might have been flattened during the war. Let's take a look inside.'

Flynt leaned on the bell at La Société Commerciale and waited for the concierge but got no answer. 'Knock up some neighbours.' Dando was quite good at that, setting off along the road, rattling letterboxes and banging knockers without success. 'They won't answer unless they see the colour of your eyes or have a concierge... the French way.'

'Let's try the pub.' They headed for the posh-looking bistro on the corner where a bored waiter was laying tables for lunch, the only customer a middle-aged manual type in a dog-eared navy blue woollen jacket that didn't chime with the ornate chandeliers and moulded frescoes. The man sat at the bar picking at a large steak tartare washed down with slugs of beer from a bottle of dark Abbaye de Leffe.

'What's he eating,' asked Dando, sliding on to a stool.

'Ground beef,' said Flynt. 'No! More like ground horse mixed with egg yolk.'

'And this in the land of the *Mona Lisa*,' exclaimed Dando. 'Looks like something, I've recycled after a heavy night.'

'The beer is good.' Flynt ordered two. 'Enjoy, while I have a go at this guy... might know something... looks as if he works around here.'

A good way to strike up a conversation with a stranger was to show you shared the same tastes. Moving closer with his Abbaye de Leffe, Flynt uttered the immortal line, 'Do you speak English?'

Swallowing a mouthful of ground horse, the man nodded weakly, '*Un peu... un petit peu.*'

That's good enough, thought Flynt. 'Work here?' The man shrugged helplessly. Evidently Flynt had already hit upon the '*petit peu*' bit of his English vocabulary.

Flynt tried again with, '*Que faire?*'

'*Concierge,*' the man replied.

'*Concierge ici?*'

The man shook his head. '*Non, le bâtiment d'à côté.*' A hand flapped towards Rue Lord Byron.

Several beers later Flynt discovered he was drinking lunch with the concierge at Number 12 Rue Lord Byron. Much more than a security guard with the key to the front door, the concierge and his wife lived on the premises in some dingy back room, their noses in other people's business twenty-four hours a day.

The offices, said the concierge, were all occupied and their letterboxes emptied daily, except for La Société Commerciale. The company never had mail, nor had he seen anyone at the office in ten years. A fifty-euro note and the twist of an imaginary key between Flynt's fingers was met with a Gallic shrug and raised eyebrows before the concierge led the way out into Rue Lord Byron, Dando following until Flynt said, 'Wait here... I'll do this bit. Have another beer... read the paper.' He threw him a copy of an English-language free sheet for local ex-pats. Dando dithered, wary of letting Flynt get the jump on him. 'Don't worry. I won't pull a fast one. It's the concierge... he doesn't like the look of you.'

The office door opened with a single turn of the concierge's pass key, opening not into the dusty time capsule Flynt expected but a squeaky clean office with desktop computer, printer and fax. Crossing to the computer, Flynt brought up the company's home page. 'Christ! They run the ferry between Brest and Île d'Iroise,' he muttered to himself. Flynt's interest moved up a gear. At his back the concierge was shaking his head angrily for having been bypassed all these years.

'*Comptes*', Flynt recognised from his days as a city editor in London, meant La Société Commerciale's accounts. '*Compte bancaire*' was money the company had in the bank. 'Wow! Look at this. They're loaded.' The concierge was poking into cupboards and drawers and missed the million-plus euro figure set against the bank balance of a very small ferry company providing a limited service, one crossing a day, and then only if weather permitted. Lobster was expensive but surely couldn't account for all those zeros. 'Where's it coming from, the revenue?' Flynt asked himself.

'*Chiffre d'affaires annuel*' – the company's annual turnover – was another surprise. The ferry's biggest earner was '*les passagers à pied*' – foot passengers. Flynt calculated that in October, not the best month for visiting Île d'Iroise, the ferry carried 168 passengers, each paying more than he did when he'd crossed for the hearing into Emilie's death. Where were all these foot passengers? They couldn't have stayed at the hotel from hell with fewer than twenty beds. It had to be some kind of tax fiddle, Flynt decided.

The concierge dragged Flynt into the corridor, muttering angrily to himself as he locked the office door. But one word emerging from the low-level grumble spiked Flynt's interest. Flynt had learned not to overreact, to feign disinterest when something was said that pressed a button. The concierge's mention of 'Gestapo' did just that. Flynt's French would be tested to its limit if he was to discover the connection between the 'Gestapo' and 12 Rue Lord Byron.

Ten minutes later he was reasonably sure he had the story. During the Second World War the house in Rue Lord Byron was commandeered by the Nazis as a district headquarters and the Jewish owners dispatched to a concentration camp. When no-one came forward in 1945 to reclaim the property it was subsumed into the French national estate and the offices relet, except for that rented by La Société Commerciale which continued to trade from the address, although the end of the war must have put paid to 'business as usual'.

'What you got... what you got?' Dando was waiting expectantly at the bistro.

'Colour, only colour. The office is abandoned... a dusty time capsule – there's a line.'

Dando wasn't satisfied. 'What else apart from dust?'

Flynt said, 'How about Gestapo headquarters during the war… picture of Adolf on the wall. The *Chronicle* will love that. Then throw in the background.'

Flynt sat Dando down at a table and asked for his *Werwolf* file. 'Have you got a highlighter?' Dando handed him an orange one. After a few moments scanning pages and highlighting sentences, Flynt said, 'There you have it – 'Gestapo time capsule'. Work in what's highlighted and you've got a feature… writing by numbers!' Dando beamed. Flynt smiled to himself.

'Thanks, Jack. I owe you big time… how about this for starters?' Dando had ringed a story in the English-language free sheet about an Algerian who'd smuggled his girlfriend into France hidden inside a petrol tank. 'You're not going to lift that crap,' exclaimed Flynt. 'They make it up.'

'Sounds OK to me,' replied Dando.

'Not for the *Chronicle*.'

'I wasn't thinking of the *Chronicle*. I know lots who'll jump at it.'

'Well, if you still want my help forget it. The French have a big enough immigrant problem without you throwing petrol on the fire.' Dando tossed the newspaper aside. 'OK, a deal! Let's go back to your place to file.'

Dando's jaw dropped when Monique shimmied towards him like a sweet sixteen year old. Flynt smiled. Because he rarely had a woman around, some hacks thought he was a middle-aged gay. At least he could count on Dando to set the record straight when he got back to London.

'Monique… Bill Dando will be here an hour or so writing his story.' Flynt winced. The *Chronicle* hack had plonked his laptop on the table beside the Bakelite.

'Let me move that out of your way,' said Flynt, running a finger across his lips and staring hard at Monique. Stepping forward quickly she carried the demon telephone off to the bedroom where, wrapped in a blanket, it was stuffed in a drawer, out of sight and earshot.

An hour later, Dando, jacket off, sleeves flapping at the elbows, was still crouched over his laptop, struggling to get past par six, despite Flynt's crib sheet.

'You got problems?'

Dando nodded. 'Six pars… another fifteen to go.'

'Let me have a look… don't worry… not an INS story.'

Reluctantly, Dando let Flynt take a gander at his screen:

'In a swish Paris suburb off the Champs-Élysées yesterday I discovered the hide-out of one of the most notorious Second World War Nazi collaborators. The room from which Paul Radenac ran his black market empire is still there – a time capsule with a portrait of Adolph Hitler on the wall inside a smart Napoleonic apartment block.

'His hide-out once doubled as Gestapo Headquarters in Paris – and is now owned by the French Government whose Intelligence services have hunted Radenac, a war criminal, for seventy years.

'Radenac, a Breton, ran his rackets from Société Commerciale d'Affrètements et de Commission with an address in swish Rue Lord Byron, amassing a fortune from trading with the Nazis but fled just days before the Allies liberated Paris in August 1944. Amazingly, the office is still there, the nameplate rusting, the door locked and bolted – until I opened the time capsule, everything as Radenac left it when he escaped.

'Before fleeing to Argentina, Radenac and his Breton renegades laid down caches of weapons and explosives for German partisans to sabotage the Allies after the war. Some dumps have still to be found.'

'Not bad at all. Apart from one too many "swish" places, it's quite good. Now run in what I highlighted. It'll fit together nicely.'

Dando said, 'I'll have to source it… the *Chronicle* is fussy about sources. Not like the *Gazette*. Remember Jenks? The most he ever wanted was a 'no comment'. If you didn't have one he'd add it himself to cover our arses.'

Flynt told him, 'Attribute everything to the Public Records Office at Kew… and a "no comment" from French police. They never say a thing.'

After Dando had dealt with a call-back from his desk, Flynt stuffed him in a taxi. 'He'll just have to find his own way around the airport,' said Flynt, pouring himself a Stella.

Monique flew at Flynt the moment Dando left. 'Don't you ever eat?' she snapped. 'There's no food in the place, not a can… not an opener.' She'd been shopping while he was chaperoning Dando, her tits bouncing invitingly as she stretched to pack away cans and some ready-made meals. Add in the beat-up look and Flynt wondered what the neighbours thought of his house guest.

'You shouldn't have gone out, not looking like that,' he said. 'They'll think I've been knocking you around. Anyhow, why the food? I don't cook, not even an egg.' For him breakfast was croissant and coffee around the corner, lunch was liquid and dinner wherever the fancy took him after the Press Bar. Sometime, somewhere the agency would pick up the tab for feeding and watering him.

Moments later Monique was smiling again, fixing Flynt with laughing eyes, face captivating and engaging despite the scratches. Their spat forgotten, he said, 'We'll eat out… that's if you're staying.'

Somewhere special, he thought. Why not the Paris Ritz, where Princess Diana had her last supper before that crash?

'But I've nothing to wear.' Monique was no different to any other woman when it came to posh restaurants.

'Buy something,' said Flynt, pulling out a fifty-euro note.

Monique's nose twitched querulously and, frowning, he handed over another.

The Ritz restaurant overlooked a garden through large bay windows, the lighting subdued and the menu expensively glossy. Flynt imagined 'cover charge' meant what it cost to read the menu. As for the wine list, the cheapest bottle would have supplied him with one a day of his usual for a month.

Monique was distinctly uncomfortable at the attention of a gushing maître d'hôtel in white tie and tails, guiding her into an ornately upholstered chair and unfurling a table napkin with the flourish of an orchestral conductor. The crystal chandeliers, the embroidered tablecloth, and bewildering array of cutlery and goblets – the hotel monogram on everything that couldn't be nailed down – unsettled Monique.

Flynt said, 'We don't have to eat here.'

'No, no,' she whispered. 'I wouldn't want to go anywhere else… it's beautiful…' Her inhibitions evaporating, she soon warmed as if to the manor born, Flynt angry with himself for dwelling on all the men she'd fucked.

But that came naturally from hard-nosed hacks with a plot that read: pick-up, use, dump, move on. News waited for no-one, certainly not relationships. But behind the bloodied eye and weeping mascara Monique's still uncorrupted innocence rattled his emotions. Without his script Flynt was as a blind man excited by the touch of a strange new skin.

Monique would never be a wide-eyed nymph. She knew what she did but wasn't much interested in doing it. Above all else her deep conviction that life could only get better was inspiring, awakening Flynt's dormant sensibilities. He might never be her John Wayne, fighting the Indians attacking the wagon train. But it felt good to pretend.

It must have been his frown that gave the game away. 'You only see the men, is that right, Jack?' Monique fiddled nervously with her white linen table napkin. 'Have you not had lots of women, Jack? It's the same. Perhaps you paid sometimes?' Flynt had, several times before AIDS frightened the shit out of him.

'Tell me about them, the women. Your apartment is empty, cold, bare.'

'You mean the furniture… suits me.'

'I didn't mean that. There's nothing personal. No photographs of girlfriends, family… you must have family.'

'We're not in touch… only weddings and funerals. I have no need.'

Monique was sad for Flynt. 'We all need someone.'

Flynt shook his head. 'I keep my personal life here,' he said, tapping his head with a hand, 'not here,' hand on heart. For once his kneejerk response sounded empty. The noise that usually drowned out personal feelings wasn't there, leaving Flynt disorientated, filled with subtle uncertainties about their relationship. It was too much for him to fathom, only that he felt born again.

'But you've been married?'

'How did you know?'

'You screw like a married man.'

How could she tell? She hadn't let him, not yet.

'What happened to your wife?'

'She's dead but we hadn't lived together for years. We were only married a few months… in the living-together sense… never got a divorce. I didn't even know where she was.' Flynt sensed that behind Monique's inquisitiveness lay genuine care.

'Were there many girlfriends?' Flynt's eyes tightened, brow creasing like corrugated iron. Was it that obvious from his care-worn persona, the apartment devoid of memories that he spent most of his time alone?

'I don't really have girlfriends – partners sometimes. Sorry… I didn't mean it the way it sounds.'

'I don't always have sex either, Jack,' Monique replied, glancing quickly over her shoulder. It was early and the only other diner had his head buried in a newspaper. 'Most men are satisfied before… they can't help themselves…' That was too close to the knuckle for Flynt who was becoming similarly disadvantaged. Monique was sounding like a nurse helping senior citizens on and off the toilet!

But how about those clients who insisted on à la carte? Monique was a very lucky girl if she got through the night with only a damp sheet. Flynt hoped he wasn't like the guy who, zipping up his fly, asked sanctimoniously, 'What makes you do it, honey?' The guy never really cared – only asked to wash away the cheap perfume and lighten his remorse for cheating.

Flynt didn't ask how Monique got into the game, she volunteered, explaining how she came to Paris from Brittany to work as a waitress. Marriage to a fisherman or farm worker, and a job in the onion fields or fish factory was about all there was for young women in her small village outside Brest.

Arriving in Paris, Monique took a flat with a woman from the restaurant where they worked. Both were paid the same, shared the same tips, but Monique's flatmate had a car paid for by after-hours earnings. It was easy money, she told Monique. The men were often old, generous and rarely troublesome, spending their time avoiding premature ejaculation. There were others, more insistent on getting their money's worth but on balance the work was undemanding. A lot of women working the streets were hobbyists, she'd said, the extra euros buying little luxuries they could not otherwise afford. Having discovered she quite liked sex, Monique joined her friend touting for trade around Paris Gare du Nord. The flatmate, however, didn't mention Jean Luc, the Corsican pimp who took a percentage – and then took Monique.

Flynt had always wanted to be better liked. Was it happening over a bottle of wine and flickering candlelight or was it the father/daughter thing? Whatever the case, Monique was rubbing the rust off body armour he thought hermetically sealed. Every man wanted a hand to hold as he slid towards the abyss, a wife, son, daughter to ease the journey into the unknown. Flynt had grown more conscious of his own mortality since the Bakelite woman started calling. It was tough for him to admit that if there was no tomorrow the only person to care was a twenty-something hooker.

Watching Monique work her way through a Caesar's salad with a plate of large shrimps on its way, Flynt felt the warmness between them was more than the professional's feigned response to his glad eye. Their conversation faltered only the once, when, returning to type, he was disagreeable with the waiter about his sirloin. 'I expressly asked for English medium,' Flynt snapped, 'no blood on the plate.' His steak was swimming in a bloodied bath. 'The French can't cook steak… not properly,' he told Monique, then asked, 'Do you eat a lot?'

Monique, who was devouring her shrimps like they were about to become extinct, was startled. '*Pourquoi?* I look fat?'

Flynt said, 'Not at all… you've a great figure.'

'And you?'

'I complain about eating. I think it's a waste of time… too busy. Deadlines don't wait.'

'Did your wife understand?'

'Not really… she wasn't interested in what I did.'

'I am. You're more interesting than anyone I've known. You talk like a newspaper… deadlines, copy, filing…'

Flynt was damned if he could remember what in fact they had talked about except that only rarely had he felt an embrace without a touch, a caress not needing consummation, his obsession with his own concerns expelled.

Even the Bakelite in the plastic bag between his feet was

forgotten until, soon after they returned to the apartment, it rang again. Picking it up quickly, Flynt called to Monique who was in the bathroom. 'Listen… the woman… the same voice.' White-faced, hand trembling, she pressed the receiver to her ear. 'The voice,' Flynt whispered, his eyes filling with desperation, 'you heard her?'

'The woman?' Monique mumbled.

'Asking for help?'

'I think so.'

Dropping on to the sofa, Flynt pulled Monique down and held her close. 'Thank Christ someone believes me.'

'I know someone who could help,' Monique replied, the words sticking in her throat.

Crossing to the window, Flynt glared at the cobbles in the street below wrapped in the dull orange glow from the street lighting. After a moment he turned slowly. 'So you didn't hear the phone ring… or the voice.' Monique was only humouring him.

Chapter 13

THE NEXT MORNING Flynt asked Monique, 'You said you know someone.'

Monique's clients were broad spectrum. Professor Paul Monchette was a psychiatrist, discreet, spoke perfect English, she said. Flynt was uncomfortable about consulting a shrink with whom he shared a woman. Would conflict of interest impair the diagnosis, their relationship with Monique difficult to place off-limits? Nor did Flynt fancy being hypnotised, in fact doubted whether anyone could put him under.

Flynt didn't need an expensive shrink habit to tell him imagination played tricks. Analysis was like a Class A drug – those who could afford it became addicted, unable to perform without a session on the psychiatrist's couch. Why pay skyscraper fees when he'd dealt with oddballs often enough to sort it for himself? Christ knows what a shrink would dig from his subconscious.

This was not the first time intuition and insight had caused him trouble – Flynt imagining something was true, someone guilty before knowing all the facts. In the past, he'd run it to ground, proving or disproving before making a judgment. This was different. He'd not checked out the Bakelite lady.

A shrink would say she was ringing in his head. Fair enough, phones were the nuts and bolts of what he did, so common he was sometimes not conscious one was ringing until told to pick it up. In Baghdad when there was a gun around every corner, he believed he saw a shooter each time a car backfired. The Bakelite was much the same. If he could imagine it did ring, the woman on the line became an extension of his day-dreaming.

'No thanks, Monique. I'll stick with self-analysis, it's cheaper.' What could her shrink friend say? Only that the Bakelite wasn't ringing in the real world; that it couldn't because it wasn't connected.

Flynt knew that people living on the edge retreated into darkness; that insanity didn't suddenly descend but advanced by very fine margins. Flynt had three triggers for his overheated imagination: Emilie's accident, then his mother died, and now his main stimulus, chasing stories, was hanging by a thread. If he had at times mistaken the repetitive sound of a ringing telephone for silence, then perhaps it also worked vice versa.

His self-analysis not entirely convincing, Flynt turned to Monique, 'Do I look mad?'

She smiled, reached out an arm and sat him down on the sofa bed. 'Not crazy-crazy, not like Jean Luc.'

Flynt said, 'Thanks for that.'

Monique replied, 'You're certainly not boring. How do you say odd in English?'

'Eccentric,' exclaimed Flynt, taking a deep breath before continuing. 'Have you noticed I take a pen and notebook to bed... not into bed... keep it on the bedside table.' She hadn't but would the next time they slept together. 'I dream a lot, write stories in my sleep. I take a note because I won't remember in the morning. Does that sound crazy?'

Monique asked, 'Are they nice? The stories you write in your sleep?'

Flynt said, 'Not complete stories... only the first few paragraphs.'

'Do you dream about me?' Monique asked.

'I haven't yet but will when you're dead. I dream mostly about dead people, people I've worked with. That must sound crazy.'

'Eccentric... that's what you called it.'

Apart from strange dreams, slightly overweight and probably

with a dodgy liver, Flynt felt well enough. 'I do get a regular check-up,' he insisted. 'They've not found anything wrong. The office pays… doesn't want me dropping dead on the job.' But that didn't stretch to a hearing test. Perhaps the Brenton woman was nothing more than an auditory hallucination and all he wanted was a hearing aid to make her go away.

'Back to the drawing board, I suppose,' Flynt muttered.

'What do you mean?' Turning up her cute nose and pouting just a little, Monique had the prettiest way of asking questions.

'Start at the beginning. Expel my phantom caller by doing what I do best, turning over stones.' Flynt was determined to track down whatever was driving him to the edge.

'My hobby could be the source of the trouble,' he told Monique, waving towards the display cabinet and his collection of antique telephones. 'Didn't I say I was a collector? Quite possible that little lot has blurred my distinction between introspection and reality.' Monique was confused. Her English was good, got even better the more she used it but not for discussing the metaphysical, or how a conjunction of events was disposed to produce an illusion.

A few minutes later they both heard the bell ring, not the Bakelite but the intercom. A gendarme was waiting to escort Flynt to the *Poste de Police* across the park from the apartment to make a formal statement. The investigation into Emilie's death was now a criminal matter after the Bretons wrecked the inquest. Flynt was expecting this but was more afraid of what might get lost in translation. What if they asked for his ID card? Flynt didn't have one, moved around so much he wasn't in Paris long enough to qualify, his British passport always good enough to get by. But France's laissez-faire approach to free movement had been blown away by terrorism, a British passport no longer the gold standard it once was. Terrorists had passports, lots. Some petty French functionary at the local cop-shop could easily decide to cover his own backside by kicking Flynt upstairs: decide he wasn't very different to the refugees and economic migrants streaming across Europe. For all practical purposes he had no country, spending most of his time on the road.

'I'll come with you,' said Monique, 'to the *Poste de Police*.'

'Please! Tell them I'm your step-father and I don't speak French. Our names are close enough to be related, at least in Britain – Jones and Flynt.'

'How do I explain the ID card?'

'Tell it as it is – that I haven't lived here long enough to have one… that I'm a tourist. If they ask about tax, say I don't work here, that I'm paid in Luxembourg. No-one at INS pays tax in France. By the time they've taken a close look I'll be long gone.'

The *Poste de Police* was a nondescript building with the nondescript detective waiting to take Flynt's statement, greeting Monique like a friend. She was a natural, flirting outrageously. Flynt guessed they were acquainted, how well he didn't want to know – only that it got him off the ID hook. His statement about Emilie's fall was a formality, the French copper only there to witness Flynt's signatures on English and French versions of the testimony he'd already given at the inquest.

Less than an hour later they were back at the apartment, Monique curling herself into a ball on the sofa, knees tucked beneath her chin.

Flynt said, 'You did well. I liked the peck on the cheek for French Plod. Nice touch. That should hold them for a while.'

Monique was shaking, pale-faced. Flynt guessed why. Before signing the statement the detective had read it over to him, in both languages. 'You pushed your wife!' Monique blurted. Her eyes flared, boring into him.

'I didn't. Emilie fell. We had an argument. She ran from the house… I was trying to stop her when she slipped. Christ, I went over the cliff too… I could have been killed.'

'Why didn't he say so, the man at the inquest?'

'You mean Lan Brevilet... because he didn't want to give evidence in French. You're Breton. You know the problem. It's a cultural thing.'

Monique looked away before continuing. 'Your wife... you loved her?'

'Yes,' Flynt said emphatically. 'To tell you the truth, I blame myself. I've always been a selfish bastard... always about me... what I want.' Flynt didn't spare himself, explaining how his globetrotting and Emilie's cultural obsessions led to their split. 'We simply drifted apart, went separate ways until...' Flynt stopped short.

Monique closed her eyes. 'I'm sending you to sleep, aren't I?' Flynt said.

'No. I was thinking about why you went back to Emilie.' She stood up, crossed to the kitchen and pulled two cold Stellas from the fridge. 'Tell me about her,' Monique said, taking a heavy swallow.

'The best thing that ever happened to me... and it took me eight years to realise it. Now I'll never get her back. All those years... lost... like the Lady in the Lake... and I never laid a hand on her.'

'The Lady in the Lake?'

'A Welsh fairy tale.'

Monique listened intently, saddened, weeping silently for his pain.

A car stopped in the street below, brakes squealing on the cobbles. Flynt took a look from the window. There were two men on the pavement opposite, studying the apartment block, too far for him to see clearly.

'Jean Luc?' He beckoned Monique to the window.

'I don't think so,' she said. One of the apartments was for sale. That probably explained their interest.

Flynt opened up his laptop. Having convinced himself of a link between the Brenton woman's last words and his mystery caller he had, as a matter of course, checked the *Gazette* web-page for follow-ups. Any day he expected to read she was dead; that life-support had been disconnected.

'Good God! That I never expected,' he exclaimed, 'a retraction and apology. They've folded. Run up the white flag.' The white flag wasn't a paragraph tucked away inside the *Gazette* but at the top of a right-hand facing page where readers wouldn't miss it. After eighteen months following every twist and turn in the Brenton story, the *Gazette* had been leaned on heavily to publish a fulsome retraction:

CORRECTION AND APOLOGY

'It has been drawn to our attention that various reports published by this newspaper during the last eighteen months concerning Mrs Helen Brenton who is presently receiving treatment at west London's Royal Hospital after a car accident have implied her life was threatened. We are happy to make it clear this was not the case and the accident was not in any way a deliberate attempt upon Mrs Brenton's life. The *Gazette* accepts the only reason for this tragic event was that Mrs Brenton's car hit a tree during a storm. Nothing we have published should be construed as suggesting we have evidence to the contrary. Mrs Brenton remains in a coma. The *Gazette* apologises for the distress this misunderstanding has caused her family, and undertakes not to repeat, or allude to it in future. The *Gazette* has made a substantial donation to Fight for Life, the charity supporting research into the treatment of coma patients at west London's Royal Hospital.'

Flynt knew about retractions. Even when a story was hopelessly wrong, the gut response was offer as little as possible. Newspapers were always in denial. But when forced by lawyers into publishing an apology, an editor's mantra was 'Getting it in today means less to pay later.' Damage limitation was the name of the game and the sooner an editor said sorry, the less the damages. It was eighteen months before the *Gazette* said sorry.

When someone featured prominently and regularly – as Helen Brenton had in the *Gazette* – the coverage became a shield discouraging adverse or inappropriate action against the object of that coverage. The retraction and apology meant Helen Brenton had just lost her shield. Not another line would be published. It was tantamount to a gagging writ.

Flynt looked across the room at the Bakelite sitting on the table beneath the apartment window, expecting it to ring. Brenton's subconscious pleading must be at bursting point. In Flynt's mind the phantom voice that offered a possible explanation for his own dilemma was becoming a 'Save Brenton' campaign. He was Helen Brenton's last chance unless he was rationalising his own madness?

Turning to Monique, his mind made up, he said, 'I'm going to London for a few days.'

'When do we leave?'

'You don't. Stay here. You can use the apartment.' Monique fixed him with a grim determination, her soft persuasive voice appealing his attempt to sideline her. Flynt surrendered easily. 'Can you be ready in an hour?' He'd grown to need her support and sympathy.

Fingering her party dress from their night at the Ritz, Monique replied, 'Not much more to pack!'

'You'll need a passport,' said Flynt.

'This will do,' she retorted. 'I have one, you don't.' She waved her French identity card, good enough for UK Border Control.

'OK, ring Eurostar and get a couple of tickets to St Pancras. You can pick up some bits and pieces for yourself before we catch the train,' he said, passing over his American Express card.

Flynt wondered why Brenton's husband hadn't run it

through the courts – why he preferred to negotiate a retraction, not sue. On the other hand, retractions were not always what they seemed – that a hack misquoted someone. Sometimes a newspaper pulled up the drawbridge to get someone off its back. Newspapers were not charities. Pursuing a line blindly could lose its attraction. Before switching off his laptop, Flynt noted the name of the reporter who broke the original Brenton story: Gus White.

Flynt stood at the window watching for the cab. 'We're off,' he said, grabbing the bag they were sharing and reaching for the Carrefour with the Bakelite. Before he picked it up it rang again. Flynt froze, and watched apprehensively as Monique lifted the receiver and listened. 'This time… you're sure?' There was no mistake, her face white as marble, her lips moving incoherently. 'Got it!' snapped Flynt. At last someone could corroborate what he'd been saying for weeks.

An hour later they were picking their way through the crowd hurrying along Platform 3 at Paris Gare du Nord to the waiting Eurostar. From the smiles Monique exchanged with the women loitering under the station clock, Flynt guessed this was not her first visit to Europe's busiest rail station.

Before the train left, Flynt rang Yates at INS to say that in lieu of his anticipated dismissal he was taking two weeks' due leave. Yates protested. Flynt promised, 'Give me my two weeks and you won't have to wait for New York. You'll get my written resignation. How does that sound? You won't get a better deal. New York knows this could wind up at a tribunal. That's why they're taking so long.'

Flynt fancied he heard a muffled cheer. 'Email your resignation now… then take your leave, permanently,' said Yates decisively.

The journey across the flat, featureless Normandy countryside was tedious, the Channel Tunnel followed by equally dreary stretches of south-east England. Why Kent was called the 'Garden of England' Flynt never quite understood. This was no holiday, he reminded Monique, stamping his feet on the carriage floor to make the point. 'Legwork, lots of it. I have people to find and questions.'

She seemed to understand until he tried explaining why the voice on the Bakelite might be Helen Brenton's cry for help. Monique's raised eyebrows and puzzled frown ended in another Gallic shrug.

Chapter 14

A T ST PANCRAS, Flynt and Monique stepped into a cold
London drizzle, the city clogged with rush hour traffic
as they headed by cab to a large Victorian terraced house in
Paddington, a hotel Flynt had used before. The only room
available opened into the lobby, a few steps from the reception
desk where the jumbo-size Pakistani manager, Rana, squatted
on a stool playing a games console.

Rana never seemed to leave his stool, clocking guests in and
out although few stayed long, some only an hour maybe. It was
that kind of place. The only thing that had changed was Rana,
bigger than Flynt remembered, burying his stool in large rolls of
fat. He greeted Flynt as though he'd never left.

There was only one way out, through the lobby, Rana
remarkably quick off his stool if someone tried to do a runner.
Stealing a look under their bed, Flynt found the bottle bank,
one quarter full of scotch, the others empty flagons of lager
from the night before. At least the sheets were clean, smelling
like a flower garden, Monique's twisted smile hinting at familiar
territory.

Around the corner from the hotel was a culinary icon –
Micky's Fish and Chip Bar, nothing to look at and easy to miss
but for the queue outside. A range of stainless steel fryers down
one side, a narrow Formica-topped shelf along the other for
stand-up diners, the queue snaked along the pavement, Flynt's
stomach groaning in anticipation. Not so Monique, pouting
with astonishment at cod and chips. The horror story every
French child heard at their parents' knee about British food was
true, sprinkled with lashings of salt and swimming in vinegar.

Monique studied her plastic plate for a full two minutes before slicing the batter like a surgeon delving for vital organs. Finding nothing worth eating and dismissing the chips with a withering frown, she exclaimed in astonishment, 'French fries!' Flynt scoffed, bending his head to the serious business of washing down his fish with a steaming cup of strong tea, occasionally interrupted by a sharp dig in the ribs from Monique, by now more interested in the clientele. 'People are looking at us,' said Flynt.

'*L'age – n'est qu'une idée*,' she said, her quick, keen eyes reading his embarrassment.

'I'm not so sure about age being only a number,' replied Flynt, 'not when it's a high one.'

Sharing a bed barely wide enough for two promised an interesting experience. Flynt anticipated a hard time holding on to all his moving parts. But with the crack about 'no country for old men' still ringing in his head, he took a cold shower before climbing in beside Monique, her face buried behind a curtain of dark hair, breasts quivering, whispering for attention under a solitary white sheet. If squeezing her thigh gently was Flynt's idea of foreplay, all he got was heavy breathing. A moment later Monique turned and, pulling Flynt close, kissed him fiercely, stifling his voice with her lips. Her head sank back and she held his hand between her smooth thighs, her belly moving rhythmically. His brain was on fire.

'I do like it,' she whispered. 'Is that why I'm a whore?'

A professional, anticipating every move, understanding the nature of the man, she urged him 'not to hurry' but the wriggle and heave was too much, her vagina closing tightly on his dick. Coming with Monique was sensuous, natural and good.

Flynt had expected her to be indifferent to sex, chilled between the sheets. Not so, at least with him. Closing her dark soft eyes she dozed in his arms, looking even more beautiful, lips full and delightful, retroussé nose, only slightly turned up. What endeared Monique to Flynt was that she was an original – a little vague perhaps, her lips slightly open affecting a thoughtful look.

When they woke an hour later she turned and said, 'You're a kind man.'

Flynt drew back. No-one ever called him kind, selfish yes, never asking for help, nor offering it.

Climbing off the bed, Monique headed for the bathroom, her breasts brushing his face in the darkness. 'Don't fall in love with me,' she whispered.

'Unlikely,' he lied. 'I'm too old for that… anyhow I've another woman… she rings often… on the Bakelite.' Monique slid into bed again, taking his head in her arms comfortingly. Flynt was delighted she cared.

'You can use the apartment in Paris for as long as you like,' he said. 'I expect I'll be moving on soon… find another job… another country. You could always tag along.'

'I can't.' Monique's head fell back on the pillow, sobbing quietly. 'I have a child.' Her eyes were moist and red.

Flynt had guessed as much when he saw the telltale scar of a Caesarean section. 'Jean Luc?' Monique nodded. 'And he sends you on the game!'

'He'll never let me go. He'll find out… and then he'll come for you.'

'Where's the child?'

'Where he won't find him… Henri is in Brittany with family.'

In their shabby room across the lobby, Flynt and Monique were at ease with each other and the world, disturbed only by the click-click of Rana playing games and the hum of the city, until the Bakelite intruded. Monique froze. Flynt dragged the phone from the Carrefour bag and on to the bed.

'Answer for me, answer,' he muttered. Monique heard the same chipped and broken message fighting the static.

'It has to be her... the coma woman. The hospital's not far away.'

The next morning Flynt was already on his mobile chasing contacts in Fleet Street, the centre of the newspaper world until it moved to Docklands. The maelstrom that once swirled around the 'street of shame' had dissipated and with it the buzz and urgency that crackled whenever hacks congregated, the bars now patronised by grey, colourless lawyer types from the Royal Courts of Justice along the Strand.

'I've fixed lunch at the Cheese. I'm meeting a reporter from the *Gazette*,' he told Monique as she dressed.

'Cheese for lunch... only cheese?' she sniffed, recalling the abortive fish and chip supper from the previous night.

That was always going to be a problem, but a charming one when Monique's English tripped over colloquialisms.

Paris had its bistros but none with whiskers like the Cheese, Flynt intrigued to see how Monique handled a slice of Olde Worlde England.

Ye Olde Cheshire Cheese in Wine Office Court, a hidden alleyway off Fleet Street, counted Charles Dickens and Samuel Johnson among former habitués. The Cheese advertised itself as being re-built after the Fire of London in the sixteenth century and was a regular on tourist itineraries, the tavern's dark wooden interior an enchanting warren of narrow corridors and rickety staircases leading to intimate dining rooms, floors sprinkled with fresh sawdust every day for ambience.

The drizzle from the previous evening was turning heavy when they squeezed into the dark oak-panelled bar, full of raincoats steaming in front of a large log fire and hanging on to pints of Samuel Smith's. Monique was captivated, her eyes fixed on the portrait above the fireplace of William Simpson, a waiter at the Cheese in 1829. Flynt imagined she expected Simpson to appear at any moment holding a tray of crisp, brown chops.

The former intimacy of the Chop Room had however been lost, the clamour of open-plan drowning conversation when Gus White arrived, panting for a drink after slipping out of a murder trial mired in legal argument at the Royal Courts of Justice.

A middle-aged general news reporter covering anything that moved, Gus smiled dubiously at the pretty dark-haired French woman Flynt introduced as an 'associate'. Not that it worried Flynt. Most guys like Gus, left with a few more turns around the block, welcomed a pretty alternative for their failed ambitions. Flynt warmed to the *Gazette* reporter, a soulmate chased by young upstarts on the News Desk querying what he wrote.

Gus covered the original story about Helen Brenton's accident. He'd quoted her friend Julia Cross about that last phone call. 'I did the follow-ups. Then they took me off the story after the paper got a solicitor's letter threatening to sue if we mentioned the telephone call again. The solicitors admitted Cross received a call from Brenton just before the accident but it was all about a 'killing on the stock market' by Brenton's husband David… that I'd misquoted her. Balls! Brenton told her "Help! He's trying to kill me"… nothing about the stock market or anything else. The problem was I didn't have a note.'

The *Gazette* decided that since the Brenton woman was as good as dead there was nothing to be gained from arguing the toss with solicitors. 'The desk told me to write a correction and apology. I had no choice.' Aggrieved at being hung out to dry, Gus welcomed the opportunity to unload his bruised self-esteem over a free lunch. In return, he gave Flynt everything he had on the story, including a photograph of David and Helen Brenton in happier times.

'And the Cross woman… you're sure she said Brenton had told her, "Help! He's trying to kill me"… nothing about the stock market?' Flynt eyeballed the man from the *Gazette*, the slightest twitch often more revealing than the answer. Gus didn't blink.

'Look, Jack, I don't make mistakes like that. I've been around too long. Neither do I make it up like some I know earning a lot more lolly. According to Cross, Brenton said, "Help! He's trying to kill me." I had the note… just lost the fucking thing. Who keeps a notebook eighteen months?' Flynt did for that very reason.

A missing shorthand note wouldn't have worried Dr Johnson, thought Flynt, glancing at the portrait of Fleet Street's champion of free speech hanging on the wall of the Chop Room behind Monique's head. She probably thought Johnson was scribbling in the attic.

'Any thoughts on who was trying to kill the Brenton woman… the husband? He seems in a great hurry to put her to sleep, permanently,' Flynt said.

'No idea mate… I just write the stuff.' Gus White was too old a hand to answer a leading question. If he agreed the husband was a suspect then Flynt would certainly be tempted to quote him as a source 'close to the investigation'. That happened!

'Were they happy, the Brentons?' Flynt tried another tack.

'It seems so… he was a big noise in a bank in the city. They had a mansion out at Kew, on the river.'

'And the friend, Mrs Cross… where did she live?'

'I thought you'd ask,' said Gus sliding across the address on a page torn from his notebook. 'They were neighbours… rich, too. You have to be to live on the river.'

'Did Helen Brenton have any worries?'

'No idea. I was about to do an update when we got the letter from Brenton's solicitors. From then on it was off limits and I was moved to something else.'

'What about Cross? Was she party to the solicitor's letter from Brenton?'

'Corroborated Brenton's so-called "killing on the stock market". That's all.'

Flynt shook his head. 'What stopped Julia Cross from suing in her own right... could have got a packet for defamation?'

'No idea,' said White, preparing to leave.

'Have you heard about the mother's injunction?' Flynt asked.

'What injunction?' The newsman sat down, antennae bristling.

'To prevent the hospital from stopping artificial feeding...'

Gus White was scribbling in his notebook. He'd not followed the story since the solicitor's letter. 'When was the injunction...? I'll look it up,' he muttered. 'Christ, how could we miss it? Cuts... we don't have the people to sit in court all day... left to the agencies... and they're only interested in the biggies.'

White had eyed a follow-up.

'No Gus, nothing for the moment. Keep it under wraps. We're on dodgy ground. Just because the husband wants to switch off his wife's lights doesn't make him a murderer,' cautioned Flynt. He didn't mention the call for help on his Bakelite. That would blow White's mind.

Gus stared at his half-eaten pork chop, gulped down a deep draught of red burgundy, before replying slowly, 'You know as well as anyone Jack that if you sit on a story you lose it.'

'But there's a life at stake, Gus.'

'She's probably brain dead already.'

'If she dies we'll never know, never stand the story up. All we've got is Cross's contested statement about the call from Helen Brenton. Your lot wouldn't run it, nor mine. We need the Brenton woman to wake up.'

'And how do you intend doing that?'

'By proving she's not brain dead.'

Gus frowned. 'You've lost me now. I wouldn't know where to start.'

'With the hospital, her consultant.'

Gus took a deep breath. 'He'll hide behind patient confidentiality… I bet you won't get close.'

'I will if I say please – say INS is doing a piece about how his treatment of coma patients is ground-breaking? He won't be able to resist. Doctors are vain, arrogant buggers.'

'But you can't… not on gardening leave.'

'How do you know that?'

'I checked you out. Been drinking too much… correct?'

Monique hadn't said a word. Now she flew at Gus White, eyes flaring, tight, small white-knuckled fists rapping the table. 'No… no… Jack doesn't drink,' she growled above the hubbub. Flynt looked around the Chop Room, grateful for her defence but not so publicly.

Gus swayed out of reach of Monique's anger. 'I suppose the hospital won't know you're on gardening leave,' he said quickly. 'OK… I'll sit tight until then.'

After Gus White left to catch up on his murder case, Flynt found a quiet corner to call west London's Royal Hospital on his mobile. He'd visited once before when a colleague working in the City had a stroke. A former Victorian workhouse for penniless families, he recalled that the original red-brick building had since become a centre for treating those in a persistent vegetative state, a sort of waiting room for long-term coma patients drowning in their bodily fluids or starved to death after a court decided artificial feeding could be withdrawn. The thought of visiting the place gave Flynt the creeps but Professor John Wilkins, head of department, was impressed that an internationally renowned news agency wanted to interview him about his work. He would see Flynt the following evening.

For eighteen months Helen Brenton had lain on her back,

breathing normally, blonde hair spilling across a pristine white pillow, her pale blue eyes locked in a blank stare while passing through regular sleep/wake cycles. But not once was awareness detected, either as sound, sight, touch or smell, despite the prodding and poking. What no-one could say, however, was whether consciousness survived at some lower level. Trapped inside her body, had Helen Brenton heard her husband, David, discussing with clinicians the switching off of life support – an unimaginable nightmare, thought Flynt. Was it possible his Bakelite had somehow become a channel for her scream in the dark?

But before Flynt tackled the consultant Wilkins, he needed to pin down the Cross woman.

A taxi dropped them near the Cross family home at Kew, one of several expensive mock-Georgian houses in a private tree-lined cul-de-sac alongside the river. A white gravel drive led from a pair of wrought-iron gates set in a high red-brick wall protecting the owners from the outside world. At the end of the drive, mock Palladian pillars identified this as the home of substantial people with a view across the Thames and a motor cruiser moored at a private jetty. Flynt pressed the polished brass buzzer set into the wall. After explaining over the intercom they were delivering a package, he and Monique were allowed to approach for an audience with a middle-aged woman, watched every foot of the way by CCTV cameras. Brusque and suspicious, the housekeeper held the front door open just wide enough to say that Mr William Cross, the owner, was selling the property. All she knew of the whereabouts of Mrs Cross was a forwarding address in Wimbledon Park, another leafy London suburb. The couple had separated, Flynt decided. There was no point hanging around.

Their next stop was an Edwardian terrace of red-brick houses, with mullion windows and wooden balconies surviving from an earlier era when no-one predicted the English would swop horse buggies for Range Rovers, and rose-filled front gardens for ugly grey concrete hard-standings with blue wheelie bins parked in the corner.

Julia Cross's elderly aunt living on Ruberry Hill was an accommodating old soul, inviting them into a large sitting room with bay window. Her niece, she said, worked at the Foreign and Commonwealth Office on The Mall and called once a week to collect her mail.

The room was stuffed with faded furniture, threadbare rugs, and gilt-framed photographs celebrating the life and times of Julia Cross from perambulator to infant performing in leotard and tutu, to graduation and wedding day bliss.

'An address?' Flynt asked. 'We're acting for her solicitors. They need her present address.'

The aunt was a wily old bird, fiercely protective of her niece. Staring at Flynt suspiciously she said, 'If you're from Julia's solicitors I'd have thought you had her forwarding address.'

'We should but it appears we don't. This happens with divorces. A couple separate, move out of the matrimonial home and forget to give their solicitor a forwarding address. It's understandable. A divorce is very traumatic, a stressful time. I've been through one… I know.' Flynt smiled.

The aunt's two-piece grey suit added a hard edge to her tone. The rain had started again and it would soon be dark. 'You were saying Julia does something at the Foreign and Commonwealth Office,' he called out while the aunt rummaged through a drawer for an address Flynt guessed she had no intention of producing. 'The offices on The Mall… covered in ivy, correct.' Not that it mattered she didn't answer. The sham search was a distraction lasting long enough for Flynt to lift a small, gilt-framed photograph of Julia Cross off a table. Monique gasped when he stuffed the picture in a jacket pocket. It wasn't the first time he'd snatched a mugshot.

Admiralty House stands at one end of The Mall, Buckingham Palace at the other, the ivy-covered building home to several hundred Foreign Office staff who exited every evening either on to Whitehall or the road running adjacent to Horse Guards Parade. Flynt had forgotten its name, only that it led towards St James's Tube Station.

That evening, before the civil service army began dispersing to the suburbs, Flynt stationed himself at the Whitehall exit, Monique at the other. Both had mobiles and a photograph of their quarry. Monique spotted Julia Cross first, a tall, attractive woman in her late thirties, wearing a smart dark suit and carrying the regulation briefcase.

'I see her,' Monique squealed excitedly into her mobile.

'Follow, don't lose her. I'll cut across Horse Guards and catch up. Just keep her in sight.'

That wasn't easy. Most of the women heading home from the office were dressed the same, and carried briefcases. And so were the men. The tide of bobbing heads and suits swept past the Cabinet War Rooms before spilling into Birdcage Walk.

'I still see her,' whispered Monique. 'Where are you?'

'Here,' replied Flynt, touching her shoulder.

'Oh… there she is,' pointed Monique, startled.

She was heading for the underground station at St James, the one Flynt used during a reporting stint in the House of Commons lobby. By the time Cross turned on to the station plaza he was within touching distance – then lost her at the ticket barrier. A regular commuter and season ticket holder, she disappeared down the escalator to some stop on the District Line before Flynt could find the fare.

'Fuck, fuck, fuck. I should have thought of that. We'll try

again tomorrow. You'll be on your own. I've got to see Brenton's consultant.'

Late the next afternoon, Monique joined the home-time tide flowing from Admiralty House, picking up Cross bobbing amongst the dark-blue suits towards St James's. Cross left the train at Barons Court and made her way along the road to the ground-floor apartment of a converted Edwardian terraced town house.

Monique was close enough to be mistaken for a stalker. She ducked into a doorway watching Cross search for her door key. But before keying the lock, the door opened, a security light flooded the porch – and Julia Cross fell into David Brenton's loving arms. The lights flicked on in a ground-floor room, then off again. Monique hung around beneath an open window. The grunts and moans were unmistakeable.

At west London's Royal Hospital, Flynt was skirmishing with Professor Wilkins. A broad shouldered man not easily intimidated, the professor welcomed publicity if it furthered his ambitions. White shirtsleeves folded neatly back to expose a Rolex on one wrist and gold chain on the other, he projected the image of a person in complete control. To this end his white clinician's coat was draped casually across a chair, discarded disdainfully by a person who didn't need a uniform to stamp his authority. At thirty, the professor was the youngest in his field and the article Flynt was writing for International News Service could facilitate a move away from a decaying hospital to a position in one of the foremost trauma hospitals in the United States. INS had got its interview, a one-to-one with Wilkins, because Flynt had said the agency was profiling Britain's 'leading coma specialist.' Otherwise, Flynt would have been bounced down the corridor as a general press inquiry.

Diagnosing a comatose patient as being in a persistent

vegetative state was tantamount to passing a death sentence. In law, the decision to stop artificial feeding was founded on the consultant's prognosis in conjunction with the wishes of the next of kin and approved by a court. In reality, if after twelve months there was no flicker of consciousness behind Helen Brenton's frozen eyes, then the final decision on whether to detach the blue crimped plastic feeding tubes was for Wilkins.

Flynt let Wilkins blabber on about his accomplishments before firing in the question the young professor most wanted to avoid. That was how Flynt operated: soften them up – then kick them in the balls.

'You must have dealt with some celebrated cases, Professor... and had difficult decisions to take.' Wilkins agreed, taking a deep breath that made him look even taller. Confident he had the measure of the INS reporter, his chest expanded with infinite pride until Flynt tossed in the first of his little hand grenades. 'Isn't there a current one... very difficult... Helen Brenton. I believe that's the name.'

Wilkins was on his guard immediately. 'I'm afraid I cannot discuss individual cases,' he replied through clenched teeth.

When it came to blowing up a roadblock Flynt was one of the best in the business, crude, not subtle, a full frontal assault man. Attack, insult, rattle, and hint at hidden 'sources', anything to frighten the shit out of the officious, self-important bastard. Not pretty. Flynt's strategy was if there was nothing to lose, there was everything to gain.

'Exactly where are patients like Helen Brenton left to starve to death, professor?' he asked almost casually. Flynt was suggesting that somewhere deep in the bowels of this former Victorian workhouse Wilkins operated a death chamber. Quite outrageous but on occasions a whack between the eyes had got him where he wanted after more conventional means had failed.

'What a thing to say,' the professor exploded. 'I understood this was to be a serious interview about very serious matters. You don't have the slightest idea of the caring, sensitive treatment these poor people receive. Decisions to withdraw artificial nutrition impose particular responsibilities on clinicians, nurses and relatives, and are exceedingly distressful for all involved. Anyhow, the final decision rests with the court which has decided that life-support can be withdrawn from Mrs Brenton.' Flynt knew his time was up – that at most he'd get one more question before Wilkins called security to escort him off the premises.

'Really Mr Flynt, I must insist you leave. In almost two years there's been no sign of any meaningful neurological recovery... but I shouldn't even be discussing this with you...'

'So why is Mrs Brenton still alive? I thought it took only two weeks for someone to starve to death.' Flynt jumped in with both feet, ploughing through Wilkins's feigned outrage.

'You're misinformed Flynt. Reporters always are. The court has said we can withdraw life-support from Mrs Brenton... I didn't say we had. For the moment she continues to be fed artificially.' Wilkins was breathing with the short, sharp stabs of a man whose back was tight against the wall. Despite the icy blast from the air conditioning he'd broken into a cold sweat. 'The panel's at the door... will you switch it off.' His breezy confidence had evaporated. Wilkins sat down hurriedly. He needed the safety of his padded chair and the white clinician's coat to protect him from another attack.

'Get out Flynt or I'll have security throw you out. You're rude, abusive, totally misinformed.' Flynt was always called abusive when he was only being assertive. 'I'll speak to your editors. You're not to publish a word. I retract everything. I promise I'll not hesitate to sue you and your agency.'

Wilkins was pointing to the door when Flynt's mobile rang. It was Monique with news of the Cross woman's steamy affair in Barons Court. Motioning to Wilkins to hold his horses, Flynt listened as Monique explained how she followed Julia Cross into the arms of a man.

'The man in the photograph I got from the *Gazette* reporter Gus White... you are absolutely sure... so he's dicking her!'

Wilkins didn't hear Flynt's 'gotcha'.

'Close the door professor before I call the British Medical Association and have you charged with deliberately misdiagnosing Mrs Brenton. Is David Brenton paying you to kill his wife?'

'Stop this!' Wilkins roared. 'I have no idea what you're talking about.'

'I'm saying David Brenton is shagging Julia Cross as we speak. They've got a pad in Barons Court. No wonder he wants to switch off his wife's life support. How do you feel about being implicated in murder?' Wilkins froze, rattled by Flynt's triumphal sneer, hands tearing at the arms of his executive chair in panic.

'That's the way the police will see it when they discover Cross has left her husband for Brenton. I can see the headline: How to kill your wife with the help of her doctor. You were almost there.' Flynt wasn't letting go until the poor sod surrendered absolutely.

'You think I want to kill people?'

'I never said that. But you must have known about Helen Brenton's telephone call saying someone was trying to kill her.'

'Only what I read. Mrs Cross denied everything... threatened to sue...'

'No she didn't... Brenton did... and you obliged by signing his wife's death warrant for the judge... all very convenient.'

Wilkins's face was gun-metal grey, his voice a stutter, every word painful. 'How do you know all this?'

'Because that's what I do... investigate... find the truth. They've probably been at it for months, even before the accident.

Did Helen Brenton know her husband was playing around? I bet she never guessed it was with her best friend Julia Cross.'

'This is terrible. I had no idea. Believe me, Flynt, if I knew I'd never have signed anything. It's terrifying, ghastly. Brenton started pressing me to withdraw life-support after twelve months, his wife's legal entitlement. His wife, he said, never wanted to live like a vegetable. I said we needed more time to assess her. My God, Helen Brenton would be dead but for her mother's letter.'

'What letter?'

'The letter she used to get a temporary injunction against the court's ruling. Says it proves her daughter is not brain dead... that she survives at the subconscious level.' The letter from her daughter was post-marked after the accident, said Wilkins.

'What else did the letter say?'

'That someone had tried to kill her.'

'And you believe this?' asked Flynt.

'Do I believe in the paranormal? Of course not! It was just a ploy to delay the implementation of the court order. The injunction is only temporary. She'll have to produce the letter at the next hearing.'

Having painted a graphic picture for Wilkins – accused of being an accessory to attempted murder, struck off, reputation and ambitions destroyed – Flynt saw the fear gripping the consultant. Wilkins saw himself as David Brenton's hired killer. Too distressed to think straight, he was dragged along like a rabbit trapped in Flynt's headlights.

'You'll be in the clear if Mrs Brenton regains consciousness, you do see that?' And so would Flynt if the Bakelite stopped ringing.

Flynt didn't want Wilkins languishing at the bottom of the deep hole he'd dug – he needed the professor to climb back up and pull Helen Brenton out of her coma.

'Little possibility of that,' muttered Wilkins. 'The coma has lasted too long.'

'How about her subconscious... might that have survived?'

'Who knows? It's possible that raw emotional feelings do exist at a lower level without any obvious signs. What is certain is that if Helen's mother wasn't so devoted it would be over. She's been under a lot of pressure from her son-in-law.'

Flynt decided Wilkins was too professionally puritanical to have any truck with the paranormal, although he'd read somewhere about physical and emotional traumas often preceding the onset of psychic abilities.

'Zolpidem... have you tried it?' Flynt knew about the drug from his own research.

'The insomnia drug... I've suggested it several times but Brenton doesn't want to put his wife through further discomfort. It has helped some coma patients regain consciousness but only for short periods, most relapsing after a few hours, except for those who were originally misdiagnosed.'

'And your diagnosis could be wrong?'

'Honestly Flynt, I don't know what to think any longer. I'll try anything, even zolpidem. But Brenton won't agree.'

'He'll change his mind,' Flynt retorted confidently, 'after I've had a word. I guarantee he'll call... agree you try the drug.'

Chapter 15

NEXT MORNING FLYNT and Monique checked out of the poky Paddington hotel with the dirty grey carpet tiles. The Royal Gate Hotel, with views across Hyde Park, had marble floors and was a ten-minute taxi ride from David Brenton's offices in the City. Flushing out the financier from behind his security doors and influential friends wasn't going to be easy.

Flynt had learned from experience not to go up against the powerful, particularly the dodgy ones, without a concealed weapon. David had brought down Goliath not only with a sling shot but a good eye for a weakness in the giant's armour.

'Dick Jennings, he'll know. Dick's got the dirt on everyone in the City,' he told Monique. She didn't understand but twitched her nose in that captivating way she had. Flynt and Jennings had worked together, Jennings delving into profit and loss for *World Business Daily*, Flynt for the *Gazette* more interested in the margins – in particular who amongst the great and the good had a woman stashed away.

'Hey Dick, it's me, Jack Flynt. How are things?'

No-one ever rang Jennings to ask about his health. 'What you want, Jack?'

'A favour. The name David Brenton, mean anything to you?'

'It may… but why?'

'Don't worry. It's not a business story… more medical…'

'Then it must be about his wife,' replied Jennings, 'on life support… in a coma after the car crash. We had a fundraiser for the hospital.'

Flynt asked, 'Brenton… has he crossed any red lines lately?'
All bankers did at some point.

Jennings paused. 'Brenton's clean, apart from rumours.'

'Any rumour in particular?'

'A share support scheme.'

That's promising, thought Flynt. Brenton was head of mergers and acquisitions at Shield Bank. During his last deal the share price of the target company crashed when during takeovers it usually went the other way.

'What happened?' asked Flynt.

'Nothing… the price settled down and Brenton closed the deal.'

'But you suspect more. Correct, Dick?'

'An off-shore subsidiary of the bank, Cayman Islands Finance, sold shares it never owned.'

'Naked selling to drive the price down… get the company on the cheap… is that what you're saying?'

'But we couldn't prove it. We had a whistleblower but he retracted. I think the bank bought him off.'

This was the kind of lever Flynt needed to get to Brenton – an allegation of financial irregularity.

'Did you put it to him?'

'No… not after our source dried up. Are you planning to?'

'Yes, but only as a tin-opener. You know what these people are like… can't get near without leverage.' One slip and Flynt would be escorted off the premises. At worst, Brenton would call the police if he discovered Flynt was posing as an INS reporter – on gardening leave, not on duty.

Brenton's six-figure salary plus bonuses had propelled him into the luxury yacht and Marbella league. His office suite even had a private bog. 'Nice,' thought Flynt taking a pee. He always found it hard to piss when someone was waving his dick in the next booth.

Flashing his press card got him as far as a PA, Brenton still several security keypads down the corridor. Flynt waited for his scribbled note about 'investigating financial irregularities' to be passed along. The wheelers and dealers of high finance only engaged with the real world when forced to by the law.

Flynt knew there was no chance of getting close if Brenton suspected the interview concerned his wife. He'd find a hundred reasons to avoid it, in the last resort get a court order prohibiting Flynt from interfering. The only way was to lie – say INS was investigating serious allegations against Shield Bank and invite Brenton to rebut them before they were taken to the Financial Services Authority. Flynt had worked in the City long enough to know that deal-makers like Brenton had a soft spot. Takeovers involved sailing close to the regulatory wind. Any suspicion a share price was being rigged was deemed a 'concert party', a criminal offence. No financier wanted that on his CV.

The man sitting behind the polished dark-oak desk in the large office bore a striking resemblance to the English 'bird-watcher' on Île d'Iroise, a caricature, the same sharply tailored dark-blue Savile Row suit hugging an athletic forty-something frame, greying brown hair brushed tight against the scalp.

'International News Service, Paris Bureau,' Brenton read, fingering Flynt's calling card. 'The City's a bit off your beat, isn't it?'

'Not really. I've worked here. The office thought I was the best man for the story, if there's one. It could be just the rumour mill again. You know the City, Mr Brenton,' said Flynt settling into a deep leather chair, strategically positioned for Brenton to look down his nose at visitors.

'Do I hear a trace of a Welsh accent, Mr Flynt? I like Wales… we have a place there.'

A mansion, Flynt imagined, with rolling acres. Lebrun the Frenchman was right – his death rattle would have a fucking accent. 'Born and brought up in the Valleys, the Welsh Valleys. No… my father wasn't a coal miner. In fact, I don't know who my father was. And oh, I can't sing.' Flynt couldn't resist biting back when typecast by the quintessential English as quintessential Welsh, his reaction to the supercilious bastards usually over the top. 'And you... where are you from, Mr Brenton?'

'From Kensington.' Not London, Flynt observed, but from prime real estate.

'Before that?'

'Eton and Cambridge, then back to London. But what has this to do with your inquiry?'

Flynt need not have asked. Brenton's pedigree was etched into every word, clear, distinct, a dead giveaway for a practised listener like Flynt. More irritating was that condescending echo – that Flynt was only filling space, his presence on the planet unnecessary.

'Please, tell me what the City is saying?' insisted Brenton. 'The merger you have in mind was completed almost two years ago. The bank has moved on.'

'I'm talking about traders,' continued Flynt, 'inventing a rumour in the morning and knocking it down in the afternoon to pocket their margin.'

'I wouldn't know about that. What have they been saying about the bank?'

'A whistleblower claims Shield Bank ran a concert party. It all seems pretty thin to me... perhaps someone with a grudge. Have you sacked anyone lately?' Flynt sat back, watching a smile creep across Brenton's good looks, relieved by the reporter's lack of enthusiasm for the story. But an allegation of a share support operation during the merger was a serious matter, even though it was done and dusted.

'Go ahead. I'll be happy to help, if possible,' said Brenton, 'although I thought this kind of operation ended when those Guinness fellows were locked up thirty years ago.'

'We had a letter, anonymous of course,' explained Flynt, 'from someone who evidently doesn't like Shield Bank. He claims your offshore subsidiary, Cayman Islands Finance, secretly sold shares it never owned – naked selling, I believe you call it – in Deep Drilling, the oil company you were after, thereby supporting your bid by driving down its share price. That way you got the company on the cheap. Well, that's what the whistle-blower says.'

'You're partly right. Shield made a killing on that deal but the bank had already disposed of Cayman Islands Finance. If it was selling short then it must have been on its own account. If you want to take this further I suggest you talk to Island Partners Trust, the new owners of Cayman Islands Finance.'

It was Flynt's turn to wobble. Not for the first time had he fabricated a story only to discover it contained a grain of truth. Brenton's reference to 'making a killing' sounded too much like Julia Cross's revised account of that last phone call.

Prevaricate, play for time, that's what a reporter did when stumped. After a few more polite but irrelevant questions to show he knew the mechanics behind takeovers, Flynt closed his notebook and said, 'That covers everything, nothing in this. I suppose I better get hold of Island Partners Trust, the new owners. Is that what you said?'

'Yes, but I'm afraid you'll have to go to the Cayman Islands. They don't have a presence in London. Not so bad, if the office pays.' Brenton beamed, pleased with how he'd handled it. 'If you do write something, Mr Flynt, you won't mention the bank, will you?'

Flynt nodded. 'Incidentally,' he said as he rose to leave. 'How is your wife? That's another story I've been following… patients in a persistent vegetative state.'

'Ah… no different really,' stammered Brenton, shaken by the sudden change of tack. 'We thought there was a slight improvement but it was imaginary.'

'So life-support hasn't been withdrawn? Is that imminent?'

'Ah… yes… But why are you asking Mr Flynt?'

'As I said, it's a story the agency is following. In fact, I saw Professor Wilkins yesterday. He seems to think zolpidem might help and can't understand why you refuse to let him use it.'

'Really, Wilkins should not be discussing such matters without my consent. This is a serious breach of patient confidentiality. I'll have to speak to him.'

'I thought you'd want to try anything if there was a chance of reviving your wife.'

Brenton exploded, his composure broken by an uncharacteristic snarl. 'So that's your game! You get in on a pretext, when you're real interest is poking your tabloid nose into my poor wife's last remaining days. This is a private matter.'

'I wouldn't say switching off a person's life-support was entirely private. A judge has to give the go-ahead.'

'And he has, a month ago… but it hasn't happened.'

'That's only because the mother got an injunction.'

'No-one believes her. Have you seen the letter… no-one has. It doesn't exist.'

'But your affair with Julia Cross does… very real… shagging your wife's best friend while she's unconscious…'

Brenton's mouth dropped open. All he could manage was an incoherent choking sound. One more push and Flynt knew he had him.

'Gives the police a motive if you try to put your wife asleep… permanently.'

Flynt's style was more Spanish Inquisition than Q&A. The trouble with his approach was that precious little room was left for retreat, the only way forward, to go for the jugular. 'Don't tell me you want Helen to die with dignity,' Flynt snapped. 'A shot of zolpidem won't make death any less dignified.'

Flynt had pressed the pressure point so hard it was sticking out of Brenton's neck, the silky smooth financier tugging at the arms of his executive chair for a weapon; afraid to utter another word in case it was twisted back at him.

'Doesn't look good, Brenton,' Flynt pushing even harder, 'the telephone call before the accident… your rush to pull the plug on life-support… the Cross woman not just waiting in the wings but in your bed… now zolpidem. Imagine what the courts will make of that little lot.'

Flynt did not particularly like the way he did business and was glad he couldn't see or hear himself in action, the process draining him of human feeling. The more bastards he subjected to this brutal line of questioning, the more insensitive and indifferent he became to human sensibilities. The Spanish Inquisition had people like him using rack and thumbscrew.

Brenton's loathing for the reporter who was kicking the legs off his life was palpable. 'I imagine you're planning to spread this across your dirty little newspaper, Mr Flynt?'

'Not one… dozens. INS is an agency with three thousand subscribers at the last count.'

'I'll sue.'

'Join the club. You won't get far. I can prove it. And Wilkins will confirm you've stopped him trying zolpidem. He doesn't fancy being an accessory to attempted murder.'

'What guarantee do I have if I let Wilkins administer the drug… that you won't mention the relationship with Julia?' The only time Brenton had known a journalist sign a confidentiality clause was when forced to by a court.

Flynt had always refused to deal. This was different, not about securing a front page splash but personal. His guts were being twisted into knots by the voice on the Bakelite – worse still, how it got there.

'Let's do it then,' he replied. 'What do I have to sign?' Brenton buzzed his PA and a few minutes later Flynt was signing what was in effect a gagging order. But what the hell! Flynt had nothing to sign away, no outlet for the Brenton story. Sacked by INS, Flynt would be considered damaged goods. No-one would touch him and anything he offered would be suspect.

'I want closure, otherwise Julia and I will have this hanging over our heads forever. We've nothing to be ashamed of. Do you know the last time I had sex with my wife? Not eighteen months ago, more like five years. Our marriage has been on the rocks for a very long time.'

Rocks, thought Flynt, picking up the telephone on Brenton's desk, were always in the bed. 'Ring Wilkins,' he said, waving the receiver at Brenton, 'tell him he can use the drug. I want to hear you say it.'

Brenton did, then handed the receiver back for Flynt to speak with Wilkins. The consultant was hedging his bets. 'Even if there's sign of recovery,' he cautioned, 'she might easily relapse. It happens with zolpidem. Her head struck the steering wheel; the impact drove her brain against the side of the skull. It all depends on the depth of the coma. Most patients who regain consciousness with the assistance of zolpidem have relapsed after a short time.'

'How short?'

'Some remain conscious long enough to recognise relatives, even talk… others only minutes.' That's all Flynt needed – time to discover whether Helen Brenton was the voice on the Bakelite.

Chapter 16

FLYNT JOINED FAMILY, clinicians and nurses outside the ward Helen shared with two other patients in a persistent vegetative state. The mood was sombre, the bed of one patient – a young woman also injured in a road accident – empty, the sheets stripped, the life-support gear removed. The blue feeding tubes had been disconnected the previous week with the agreement of her parents and she died seven days later. Zolpidem had not helped.

Only David Brenton and the mother-in-law who loathed him were admitted to the ward with Wilkins and a nurse, together with an independent clinical observer.

Flynt was permitted to wait in an adjoining room, to observe the administration of zolpidem through a glass partition. Wilkins and the hospital knew full well that if the treatment worked it became front page news around the world. Publicity like that was sure to help fund the care of other patients. Nevertheless, Flynt was asked to sign an undertaking of confidentiality, surrendering to Wilkins and the hospital the absolute right to approve or block anything written for publication. Not that this worried him. His hands were never tied. In Flynt's world the person with least scruples more often than not won the race to get the page one splash.

The treatment, Wilkins explained, would be over a period of five days after which it would be suspended if there was no discernible change in Brenton's condition. Flynt understood Wilkins's anxiety. Zolpidem was a double-edged sword, a sort of truth drug. If a patient diagnosed as 'brain dead' did regain consciousness, the clinician was exposed to a charge of misdiagnosis in an increasingly litigious world.

Flynt was expecting to see someone hovering between life and death, an ashen face at the end of a plastic tube. Not for a moment had he imagined Helen Brenton's ruby cheeks, pale blue eyes, blonde hair neatly combed, eyes wide open, staring into the unknown, not blinking, quite motionless. Rather than the ante-room to a morgue, the ward seemed strangely vibrant, the woman lying there more alive than some of the paper characters who filed through Flynt's world. Surely, a simple kiss on the cheek would revive the sleeping beauty. How could the Brenton guy play around when in happier days this woman was waiting at home? Trapped inside a body that never moved, behind eyes that never flickered, did Helen know the bastard wanted to starve her to death? From one look at Helen Brenton, Flynt was convinced that from her rich and complex internal life she had reached out to him to save her from her husband's murderous intentions. Wilkins had told Flynt of several well-documented accounts of coma patients who, on regaining consciousness, told of how they were trapped inside their bodies, yet fully aware of what was happening around them. It truly was the stuff of nightmares, unable to speak, lift a hand in protest, fearing that each time a nurse fiddled with the blue feeding tube might be the last.

'What next?' Flynt asked after Wilkins gave Helen her first shot of zolpidem.

'We wait. Nurses will monitor the situation around the clock, checking blood pressure, heartbeat, regularly. The first sign of an improvement could frankly be anything – sweating, faster breathing, increased blood pressure,' explained Wilkins. Consciousness, he reminded Flynt, would not return like the flick of a switch. The process went through several phases. Moaning was a good sign, so was response to pain. No, they would not be sticking pins in her although the standard test, applying pressure to the fingernails and the bony ridge above the eyes still sounded primitive to Flynt.

'And she'll help,' added Wilkins, nodding towards Jane Long, Helen's feisty mother, kneeling at the bedside, holding her daughter's hand and praying. 'She's been here constantly. If anyone sees a change she will.' On a stand beside the bed, in direct line of sight were photographs of the Brenton children, and other mementos, including a small blue handkerchief, Helen's night-time 'comforter' as a child. Jane Long had tried everything to revive her daughter, railing at her to wake up when artificial feeding was withdrawn from the other patient. Holding her daughter's hand, she'd screamed, 'You'll be next. Start fighting, don't you dare give up now. I've had enough of this. Smile at me, damn it! Come back to me.' Day after day Mrs Long had sat there, washing and combing her daughter's hair, talking about family and friends, while fighting off her heartless, treacherous son-in-law.

After the fourth dose of zolpidem, Helen's mother felt her daughter's fingers straighten in the palm of her hand. The slightest of movements, barely discernible, it grew steadily stronger until Helen was squeezing gently in response. Eyes that were trance-like opened wider and turned, smiling at the photographs on the stand beside the bed. Then she slept, a real, deep sleep, the first since the accident.

A ripple of excitement ran through the hospital, Brenton's recovery giving hope to others. Wilkins was massively relieved, embarrassing Flynt with his gushing gratitude.

'She's dreaming,' Wilkins told Flynt cheerfully. 'I don't believe her dreams ever switched off. Blood pressure is fine and so is the pulse rate. Whether it's the drug, or the mother, I can't say. But it's absolutely remarkable. Thanks don't seem enough, Flynt. You put me through hell but you were right to do so.'

'But for how long?' Flynt interrupted.

'She won't relapse. This is natural, healing sleep, I'm certain.'

The next afternoon Helen sat up and smiled at her husband David as if he had never left her side. Flynt shook his head in disbelief. Later she was chatting to family members, even watched some television, but the man who made this possible wasn't allowed near. Collaring Wilkins in the corridor, Flynt asked impatiently, 'Just one minute for one question... about the telephone call she made before the accident, that's all I ask. I'll go then. You owe me... and I can't write anything without your say-so.'

'Why does it matter now what was said on the telephone? Look at them... they seem very happy with each other. Her memory is pretty good as regards events before the accident. She's unlikely to behave this way if her husband wished her harm.'

'For me this is personal... nothing to do with any story but it matters more than you will ever know,' pleaded Flynt. 'For Christ's sake man, let me ask the question.'

Wilkins found Flynt difficult to resist. But would his aggressive line of questioning cause a relapse?

'You're a terrifying man, Flynt,' said Wilkins. 'It's not so much the questions you ask but how you ask them. You're remorseless. You wore me down. Helen couldn't face it, not so soon. She's only now remembering.'

For once Flynt thought hard before replying. He had another tool in his box – charm, in abundance for situations like this. 'Hard man, soft man... you've heard of that, Wilkins?' replied Flynt. 'All you've seen is a disagreeable bastard cracking a hard nut, you! I am quite capable of compassion, sympathy, if that works better. Just give me the chance.'

Wilkins still shook his head. 'What if Helen Brenton can't

remember or doesn't want to… you'll revert to type… be the hard man again… won't you?'

'No way… just one question, that's all I'll ask. If I don't get an answer, that's it, I'll walk away. You don't really think I'd want to harm her, not after everything the woman's been through,' smiled Flynt, charming the bird out of the tree.

'You'll give me that assurance?'

'Certainly… then I'll be gone, out of your lives forever, promise.'

Wilkins waited for David Brenton to leave before leading Flynt into the ward where Helen was chatting happily to her mother.

While the mother greeted Flynt as her daughter's saviour, Helen barely acknowledged his presence until obliged to do so after Wilkins reminded her of Flynt's sympathetic support for her treatment. Flynt might not have existed – Helen irritated at having to break away from her mother to engage with someone she evidently preferred not to know. At last acknowledging his presence with a smile as thin as tracing paper, she raised her steely blue eyes, and snorted genteelly. 'Mr Flynt… my husband has spoken about you. I am so grateful,' promptly resuming the conversation with her mother.

Christ, she's dismissing me, thought Flynt. The defenceless soul who had stared at him through empty eyes was now a quite different person, self-assured, arrogant. Once conscious she'd reverted to a type that placed Flynt's station in life several rungs down the ladder. Having been rewarded with her miserly thanks, he was expected to leave. Helen Brenton was as disdainful as her fucking husband, thought Flynt, sorely tempted to revert to his other type.

Instead, he pressed on with the question he was aching to ask but already sensed the answer. Back in the real world, the

Brenton woman was not one to shop her husband, no matter what he did or didn't do.

'The last thing I want is upset you, Mrs Brenton, but can I ask about your friend Julia Cross and the call you made to her on the night of the accident?'

She smiled weakly at the mention of the name. 'Oh yes, Julia. Not such a good friend,' she replied with more frankness than Flynt expected.

'Why do you say that?'

'She was having an affair with David, still is… has been for several years. I wasn't really interested, Mr Flynt.'

'But you did call her on the night of the accident and did you say, "Help! He's trying to kill me."' Flynt's voice pleaded for a yes.

The question hung in the air. Helen Brenton made Flynt wait. When the reply came he wasn't surprised.

'Yes, I did telephone Julia but if I remember correctly, I said something about David having made a killing. It was on the stock market, some oil deal, I believe.'

The answer was there, on the tip of her tongue, waiting to spit in his face. What had the cheating husband promised in return for an alibi?

Question asked, Flynt hesitated, wondering whether to toss in a little hand grenade but decided not to bother. There was no mileage for him in exposing the tangled love life of the Brentons. The coma was another lead that had run aground – unless, of course, the Bakelite never rang again. If the woman's cry for help had been a projection of Helen Brenton's subconscious, she'd ring off now that she was wide awake. He could only wait. But Flynt who'd followed many a story down a cul-de-sac sensed he'd found another.

Leaving the ward, he headed for the hospital exit, Wilkins on his shoulder, beaming, quite unable to contain his excitement. 'A world first,' he muttered, the consultant already basking in the acclaim he was anticipating. Instead of destroying his reputation and career as seemed possible at one point, the Brenton case would propel him into the front rank, thanks largely to Flynt's intervention

Flynt was stepping through the exit door when Wilkins held him back. 'Just one question,' he insisted. 'I'll say it again… you were instrumental in Helen Brenton's recovery. While I neglected to question her husband's decision not to use zolpidem, you did and won. How you persuaded him I'd rather not know. Without your intervention she'd still be in a coma so why the obsession with a silly telephone call? Why not take the credit for what you achieved?'

With a last glance at the consultant Flynt mumbled, 'A loose end. I don't like leaving loose ends.' But he had – a very large one!

Chapter 17

THE SHINY, FUR-TRIMMED, brown-leather bomber jacket loitering outside the wrought-iron gates of the Royal Hospital locked on to Flynt heading along the pavement towards the Tube station. Flynt didn't hear footsteps or see a shadow, nor spot the black saloon car pull away from the kerb, but sensed a tail. A crime reporter he knew swore you could smell a professional tail because Special Branch 'watchers' rarely bathed.

At the station plaza Flynt studied the map of the London Underground to figure how best to get to Docklands. Before stepping on the elevator he turned and sniffed the air – nothing, only a black saloon lingering just beyond the entrance.

Flynt had a score to settle. Gus White had given him a bum steer by juicing-up Helen Brenton's last words, never expecting the coma lady to make it through the endless night.

The watering holes might have changed from Fleet Street to Docklands but by eight in the evening they were still awash with reporters burying the end of the day in a torrent of noisy self-adulation lubricated by as much beer as they could swallow before their last train. There were a dozen such bars, each an off-duty extension of a newspaper. The *Gazette* pub was the Red Lion, standing room only, no seats, just a long bar down one side and a shelf on the other for thirsty hacks to plonk their pints. Outside, under a large yellow parasol, the great unwashed, the smokers, sheltered from the wind and rain before hurrying back to dip their frozen toes in large malt whiskies.

Flynt spotted Gus White through the gaggle of reporters, his back to the crowd, leaning against the bar and leering at the barmaid who didn't have much to offer but neither had White.

'You bastard,' Flynt growled, snatching at White's shoulder. 'Coma Woman's Last Words… you made 'em up.' Shaken by the savage assault on his rear, White turned, pushing his assailant aside.

'What did you say?' he croaked through a squall of beer fumes. 'Oh that. The Brenton story,' he added, recognising Flynt. 'For Christ's sake, Jack, forget it… it was only a little one… no harm, no-one got hurt.' Pressing a finger against his lips, White offered Flynt a pint. 'Live and forget. You've done the same, haven't you Jack?'

'Never,' shouted Flynt slamming a fist into White's fat beer gut. The *Gazette* reporter dropped to his knees, spewing his last pint across the floor. The hubbub in the bar cut to a murmur, the crowd of reporters parting as Flynt elbowed his way to the door. That, he told himself, was the first time he'd left a pub without a drink. But he didn't get far, his escape blocked when the passenger door of a black saloon parked at the kerb flew open across his path. Levering himself onto the pavement, a Special Branch officer in a shiny brown bomber jacket said, 'A word, Mr Flynt, we'd like a word.'

'And who wants a word?'

'Counter Terrorism Command, sir.' The man flashed a warrant card. It might have been his bus pass.

'Not Special Branch, aye?'

'Not since 2006… we were merged.' Flynt swayed backwards, away from the man's bad breath.

'You want a word… about what?'

'I can't say, sir…'

'I know… you just watch…'

'Our instructions are to escort you…'

'To Thames House… MI5?'

'Paddington Green.'

174

'The same... for questioning terrorists. You're not suggesting I'm one?'

Fetchers and carriers said nothing, they only watched while munching stale sandwiches and drinking cold coffee. Flynt would play along, not protest his civil rights until he got to the main man.

'No brown paper,' he said, climbing into the back of the Ford Focus.

'Brown paper, I don't follow.' At last a reaction!

'I was told you people lined the interior with brown paper. Isn't that standard... so suspects can't plead they were framed... say they picked up the Semtex on their pants on the transfer to the nick?'

The interview room at Paddington Green was square, not covered with brown paper either but with symmetrical, white tiles. The purpose, according to rumour, was to focus the attention of suspects, not allow it to drift away from the interrogation. Flynt had seen judges do the same, focusing on a spot on the ceiling or wall of a courtroom to deliver a fluent judgment.

The room was ten by ten feet, an underground cell with audio-visual – CDs for easy listening between spells of interrogation after a Member of Parliament complained Paddington Green was inhospitable. The pencil and paper on the table could be useful, thought Flynt, when he blew the bastards up for false arrest, of course, only figuratively!

The door opened and two suits entered, one double-breasted pin-striped, banker-type, hair slicked back across his scalp, the other a heavyweight in a loud green check.

'Bloody hell,' exclaimed Flynt, throwing up his arms in mock surrender. 'Don't hit me, don't hit me... promise, I'll sing like a canary.' The 'twitchers' were back from Île d'Iroise. Leaning across the table, a hand cocked behind his ear, Flynt smiled, 'Not a twitter, fellas... no birds down here.' Plod and Son hadn't pulled him in for nicking Julia Cross's photograph – or to congratulate him for saving Helen Brenton's life. He was there by invitation. Not many hacks got one. Flynt would make the most of the anti-terrorism squad's hospitality for a look around.

'Introductions... please fellers.'

'I'm Mathias,' said the Brit. 'My associate is Donovan.' It wasn't necessary to add MI5 and CIA. Flynt took that as a given.

'Do you still have it, the plastic bag?' Mathias put on a cold, polite smile. 'The Carrefour bag? You had it in Paris and St Pancras.'

Flynt said, 'Isn't that the kind of thing you guys do – know where stuff is?'

Mathias wasn't playing games. 'You moved out of the hotel in Paddington,' he said.

'But only around the corner to the Royal Gate,' said Flynt.

Mathias asked, 'Has it rung again, in London?'

Flynt ran the flat of his hand across his scalp, resisting the temptation to punch the air. They'd heard it – that first night at Hotel du Port. His mind wasn't playing tricks. The follow-up question would be something like, 'Can we take a look.' Why shouldn't they. No-one was better equipped than MI5 to discover why the Bakelite rang. To Flynt's surprise, Mathias dropped the subject, asking instead, 'How well do you know the Brevilet brothers?'

'Only that they've put my life on hold with their bloody language protest. You saw what happened, what they did to me.'

'Oh yes, their beloved lingo,' exclaimed Mathias. 'The younger brother – Lan, I believe – at the very spot your wife fell in the middle of the night and holding a flashlight to make sure he didn't miss a thing... very convenient. Then they hang you out to dry.'

'He was looking for lost sheep… that's what he would have said if the magistrate gave him the chance.'

Donovan's first contribution to the Q&A rocked Flynt.

'The Brevilets don't keep sheep… they don't have any livestock, not even chickens. We're not sure what they farm, if anything. Nor do they fish. Nor are they crew. But they have the ferry.' Lebrun had said the big rasping American didn't have a sense of humour. He wasn't joking.

'In fact, who is Herve Brevilet?' asked Mathias.

'My wife grew up there… remembered him as a kid.'

Mathias said, 'Yes, we've seen his birth certificate. Born on the island in 1960 it says, and his brother… both on the family farm.'

'So what's the problem?'

'His father is stated as being "deceased, lost at sea"… no name. Strangely, the younger brother's biological dad is also "deceased, lost at sea." Both took their mother's maiden name… Brevilet. And, yes, the birth certificates are genuine, and in French. No language hang-up there.'

'So the Brevilets are legit.'

'So is the extended family. Our people have identified twenty or so from French National Archives… could be more. Give 'em a form and they'll fill it in, pronto. Not the others.'

'The others?'

'Those who don't exist, at least not officially… have never registered a birth or death, nor participated in any census all because of the language hang-up,' said Mathias. 'They sit on the quay mending their nets, not talking to strangers… hanging on to their language like a life jacket.'

Flynt nodded. 'Probably is for them. But I agree… not fun people.' He was thinking in particular of mine host at Hotel du Port with her greasy apron and few words.

Donovan half smiled. 'The old crone at the hotel is Madame

Brevilet, the mother. The hotel's been in the family since the end of the last war.'

Flynt sat quite still, not pushing back as was his style but wondering why Mathias was telling him all this. Was this an interrogation or a briefing? The American was clearly impatient to make more progress and of the type not averse to a spot of second degree, but he wasn't running the show. Flynt guessed it was being orchestrated by someone from behind the large mirror on the wall opposite. Whoever it was knew that in Britain hacks wore a 'don't mess with the Press' notice around their necks.

Plod and Son were unusually civil and respectful, Mathias in particular cheerfully swapping info. Successful interrogations were like interviews, about holding the high ground. Flynt had a set of stock responses for that purpose, his favourite, 'Don't bullshit a bullshitter.' No need. The pair had surrendered the high ground voluntarily.

A bleeper sounded in Mathias's jacket pocket. Nodding to each other they headed for the door. 'We'll be back – listen to the music,' said the American. 'Fly Me to the Moon' was Number 1 in Interview Room 3 and on its way around a second time when Plod and Son returned accompanied by a distinguished, older individual with silver hair and a weak smile. After introducing himself, Jerry Townsend said, 'I was impressed with how you handled David Brenton.'

Flynt accepted the compliment with a slow nod. How did MI5 know about his conversation with Brenton in his executive suite at Shield Bank... and why another sudden change of tack? Perhaps interrogators were taught to jump about to soften up a subject for what was to follow.

'I thought some of Brenton's answers concerning that share support scheme were a bit thin – well worth a closer look,' said Townsend. 'Not for us but I'll see it's passed on.'

Flynt got the message. Townsend was saying there were no

secrets from MI5; that he'd be calling the shots from then on. Townsend was the man to give the nod if Flynt decided to pull the plug on their little chat by pleading unlawful detention. But having suffered the agonies of the Brenton dead end, he wasn't ready to surrender his handle on what was shaping as a new lead.

Townsend began with an apology. 'I hope we haven't upset you by mentioning your wife. Our friends in Paris are taking care of that.' Mathias flushed painfully. Donovan was amused. There must have been a very British spat behind the scenes.

Townsend continued, 'We are interested in the telephone that appears to defy the laws of physics by ringing when it shouldn't. I've not heard it personally but my friends have.'

Flynt was convinced Townsend was about to ask for a gander.

He didn't.

'Has it occurred to you Mr Flynt the calls are for you and you alone, that if we were to confiscate the phone, as we could quite easily, and pull it apart the caller might never ring again?'

'That suits me fine. It's driving me crazy. Until your guys said they'd heard it I thought I was.'

'But they've not heard the voice... no-one has apart from yourself.'

'My girlfriend has.'

'The young Monique. Are you sure she's not saying what you want to hear?'

That was always a possibility. Monique had told a porky to humour him, why not again?

'It is not our intention to seize the phone,' Townsend continued, 'at least not immediately. That's not in the best interests of national security.'

So this was a security matter. Who in God's name did MI5 think was ringing? What about the message? Flynt wondered whether it was some kind of terrorist code. But that wouldn't explain how it came to ring.

Townsend offered an explanation. 'Technology has moved on Mr Flynt. If terrorists are able to use a mobile phone to detonate a bomb from the other side of the world, don't you think technology can generate a signal to ring your little bell?'

'Demonstrate,' said Flynt, 'assuming you have that technology.'

'That's the rub. The bell and voice are produced by separate mechanisms. We had a similar experience some years ago at our embassy in Tehran. Pulled the phone to pieces prematurely, found nothing and lost the link to the source. The phone was re-assembled but never rang again. We don't want a repeat of this, not before we find the source and analyse the message.'

Townsend ploughed on, not stopping to take a breath. Evidently, the situation was frustrating MI5 at least as much as it did Flynt.

'On the other hand now that Helen Brenton is back in the land of the living it might never ring again. If that was to happen it opens up a whole new ball game, as our American friends would say – that someone could communicate through their subconscious.'

'What next... what do you want from me?'

Townsend said, 'We want you to take the calls, note the circumstances – in particular where you are at the time. That will help us identify the source. And there's this...' He handed Flynt a micro recorder with a rubber sucker at the end of a lead to clamp to the side of the Bakelite casing. 'There could be some subtle changes in the message, a hidden code.'

'There have been some changes. The last time the caller rang before Helen Brenton came out of her coma I thought she wanted to say more but got cut off.'

Townsend took out a white linen handkerchief and wiped his lips, then looked at it as if expecting to see blood.

After wiping his lips a second time, Townsend carefully folded the handkerchief and stuffed it inside the sleeve of his jacket. 'I'm told,' he said, a touch of weariness in his voice, 'that you're no great fan of the security services... that we're too public school for the boy from the *Varllays*.' The sarcastic crack riled Flynt who couldn't remember ever expressing an opinion on MI5. 'We keep Britain safe,' Townsend reminded him, 'allow you more freedom and better conditions than any other country in the world. The old school tie works for Britain.'

Contempt shone in Flynt's eyes. His only loyalty was to freedom of the press.

'And get a new plastic bag before the Carrefour falls apart,' Townsend added.

Leaving Paddington Green Flynt was careful to look around every corner. After the third corner he stopped and turned. The black Ford that picked him up in the Docklands was still there. Flynt walked towards it. The driver pulled into the kerb and parked on a double yellow line. Flynt tapped his window. The pasty-faced 'watcher' tried to look surprised.

'To give you time to take a bath,' said Flynt, 'I'm heading back to the hotel to pick up my woman and take her for a steak at Simpson's-in-the-Strand washed down with a bottle of Aussie red, maybe two, followed by cheese, British, of course. After brandy with espressos, it'll be back to the hotel for a fuck. No, you can't watch.' The astonished 'watcher' cracked. The look on his face made Flynt's bloody awful day a little better.

MI5 and pals must have been on his tail since the Bakelite rang at Hôtel du Port. Pushing his way along Oxford Street, Flynt felt even more confused. Was Townsend really suggesting the Helen Brenton experience meant communication with the subconscious was possible, could be used in the interests of national security? The notion rattled around Flynt's head like a snooker ball looking for a pocket. Flynt found it hard to believe. More likely he was the unwitting party to some kind of terrorist plot. That's why MI5 wanted him to record the calls so that it could trace the source.

Monique was standing guard over the Bakelite when Flynt opened the door of the hotel room overlooking Hyde Park. Crossing to his bag lying on the bed, he pulled out the bottle of scotch that travelled with him for emergencies. 'An emergency,' he told Monique, filling a tumbler. Monique watched, dressed to kill, waiting to be taken for dinner at the hotel's à la carte restaurant. Flynt's only interest was the scotch bottle, tossing a couple of ice cubes into the tumbler, and topping up again before wriggling out of his jacket and settling in an armchair for a session. By the end of the bottle he figured the Bakelite should be ringing like crazy.

'Want one?' he said not bothering to look up. Nothing would distract him from hunting pink elephants. Without asking, Monique knew it was a bad day – that Brenton was not the woman on the phone. 'She's back in the world of the living, OK, but denies everything,' Flynt volunteered. 'Agreed she made a call to the girlfriend before the accident but nothing was said about anyone trying to knock her off. The *Gazette* spiced up the quotes... Gus White admits it.'

'Have you tried Cross?' Monique asked.

'No point. Brenton knew all about the affair... wasn't interested. I'm screwed both ways. If the Bakelite woman doesn't ring again I might not be mad but the implications are mindblowing... subconscious communications and all that toss. If there's another call, I really don't know what to think. Has there been?'

'Yes,' said Monique, 'twice.'

'When,' he exclaimed, pouring himself a refill. He had his little chat with Helen Brenton around two that afternoon. According to Monique the Bakelite lady rang, much later. Flynt's hopes of finding a credible explanation were drowning amongst the ice cubes in his glass.

'At least you're not…' Monique hesitated.

'Mad, is that what you're thinking?'

'I've heard her… remember?'

'Perhaps I've infected you too.'

The bottle of scotch was half empty. The pink elephants should soon be joining the party. He swore the black Bakelite was smiling at him from across the room, tempting him to drink himself to death. Monique agreed, knocking the glass from his hand, the amber liquid spilling across the snow-white bedroom carpet. Instinctively, he reached out to protect his bottle, but too late. Monique kicked over the table, Flynt dropping onto his knees trying to catch the precious fluid.

'Idiot… you're like a mad dog scratching in the dirt. If you want to kill yourself, there's plenty here,' Monique screamed, throwing open the door of the minibar. Flynt climbed to his feet and staggered to the bathroom, bouncing off the wall. Moments later he had three fingers down his throat and threw up. That's what drunks did to free up capacity.

Wiping his face with a towel, Flynt stared blankly at the mirror on the wall, Monique railing at his back in French. The Gallic torrent was shot through with real concern.

'I'm hungry. I want to eat,' she said suddenly. Flynt fished out his wallet and threw a few large notes on the bed.

'Are you coming or drinking?' her voice loaded not with contempt but pity. Flynt replied by diving on the bed to dream of pink elephants. Occasionally, Monique flickered into focus, driving the elephants away from a very large black Bakelite phone sitting at the edge of a grassy plain. Suddenly, the phone rang, jolting him awake. His eyes heavy, he scrambled off the bed, snatching up the Bakelite but nothing, no voice, not a sound until it dawned on him Monique was at the door returning from her meal.

'She's rung again, the woman?'

Shaking his head, Flynt fell back on the bed, desperate for sleep but afraid to dream. Burying his head in his hands, he felt Monique's arm slide around his shoulders, holding him like the child he never was.

'You'll feel much better when we get home… everyone does.' Monique's whisper was a shield against despair, against the pain of not knowing. Head bowed, eyes chasing empty shadows, Flynt knew it could get a lot more complicated after his tête-à-tête at Paddington Green. Until he found a real-world explanation for the ringing Bakelite he'd do what he did best – chase other people's problems, let them prevail over his own. He'd work the bloody thing out of his system!

He woke hung over, eyes gritty, still half pissed. Someone had driven a spike through the back of his head. After a long cold shower and plenty of strong black coffee, they were in a cab heading for St Pancras. Monique was right. He needed the familiar feel of his Paris apartment.

Chapter 18

EUROSTAR WAS EMERGING from the Channel Tunnel at Calais when Flynt got the call from Yates in the Paris Bureau.

'Where are you?'

'On the train… just left the Tunnel. Why ask? I don't work for INS, remember? I quit before I was sacked. So what do you want, Yates?' Flynt guessed from the pause at the other end that Yates was searching for an easy way out. There wasn't one. 'You've won. New York has allowed your appeal… my fault… would you believe it! I should have put it in writing… the final warning. They're shit scared… afraid to go to court. You're back on the payroll.'

'I'm on leave… another week.'

'By Sunday I want you on that island of yours.'

'Île d'Iroise?'

'The French are sending a fucking gunboat.'

'What! When did this happen?'

'Now… the papers here are full of it. Islanders refuse to speak French… tear up constitution, Napoleon very unhappy – Island at War. How come you didn't write that when you went for the inquest? You did see the story?'

'I had other matters on my mind, don't you remember?' Flynt hissed. That said, Yates was having a go at him for good reason. He'd broken his golden rule: never become part of the news, write it.

'AFP, Reuters are all running it. I had to pick it up. New York doesn't like that.'

Before Flynt could hang up, Yates snapped, 'A situationer… the island, the people… for tonight's schedule. You know the kind of stuff. How they're a bit odd… Amish-like… withdrawn, isolated from the mainstream, speaking their own language.' For Yates, the Amish were a yardstick by which he measured unconventional behaviour.

'Write it on the train,' Yates insisted, 'and don't forget the Amish line.' That's what bureau chiefs did – build up subscriber interest in a story. 'Any chance the Amish descended from the same ma and pa as the Bretons? They're all Europeans.' INS subscribers in the Amish heartlands in Pennsylvania and Delaware would buy that.

'Yeah, yeah… I hear you… but what about communications…'

'You've got a cell-phone.'

'I meant on Île d'Iroise. No signal.'

'Well, take the satellite for filing… that's all, not for personal use.'

Flynt rang off. He had an hour before Paris – an hour to write a two-thousand-word situationer.

'You're smiling,' said Monique.

'This is what I do, what I'm comfortable with.' Flynt opened his laptop and started writing about Île d'Iroise's rocky coastline, waves crashing against high cliffs buttressing barren moorland; islanders, their hands in the soil and the sea, praying on Sundays and fighting the French on Mondays. Not forgetting the Amish, of course, both isolated from mainstream society and its wicked ways. In fact, there were similarities between them; both communities devoted Christians hiding from the twenty-first century, the Amish inside it, the Bretons on the fringes – The Lost Tribe of Europe! Flynt had his angle, dressing it with stuff about people like the Jalenes, the elderly couple who wouldn't open their door for Emilie and Flynt – and islanders hiding in trees to avoid strangers, fearing the corrupting influence of French on their values and ideals. For them the Nazi occupation of the

Second World War would have been a cultural threat more than a mortal one, the islanders reputedly executing what remained of the German garrison and throwing their bodies in the sea before reinstating their cordon sanitaire. Flynt quoted 'sources' because for all their hostility towards outsiders, their fierce defence of their cultural heritage, the Île d'Iroise Bretons – the majority at least – seemed more pussycat than street fighter, their struggle essentially cerebral, preferring retreat to confrontation.

Flynt omitted from the backgrounder the bits and pieces that didn't chime with his portrait of a tribe living on the edge, clinging to the past. The DVD on the shelf in Herve Brevilet's farmhouse kitchen was perhaps the most puzzling. *Das Boot* hardly fitted with a society that killed Germans, had neither television nor radio. But the Brevilets and their neighbours in dirty-brown dungarees seemed more artful than the ragged, sullen fishermen bent over their nets around the harbour at Tourmant. The money piling up in the accounts of the ferry company from phantom visitors Flynt decided to leave for a follow-up. Someone was clearly on the fiddle. Not the fishermen, unless they, too, were taking lavish cruises. While the Amish were left to plough their own furrow in Pennsylvania, this lot were on their knees. Flynt's lasting images were of the pasty-faced little girl begging on the quay – and the Jalenes polishing a khaki-brown Nazi staff car hidden beneath a yellow tarpaulin.

Flynt sat back, searching for a final paragraph. 'Have you ever been to Île d'Iroise?'

Monique shook her head. 'It was always too far for the day and nowhere to stay when you got there. Some friends camped but never stayed long. The islanders weren't very friendly... *interdit* signs everywhere. You're not allowed to leave the main footpath.'

'A Lost Tribe... that's the line I'm taking... or would you say it was over the top, exaggerated?'

'They're certainly isolated.'

Personally Flynt felt the islanders should follow the evolutionary path, not fight it – get themselves a semi-detached, television and washing machine. But he never wrote opinion. Instead his final paragraph was about their resilience which no-one could deny:

'Lost Tribes are usually described as "unconnected" when in fact they are on the run from civilisation – indigenous groups taking a conscious decision to avoid an outside world intent on destroying their cultural heritage. The islanders of Île d'Iroise are not unlike those "unconnected" indigenous tribes of the Amazon – the Atlantic a vast blue wilderness pressing upon this surviving speck of Breton culture defended not with curare-tipped arrows but by resolution and endurance.'

Emilie would have approved, thought Flynt – not forgetting to press the send button the moment he got a signal at Paris Gare du Nord.

'What next?' Monique asked in the cab back to the apartment.

'Wait, see if it rings.' He explained about the rubber sucker for recording calls on the Bakelite. 'I'll set it up and then we wait. If I'm not there make a note of the time, how long the call lasts, what she says, whether she sounds any different.'

Flynt knew something was wrong the moment he opened the door of the apartment on Rue de St Michel. Someone had forced the lock on the display cabinet. The ebony-handled telephone picked up in Gaza always sat at the centre of the top shelf, the exhibits arranged in order of interest. It had been moved but nothing was missing. The intruder must have been after the Bakelite which was rarely out of Flynt's sight in London. Monique watched over it when he was chasing after Helen Brenton.

Not for the first time Flynt pulled out a screwdriver and

poked inside the Bakelite, hoping he'd missed something. Monique watched – she'd only ever known cell-phones. 'The bell,' Flynt explained, 'is triggered by a signal coming down the line from the exchange. The signal causes this lever to vibrate against this.' Flynt pointed the screwdriver at two small brass dishes. 'But that can't happen unless there's a signal and there can't be a signal if the phone isn't connected,' he explained, waving the frayed cable in Monique's face.

'Where did you get the phone?' she asked.

'From Boris, a friend of my mother's at the time.'

'Sounds Russian?'

'Estonian… he knew I collected old telephones. He brought it back from Tallinn after they kicked the Russians out in 1994.'

'And where did he get it?'

'No idea… Boris never said…' Flynt had returned to Quarry Hill for his annual visit, carrying a sack of presents for the assorted nephews and nieces.

After they were handed out, Boris said, 'And I've got something for you,' explaining that the phone was from Tallinn. Flynt assumed Boris had picked it up in a junk shop.

'I need to speak to Boris,' Flynt mumbled to himself. 'God knows where he is… rotting in some Estonian prison, I'd guess.' Without another word he flipped his mobile open and rang Quarry Hill.

'Dafydd… it's Jack… I need your help.'

'Only time you ring, Jack… when you need something…' He sounded bitter, staring at life on the dole at forty. Wales always drew the short straw, the good times never reaching huge swathes of the country, and ill prepared to weather the storm when the English house came crashing down.

'You'll have to be quick… I've got a meeting,' Dafydd told his brother.

189

'Still plotting the revolution... what are you calling yourselves nowadays?' replied Flynt unable to resist a crack at the plethora of groups that came and went like the tide, never offering much more than rhetoric. 'I need to contact Boris... do you know where in Estonia?' Flynt asked.

'He's not... he's here.'

'You mean in Wales?'

'Exactly... sitting beside me watching tele. Boris came back after Mam's funeral. They can't kick him out again. Estonia is part of the European Union. He's very happy... won't get rid of the bugger until they stop his social.'

'Can I have a word?' Flynt asked impatiently.

The Slav's fractured English was unmistakeable.

'Remember the phone you gave me... the one from Tallinn? Where did you get it?'

Boris hesitated. 'No matter... it's a nice phone... very old... you no want it?'

'I'm grateful Boris... I just assumed you bought it from a pawnbroker... a shop.'

A longer pause. 'Come on Boris, you can tell me... we're family.'

'From KGB...'

Flynt took a deep breath. 'You were in the KGB?'

'No, no...' replied Boris. After Estonia declared independence Soviet property was confiscated if it hadn't already been looted. Boris did his looting at KGB headquarters in Tallinn. The black Bakelite was a souvenir, he said.

'You're saying it belonged to the KGB?'

'Yes... it was in the office... on a shelf. But never worked... I bought a cell-phone.'

Hanging up, Flynt couldn't imagine the KGB, or its successor organisation, breaking into his apartment to retrieve their property unless it was something very, very special.

'Mrs Squire… she might have heard something… always listening.' Mrs Squire, his elderly neighbour and landlady, was forever complaining about the slightest noise, even Flynt's snoring. She had lived there until her English husband died and afterwards moved in with the widower across the landing. Paranoid about the few ancient sticks of furniture she'd left for Flynt to use, Mrs Squire had one ear glued to the party wall counting bottles he uncorked.

'Let's see if the old bat heard anything,' he said.

A sprightly eighty year old who took her dog to shit on other people's doorsteps each morning, she knew everything that happened in Rue de St Michel. In their friendlier moments, Flynt always said she'd make a great reporter, which seemed to please her. Apart from that, Mrs Squire thought him a noisy nuisance, wilfully destroying her furniture as he lurched drunkenly around the apartment.

Yes, she had heard a noise but didn't say what, her interest fixed on Monique. Must be his daughter, maybe niece was what Mrs Squire would be thinking, thought Flynt… too young to be anything else.

'Noise, you ask about noise? Mr Flynt you are a very noisy person. Sometimes I regret granting you a tenancy. You will have to pay for any damages. That's in the contract, you know that.' Flynt did, every last teaspoon to be accounted for according to the inventory agreement. 'You were drunk again Mr Flynt, that's what your friends said.'

'What friends?' Flynt asked.

'The two who answered the door when I complained… two nights ago… can't you remember… or were you too drunk…?'

'No, I was in London.'

Mrs Squire sniffed disapprovingly, not believing him. 'The men in the apartment,' Flynt asked, 'can you describe them?'

'One was young and fair, the other older but bigger… had

large hands, like my dentist... both were rough looking... country people.'

'And they spoke French?'

'No, Breton.'

'Now, how would you know that, Mrs Squire?'

'Because I'm Breton. I lived in Brittany before I came to Paris.' With one last look at Monique, she closed the door in Flynt's face. His neighbour might have imagined the noise – she often did – but not two real live Bretons. It was then the Bakelite rang again. The recorder clicked on but as far as Flynt could tell, the same voice, same message.

9th, 17th and 18th arrondissements meet. In the Thirties it was Henry Miller's favourite coffee stop and hang-out for writers and artists before the busy intersection was choked by exhaust fumes. Sidestepping the traffic honking through Place de Clichy, Flynt found Lebrun waiting in one of Wepler's private booths beneath a funky chandelier, his back resting against the soft leather upholstery. 'I've got more questions,' said Flynt, indicating the Bakelite in the Carrefour bag as he settled into the seat across the table.

He ordered oysters, Lebrun a Croque Madame, an open ham and cheese sandwich with a fried egg on Poilâne bread. The steadying influence of a glass of red wine checked Lebrun's shakes long enough to handle a knife and fork.

After they'd finished with the small talk, Flynt bent down and lifted the Bakelite on to the table. Lebrun frowned. 'You seem to take it everywhere my friend… perhaps that's the problem… the ringing is up here,' he said, tapping his forehead.

'It does ring,' Flynt insisted.

'I suppose it might… when repaired,' said Lebrun, holding up the loose flex. 'These early telephones were very simple devices but need junction boxes to work.'

'I've told you about the voice. It sounds crazy but she's as real as your Croque Madame. I've lost count of the number of times… on Île d'Iroise, in London and back at my apartment… and my girlfriend has heard it too.'

Lebrun reached across and lifted the receiver… still nothing. 'You say you have a conversation… with a woman?'

'Not exactly. She has a message for me – "Help! He's trying to kill me". Then she rings off. Not knowing is devouring me.'

Lebrun smiled. 'KGB,' he muttered. 'On the phone last night you said it once belonged to the KGB…'

'Yes… looted from KGB HQ in Tallinn… that's in Estonia.'

'I know where Tallinn is. I worked there during the Soviet

Chapter 19

L EBRUN WAS AWAKE, listening for a sound to break the
monotony of the night when Flynt called. Answering the
telephone at his elbow was the one thing he managed with an
atom of alacrity.

'It's Jack Flynt… sorry to ring so late. How are you?'

'As you might expect… slow, still very slow. I was questioned
by a gendarme this morning for loitering with intent inside the
launderette. I couldn't get the euro into the slot. And you?'

'OK… sort of. Remember you offered to help if I had mo
problems with that bloody telephone. You probably think I
mad.' Lebrun's silence sounded like confirmation. 'Did I ever
you I collect telephones?'

'I believe you did.'

'Well, it seems that this one… the black Bakelite – th
I carry in the Carrefour bag – once belonged to the KGB
hoping you might know an expert… someone to take a
look.' The grunt on the line meant Lebrun was intereste
another thing… La Société Commerciale… what more
know about the company?'

'I thought you were never going to ask,' sighed Leb
looked inside their office but didn't write a word. In
man from the London *Chronicle* said it's a time caps
Radenac left it in 1944. You know that's not true.'

'He wrote what I told him… damage limitation
I'm more interested in the bigger story. I know the
still not sure what it is.'

Lebrun agreed to meet Flynt the next mornin
Wepler on Place de Clichy, a busy crossroads

period, a fascinating city, even then. Did you know it was a member of the Hanseatic League, a sort of Middle Ages Common Market?'

Flynt didn't, nor did he care, anxious to move on without the history lesson.

'We're suspicious people, you and I, doubting everything and everyone, seeing only the bleakest landscape,' remarked Lebrun.

That was no bad thing in their line of work, thought Flynt, adding, 'Except when it blinds you to reality… and I won't see a shrink if that's what you're driving at.' Flynt stamped the parquetry floor, hard under his feet. Next he throttled a slice of lemon over his last oyster.

Lebrun reached for his glass of red wine, his hand as steady as a rock. 'You see how it helps,' he said cheerily, taking another sip, the dark rings around his eyes fading, the usually ashen cheeks touched with colour.

'The phone bell sounds… that's for sure,' continued Flynt. 'If it's not a pink elephant – my girlfriend will vouch for that – not a ghost, and I'm not off my rocker, then the voice on the line must be real. Where it comes from, how it got there, Christ only knows and he's not saying. Can you recommend someone, an expert, to take a look?'

'Perhaps you've mistaken a neighbour's ringing telephone for the Bakelite.'

'She doesn't have one. Uses my mobile, it's cheaper.'

'Your story is simply not credible, old chap.'

'MI5 wouldn't agree. I had a visitation in London. Well, they pulled me in for a chat.' Lebrun stopped poking his Croque Madame and took another swallow of wine.

'What do you mean exactly?' He set his glass on the table.

Flynt folded his hands behind his head. At last he had Lebrun's serious attention.

'The two bird-watchers from the inquest were there and their boss Jerry Townsend. I assumed he was the head man. He ran the show after a few preliminaries. The bird-watchers had heard the Bakelite ring at Hôtel du Port.'

'I know Townsend… thought he'd retired. The others were Toby Mathias MI5 and the American is Charles Donovan of the CIA. And did they find your telephone interesting?'

'They didn't even look. Instead they gave me something to record the calls while they try to trace the source.'

'And your wife… did they ask about Emilie?'

'To apologise for mentioning her.'

Lebrun sat back and, removing his spectacles from tired eyes, knocked over the wine bottle at his elbow.

'Don't worry, I'll get another,' said Flynt, avoiding the red stream draining off the table. In his experience, French waiters were generally idle, miserable sods, smiling only when scrounging for a tip. Welper's man, sensing work, turned his back and was heading for the kitchen when Flynt yelled, *'Garçon, ici, ici.'* After Flynt had dispatched the 'boy' with an ironic 'thank you, mate', Lebrun said, 'A torso, that's all you saw… a torso in a simple red dress and wearing a plain wedding ring… available from any jeweller. Red has always been a popular colour…' He meant Emilie's dress, the one she wore when she fell. Lebrun was at it again, letting loose a hare and seeing where it ran.

'My niece had a red dress too,' he said.

'Your niece and thousands of others wore red this summer in Paris, so what?'

'But they weren't on Île d'Iroise.'

Flynt fixed Lebrun with an apprehensive stare, the crippled old man very much the surprise package, one moment searching for the ghost of his dead wife, the next working with French intelligence. Lebrun might be on sick leave after his stroke but he was most definitely still on the Deuxième Bureau payroll.

'I tried to persuade Elise not to join the Bureau but she

wouldn't listen.' Lebrun's head dropped on his chest, his sorrow palpable.

'How old was she?' Flynt was already a jump ahead.

'Thirty-five... still young.'

Emilie was thirty-six. Flynt knew that could be a coincidence.

'Was Elise married?' He was thinking of the wedding ring.

'No... but Elise was on Île d'Iroise when your wife disappeared, investigating the incident involving the patrol boat. One moment there, the next gone, the boat I mean. You've seen our telecommunications array on the headland. The station had it on radar but not what sunk it.'

Flynt waited for Lebrun to feed him another line. Instead the Frenchman sat quietly, wrestling with his tortured thoughts.

'The wedding ring,' he said eventually. 'It could easily have been put on the finger after the body was found.'

Flynt's jaw dropped. He ran a hand across his scalp. He wasn't often stumped for a follow-up. All he could manage was a jittery, 'Why do you say that?'

'The bureau has confirmed it with the mortuary,' Lebrun said. Flynt recalled the mortuary attendant's surprise when the ring slipped easily off Emilie's finger.

Lebrun said, 'If the corpse had been in the water any length of time the ring would have become embedded in the flesh. The attendant didn't need to remove it surgically from the finger for you to examine. I believe you asked for a closer look.'

Flynt slammed the table angrily. The waiter had still not delivered their replacement bottle of red wine.

Lebrun said, 'You're mad at me not the waiter.'

Flynt said, 'Because you seem to have the answers.'

Lebrun said, 'Not yet. We're waiting to compare the DNA results. We should have had them sooner but we couldn't find your wife's brother, George Quatrevents… he's been working in America… a fashion photographer.'

Flynt rarely showed surprise but Lebrun had grabbed his balls. Emilie never said she had a brother.

'Well, you've met him… at Hôtel du Port… the short happy fellow with two pretty young women, his models.'

'I thought he was gay.'

'Probably is, probably why your wife never said a word. Good Catholics don't like that kind of thing.'

Flynt was asking himself why the Deuxième Bureau wanted to compare DNA results when the waiter finally arrived with a bottle of red.

'What results,' Flynt asked Lebrun.

'To compare the DNA taken from the remains the Brevilet brothers recovered from the sea with my niece's DNA.'

'But why?'

'Haven't you worked that out by now?'

Flynt sat back and emptied his glass. 'What do you expect the DNA to prove,' he stammered.

'Who was pushed off the cliff.'

'I didn't push anyone…'

'I'm not saying you did but someone wants us to believe the remains you identified were those of your wife and not…' Lebrun paused, afraid to finish the sentence.

'Your niece! You mean she's also missing?'

Lebrun nodded painfully. 'She has been for a month.'

If the torso fished out of the sea by the Brevilets was Lebrun's niece, then Flynt must have chased after the wrong woman – mistaken Elise's red dress for Emilie's. Flynt wouldn't wish what happened next on anyone but DNA could prove Emilie was still alive.

'If Elise wasn't running from me, then who,' he asked.

'Perhaps she'd been looking where she shouldn't.'

The sentence was an invitation for Flynt to say, 'The Bezen Perrot.' He didn't. The broken old man sitting opposite had a new obsession: to find his niece's killer.

'I'm back on Île d'Iroise at the weekend. The papers are full of it. Your lot are sending the navy to remind the Bretons to speak French.'

The Bakelite was why they'd met – to ask Lebrun for a name, someone who knew about KGB telephones. Lebrun thought for a moment. 'Dubret, Alexander Dubret, was with Renseignements Généraux – installed most of our bugs, did the sort of stuff that's not supposed to happen. Good man... very bright. If Alexander Graham Bell hadn't invented the telephone, Dubret would have. You have your mobile? Here's his number, you dial, and I'll talk. The old fingers not working like they did.'

Dubret agreed to meet Flynt for lunch the next day at Club Téléphone de France where he was curator of the telecommunications museum.

'La Société Commerciale... you were asking about the company,' said Lebrun, getting up to leave. 'It's still a going concern – the company at the centre of a black-market empire run by Paul Radenac in Paris during the Second World War.'

'I gathered that from the accounts... has a hefty bank balance stuffed not with lobster but fare-paying *passagers à pied*.'

The sharp intake of breath, the anger flaring in Lebrun's eyes reached way back. 'Radenac founded the Bezen Perrot,' he retorted, 'the war criminal who hanged my father.'

'You've already told me. Radenac must be dead and buried,' Flynt replied firmly.

'We'll see... tonight. I'll show you what happens at Number 12 Rue Lord Byron. We'll need a car. I can't hang around corners any more. Use my black Citroën.' Lebrun handed Flynt the keys, adding, 'Pick me up at two outside Wepler.'

Number 12 was in darkness when they parked across the road. 'What are you expecting?' Flynt asked.

'People arriving for work.'

'It's only a small office… can't be many.'

'Two, I would say… usually two, not always the same two.'

'Why at this time?'

'The islanders fish, don't they? The ferry takes their catch to the mainland. Fish markets are opening all over Europe at this very moment. Fish are sold by auction over the internet. That's how it's done nowadays.'

Lebrun pulled a small printed timetable from his jacket pocket and handed it to Flynt. 'The ferry schedule… sailings arranged by La Société Commerciale to suit the European fish auction.'

'The ferry also carries people,' Flynt told Lebrun, 'thousands every year according to the company books. From what I've seen La Société Commerciale earns more from passengers than fish… much more.' From Lebrun's puzzled frown Flynt guessed he'd not seen the company's books. 'What would you say if I told you the ferry carried 164 passengers to and from the island in October?'

'In October!' exclaimed Lebrun rubbing a hand over his jaw. 'You've been there… seen what's on offer… one hotel with rotten food and rooms… and the weather. You must be mistaken.'

A black Citroën similar to Lebrun's drew up outside Number 12. Instinctively, they slid low in their seats watching as two men got out, one tall and bearded, the other older, square shouldered.

'Herve Brevilet,' whispered Lebrun, 'the older one. The other I don't know.

'I do,' said Flynt. 'I saw him at Brevilet's farmhouse the night Emilie fell… well, disappeared. He's Herve Brevilet's neighbour.'

Raising his head above the steering wheel to get a clearer view, Lebrun added, 'They're using the same office. After seventy years this is too much of a coincidence.'

'You can't say that,' said Flynt. 'I'd love to write it but selling fish is a legitimate business.'

Brevilet and his companion let themselves into the lobby. A light clicked on in the third-floor office. 'They'll start selling their catch through the internet auction, their own catch and others… La Société Commerciale is the agent for a group of fishing co-operatives.'

'That's what I mean,' said Flynt. 'A legitimate business.'

Flynt studied his companion, physically wrecked, but mentally more alive than most. 'You're enjoying this, aren't you… the thrill of the chase again?' A fierce determination swept across the Frenchman's face. He'd hunt the Bezen Perrot until he found the last man standing.

Lebrun said little on the drive back to his apartment around the corner from Wepler now in total darkness. 'I told you Rouselle wouldn't let it go,' he said eventually, 'that he'd send a gunboat, force them to speak French.' Not a gunboat but the customs cutter *Tapageuse,* expected to arrive at Tourmant on Sunday, he added.

'Will you be there?' asked Flynt.

'I wouldn't miss Halloween on Île d'Iroise when those murderous sods of Bezen Perrot come out to commemorate their dead.' In the condensation dribbling down the car's windscreen Flynt saw Lebrun's eyes fill with loathing, unable to forget his father's decomposing body swinging from a lamp-post – and the sea pounding a mutilated corpse, possibly his niece.

Lebrun was levering himself from the car when Flynt called out, 'I had intruders when I was away in London. They were looking for the Bakelite. From my neighbour's description it could have been the Brevilet brothers.'

'Check your CCTV.'

'I don't think we have CCTV.'

'Is it a new building?' Flynt nodded. 'Then CCTV will be built-in. Give me the name of the owners, the address and I'll have it checked. Why didn't you call the police?'

'Nothing was stolen.'

'I see,' said Lebrun stumbling through the darkness towards his apartment.

Chapter 20

RUNNING A SECURITY consultancy in an age when a bug planted in a company boardroom could be activated by a mobile phone from the other side of the world kept Dubret fully engaged. In addition, he was a volunteer, unpaid archivist at Club Téléphone de France's museum of telecommunications paraphernalia.

The Frenchman spoke perfect English as well as several other languages, as might be expected of a person who'd spent a large part of his life eavesdropping on foreign embassies. Flynt had thought of taking Monique along for back-up but couldn't. Club Téléphone de France was for gentlemen only, the second and third floors devoted to museum pieces, one for artefacts, the other for elderly gentlemen entertaining each other.

The club occupied a sixteenth-century Renaissance town house with an imposing façade of tall, narrow mullion windows set in stone. The entrance was across a courtyard that once echoed to the wheels of horse-drawn carriages clattering over cobbles. Exclusive to those in the telecommunications industry, it was the nearest Paris had to a London gentlemen's club. Flynt waited in the foyer at the foot of a winding white marble staircase while a liveried doorman collected the archivist. Short and round with grey, happy eyes in a smiling florid face, Dubret was of the age that would never be persuaded that exercise was good for you. For him it was a boring obstacle en route to his final goal – to enjoy life's rewards before dying with a smile on his face.

'Lunch, you will join me?' he invited, taking Flynt's arm and guiding him into an oak-panelled dining room purring with contentment. Dubret stuck close to the club and colleagues from the past, rarely missing a day without breaking bread with one or the other.

Once settled over their cream of mushroom soup he listened quietly as Flynt ran through the story of the Bakelite and its chequered history from Tallinn to Paris, Dubret only interrupting when the voice on the phone was mentioned.

'I've never known a ghost make a telephone call,' Dubret remarked. 'A telephone that rings when it shouldn't is not as unusual as you might think. You must have heard a phone ring but there was no-one on the line? So you assumed…?'

'A wrong number or the caller got impatient and rang off.'

Dubret said, 'An external source could activate the phone bell but not explain the woman's voice.'

Wiping a dribble of soup from his chin, he asked, 'What other culprits do we have? Electric storms cause serious telephonic interference. I'm sure you've heard house alarms going off like crazy after lightning strikes. In fact, on average one person a year dies in France after being zapped by an energy surge while on the phone during a thunderstorm. It is easy enough to demonstrate how an external signal or power source can set a phone bell ringing even when not connected to a junction box.

Townsend at MI5 had told Flynt much the same.

'But this doesn't explain the woman's voice, the same voice, the same message. You have the telephone with you?' Dubret asked.

'Yes, in the plastic bag,' said Flynt, plonking the Bakelite on the table amongst the cutlery.

'That's not a telephone,' snapped Dubret.

Lifting his head like a startled cockerel, Flynt waited, spoon poised over his mushroom soup. 'My best guess is that what you think is a telephone is in fact one end of a transmitting device. We'll see, but that still doesn't explain the voice, same woman and same message... a recording maybe. We'll take a closer look... but first the meal, then the workshop. I've one in the attic for repairing exhibits. Lebrun says you collect telephones. You'll be impressed with our collection, and all in perfect working order.'

The service in the dining room was painfully slow, partly on account of it being delivered by waiters with a limp or having a hand that failed to function properly, all casualties of the telecommunications industry, explained Dubret. The club's policy was to offer those its industry crippled a job serving at table.

The beef stroganoff convinced Flynt that Dubret either suffered chronic indigestion or had a steel-plated constitution, the archivist dispatching the main course with the enthusiasm of a starving man, before attacking the cheese trolley, every morsel washed down with Burgundy, except for those deposited on Flynt's jacket.

The club was like an officers' mess. No money was seen to change hands, the diners signed in and out by an old crone perched on a stool behind a lectern at the entrance to the dining room. A nod of the head and the bill was duly added to the member's account. Names were unnecessary, the cashier having sat there long enough to recognise everyone. The ritual was repeated in the bar where Dubret and Flynt had large brandies before climbing the staircase to where the marble ran out and a rickety wooden ladder delivered them to Dubret's attic workshop. Switching on the light and clearing his workbench of a confusing clutter of tools, telephone parts and pieces of flex, Dubret said, 'Let's see it then... the telephone that rings mysteriously.'

'So you do believe me?'

'I have to. I know of no reason why you should invent the woman. You seem perfectly sane… perhaps a bit obsessive. I have always found that events have a credible explanation, Mr Flynt.'

Dubret removed the base plate and poked inside. 'An Ericsson 400 rotary dial,' he muttered. 'Manufactured about 1940, rare but not rare enough to be worth a great deal… and a bit of flex for connecting to the junction box except there's no box… so no dialling tone, dead.'

Rubbing his eyes, Dubret took a closer look at what seemed to be a nut. Flynt knew it was a nut. He'd tightened it several times when carrying out his own investigations. Dubret fiddled until the nut and washer fell apart.

'Ha-ha! Surely not! I haven't seen one of these little fellers for some considerable time,' Dubret muttered jubilantly.

'Seen what?' Flynt asked.

'This was,' said the Frenchman, dangling what appeared to be a shiny silver washer on the end of his screwdriver, 'an amazing invention by the Soviets… years ahead of anything we had.'

'What is it?' Flynt asked again.

'A bug from the Kremlin's top drawer. Where did you say you got the rotary dial?'

'From Tallinn in Estonia… from KGB headquarters. Not personally… I mean the guy who gave it me.' Flynt shuffled uneasily, feeling both relieved and foolish. The jovial, rotund Frenchman with bits of food glued to his red-and-white striped tie had taken less than ten minutes to solve the problem haunting Flynt for weeks. 'I should have seen someone sooner…'

'Not anyone… me, Mr Flynt. Few people would recognise it… the British never did when they found one planted in their embassy in Tehran… thought it was a washer, as you did. Remarkable…' said Dubret, holding the tiny disc between finger and thumb like a precious stone, so small, so inconspicuous.

'This,' said the Frenchman with a note of reverence, 'is The Thing, in fact a more advanced version of The Thing I found during the Cold War.' He'd been loaned by French Intelligence to sweep the US Embassy in Moscow for bugs following a series of embarrassing leaks. 'The embassy was a colander… full of holes. The Thing was hidden behind the eagle in a wooden replica of The Great Seal of the President of the United States on the wall of the main conference room. The replica was presented to the embassy by Soviet schoolchildren as a gesture of goodwill. The Thing – a passive resonant cavity bug activated by remote transponder – recorded and then transmitted to the KGB every word spoken in the conference room for more than six years before I found it. This,' he said holding up the tiny metal disc, 'was bugging every call made and received on the phone… at KGB headquarters in Tallinn, I believe you said.'

Flynt had got the drift. 'But the aerial… wouldn't it need one? I don't see an aerial.'

'Here it is,' said Dubret, pointing to a grey hair. Flynt had mistaken it for his. He'd fretted over the Bakelite long enough for plenty to fall out.

Dubret chipped away a corner of the Bakelite's casing. 'Not a hair but a tiny radio antenna. See how it's wound inside the casing… as fine as a human hair but a metre long. Even more remarkable The Thing generates its own power by harvesting energy from unused radio frequencies. There is no limit to its effective life.'

After a few more minutes examining the device, Dubret said, 'I had a call from Lebrun. He says the British are interested… have asked you to monitor the calls.'

Lebrun was at it again, spreading intelligence around. 'I've been asked to record the calls,' said Flynt. 'MI5 didn't want to pull the phone to pieces, not yet... afraid the caller wouldn't ring again and they'd lose the source.'

Dubret smiled. 'That's what went wrong for the Brits in Tehran. Their bug was planted in an embassy phone, activated by a signal from an external transponder via a connection to a landline. When they messed with it they broke the connection, never found the source. Your KGB bug would have functioned the same way until it was disconnected by your friend in Tallinn. That broke the link with the transponder.'

Flynt asked, 'What's a transponder?'

Dubret replied, 'The word is a contraction of "transmitter" and "responder." That's why I said at lunch you don't have a phone but a device transmitting recorded data. I don't know how much you need to know about the technology but a transponder emits an identifying signal in response to an interrogating signal, the frequencies of both pre-assigned before the bug is planted. At the transponder end, possibly thousands of miles away, a sensor decodes and transcribes the transmitted data, a telephone conversation, perhaps a confidential discussion. Magnetic labels on credit cards work on the same principle.'

The tiny device fitted inside the Bakelite, continued Dubret, transmitted conversations recorded at KGB headquarters in Tallinn to whoever was listening at Moscow Central. When the Russians quit Estonia the link was broken and The Thing had no route back to the mother ship.

'Poor Thing goes to sleep, a deep sleep until a burst of microwave or ultrasound tickles its bell in your apartment. But The Thing is still not happy! Without a connection to a landline poor Thing can't deliver its data which gets caught in a loop, malfunctions, escaping sporadically when, whatever, triggers its fancy, causes the bell to ring, driving you crazy each time you pick up the receiver.

Flynt said, 'What about the voice?'

'That's the last conversation recorded on the phone, played back over and over again until cutting out when the signal is lost,' said Dubret. 'That's why you think the caller has rung off.'

'Where does the signal come from to excite my dear little Thing?' Flynt patted the Bakelite on the head.

'The French communications array on Île d'Iroise has more than enough equipment to wake up Thing – cause its tiny diaphragm to vibrate expectantly. A games console could also do it, even a radio cab.'

'Tanna…!'

'And who is Tanna?'

'Long story but he was on his console when the Bakelite rang in London… he's always playing games.'

Dubret hadn't finished. He'd explained what caused The Thing to get its knickers in a twist, and how the voice got there but had no idea who the woman was.

'The voice is intriguing,' said the Frenchman

'The language… English!' exclaimed Flynt. 'Why not Russian, if the call was recorded in Tallinn?'

'I have no idea… only that whoever she is, she's probably dead. My guess is Estonian circa 1994 when the Soviets pulled out. Perhaps the KGB was bugging itself – watching its back – then neglected to remove the bug.'

Flynt said, 'But she's speaking English, not clearly, but certainly English.'

Dubret said, 'The last person either to ring this phone or make a call from it spoke English. No way of telling at the moment from the play-back whether the recording was incoming or outgoing…' Dubret paused. 'It could be the disc was clean and this was the first and only call made or received. I'll need to take a closer look, get rid of the background interference.'

Flynt said, 'The static?'

Dubret replied, 'It shouldn't have static when activated by a transponder. I've said this wasn't data flowing down a telephone line. The only purpose served by the landline connection was to receive the signal to switch on coded data transfer from Tallinn to Moscow Central. In which case there shouldn't be static interference. What you think of as static are channels, beamed from other transmitters. Bandwidth is like a narrow pipe. When too much stuff tries to get down it floods… that's static.'

Flynt said, 'But you're sure it's not repeated calls?'

Dubret's answer was to stick his screwdriver inside the Bakelite again. 'I'll call you or Lebrun when I have more.'

'How long will it take,' Flynt asked.

'Another hour… maybe longer.'

'I'll wait.'

'But not here, in the bar.'

Several lagers later a footman appeared, beckoning Flynt to follow. Dubret was crouched at the far end of his workbench beneath a strip of orange florescent lighting. Flynt heard the click of a button being depressed. A recorder sprang to life.

'Help! He's trying to kill me… there's nowhere to hide.'

The recording, cleaned of the background interference, was clear, the voice spilling from the darkness hitting Flynt like a punch in the stomach. His knees wobbled, he rasped, 'Emilie…' Reaching out a hand he steadied himself against the edge of the workbench.

'And there's more… the man who intercepted the call,' said Dubret.

Herve Brevilet rarely said anything when they'd met on Île

d'Iroise but behind the voice on the recorder Flynt saw the rugged good looks of the Breton who was never far away from Emilie at Port Maria.

'What's he saying?' The conversation had started in English but switched to French.

'Nonn... who's Nonn...? Your wife asks about someone called Nonn,' said Dubret.

'No idea... only that St Non was the mother of St David, patron saint of Wales. What else?'

'The man tells Emilie not to mention anything to you.'

'I get a mention!'

'Twice...'

'And Emilie... what else does she say?'

'Nothing... rings off. And, by the way, the interference I thought was caused by scratches on The Thing's diaphragm, you were right, it's static. Lebrun also rang, a moment ago. He said to tell you the DNA results confirm the woman you identified as your wife is in fact his niece Elise. He's taking it badly. Elise was all he had, no children of his own.'

Grim-faced, Flynt watched Dubret piece the Bakelite back together.

'The static on the recording can only mean the phone must have been connected to a landline when your wife rang. Was it?'

Flynt was heading for the door when suddenly he stopped and turned back to Dubret.

'Just the once, and only briefly,' he said, frowning through an embarrassed smile. 'I'd clean forgotten... I'd taken the Bakelite to Île d'Iroise to see if I could get a dial tone. The house had a junction box connecting to the mainland through the local exchange in the hotel but was not used. I had this crazy idea about connecting up the Bakelite to ring the office... can't get a mobile signal on Île d'Iroise.'

'Was there a dial tone?'

'Yes… yes… but I never made a call… didn't need to. After Emilie fell… well, I thought she had… I spent the night with some Bretons at their farm. We made another search the next day… found nothing. Then I went to Port Maria, packed the phone in my bag and left.'

Dubret said, 'The call from your wife was the last recorded conversation. I think she rang Port Maria from somewhere, wanting to speak to you but was answered by this Brevilet person. He could be the one who wants us to believe you pushed her off the cliff.'

An hour later Monique sensed from Flynt's twisted smile, the hooded eyes, it was payback time for someone.

'The voice on the phone is Emilie.' Flynt looked at her full between the eyes. 'She's either alive, hiding, or some bastard's killed her!' He knew his outstretched hand must feel like a wave goodbye for Monique.

'What happens when you find her…?'

'I don't know… only that Emilie is desperate for help, hiding somewhere, afraid.'

'You still love her?' As soon as the words were out of her mouth Monique wished she hadn't asked.

Flynt's laugh was hollow. 'Did I ever? If I did it was a very short love story,' Flynt said, laying a hand on Monique's shoulder. 'I can't say, not yet… I'm not thinking about us.'

They stood together not knowing what to say but feeling it wasn't over yet, her hair soft against his face. Flynt drew her close in a long, slow, clinging kiss, Monique's dark eyelashes twitching like butterfly wings. After a time she pulled her head away. Monique who with a gesture could change direction like the wind, said, 'I love to dream. Everything is happier in dreams… you'll take me with you to Île d'Iroise to meet Emilie. Help me, Jack. Then I'll go. Oh, yes! There's something I want from you… something that will always be Jack Flynt… the phone that rings at night.' Brushing aside the silky black hair lying along her smooth white cheeks, Monique closed the bedroom door, leaving Flynt empty, staring into space.

Chapter 21

'DIVING STATIONS, MR Davies.'

The Executive Officer frowned. 'Do we really need to, sir?'

'We're inside the French twelve-mile limit by invitation... on condition we don't show ourselves. The French are sensitive... they have an election coming up.'

The *Halifax* was bucking and rolling through a westerly streaming in from the Atlantic. The skipper, Commander Bob Tracey, had tried to ride it out until the jagged curtain of rain and spray whipping across the bridge poured the ocean down the conning tower. The klaxon sounded three times; the anonymous voice intoning over the intercom sent the submarine's crew into dive mode. By the time the storm ran out of steam, the *Halifax* was as close to the Brittany coast as it dared to get.

Turning to his dive officer, Tracey said quietly, 'Periscope depth.' The helmsman felt a gentle squeeze on his shoulder, a reminder from the skipper to hold steady at 100 feet. Inside the sonar shack the only contact was a shoal of fish swimming across the bow.

Commander Tracey had thought his last assignment was a desk job at US Navy headquarters in Norfolk, Virginia, until his pension kicked in and he was kicked out by navy downsizing. But before turning for home and de-commissioning, the Los Angeles-class nuclear-powered submarine was ordered by COMSUBLANT (Commander Submarine Force, US Atlantic Fleet) to investigate an unidentified sonar contact reported by Spanish trawlers in the Bay of Biscay.

Tracey shook his head after reading the order from COMSUBLANT for the umpteenth time. The Bay of Biscay was larger than England, and one of the world's busiest shipping lanes, full of sonar contacts, some from the wrecks that never made it back to Spain with the Armada. Why couldn't the French look themselves? Tracey had learned never to argue with Norfolk and was searching the shallower waters along the Brittany coast for the source of the mystery 'pinging'.

Sonar surveillance had changed since he first patrolled the watery corridors of the Cold War, shadowing Soviet spy ships disguised as fishing trawlers. Then, identifying acoustic signatures depended largely on the skills in the sonar shack, the most experienced operators able to count the blades on a propeller shaft.

After sweeping the horizon, Tracey muttered, 'Nothing, take her deeper,' folding the periscope into its casing. 'All vents open,' he ordered. The *Halifax* dipped her bow as the main tanks flooded. The helmsman shifted the rudder like a pilot landing a Boeing 747, except this was no flimsy airframe but an 18,000-ton steel tube wrapped around a nuclear power plant, three inches of steel separating the crew from an ocean-going nuclear bomb. A wrong move by the dive officer, his eyes glued to the bank of monitors blinking on the wall opposite, could send the *Halifax* ploughing into the seabed.

After levelling off, Commander Tracey moved further along the coast before returning to periscope depth for another look, his face pressed hard against Number 2 scope, a pinpoint of daylight glittering in his eyeball. 'Surface,' he ordered lowering the periscope. Still nothing, reported the lookout from the bridge except for the silhouette of a container ship crossing the distant horizon.

Tracey dived the ship again, the hull awash, the bow dipping beneath the waves leaving a trail of bubbles. 'Scope under,' Tracey announced as the *Halifax* disappeared into a world as silent as the grave.

'Passive sonar is on,' someone called out. Tracey bent his head over a chart spread across the metal table at his waist. In the sonar shack, two crewmen bathed in a dim blue light had their hands clamped tightly around headphones listening for a 'ping-ping'. If contact was made, the concentric circles radiating across their screen should pinpoint the submarine's distance from the source. But first they had to distinguish between an ocean full of naturally occurring sounds, whirring propellers on the surface, and the noise emitted by the submarine's own engines. The hydrophone array towed by the *Halifax* could detect a dropped wrench aboard a ship, a noisy hatch cover, even a door creaking on its hinges. Sonar effectiveness deteriorated, however, the nearer the *Halifax* got to the cacophony of extraneous land-based sounds on Île d'Iroise.

'Sir,' said the chief sonar operator, eyes still glued to his screen, 'I've got something but…'

'What's the problem?' asked Tracey.

'This,' replied the chief, removing his headphones, the 'ping-ping' echoing around the sonar shack. The signal wasn't theirs bouncing off a target but incoming and like nothing the chief had heard before. Ashore, he'd have said it was a ringing telephone.

Tracey stepped across to the chart table and shouted, 'Mark!' The chief bellowed back the co-ordinates for the contact. 'Compare,' muttered Tracey, calling for the incoming signal to be triangulated. 'Weird… the target is shore-based, not moving,' he said.

'A ship that's run aground, maybe,' suggested the Exec.

'COMSUBLANT would have known that.'

'Bent!' exclaimed the sonar chief. 'We're at 200 feet? The

signal bends in the shallows where warm surface water meets cold.'

Tracey took another look at the screen. The source should have been clearly shown among the monitor's concentric circles... nothing, but a definite 'ping-ping'.

'We haven't made a contact... we're being pinged. Whatever is out there has found us!' said Tracey. 'Let's see if we get a response from active sonar.'

'It'll reveal our position, sir,' cautioned his Exec.

'I know Davies... but we're not at war, not yet.'

'I've got it, sir.' The sonar chief had his hands clasped tight to his headphones. 'We're being pinged from the coast of the island.'

'Run it through the computer,' Tracey ordered, 'Let's see what we have.' The database compiled by the US Office of Naval Intelligence had thousands of underwater sound signatures. 'Nothing,' said the sonar chief checking the printout. 'Best guess – a diesel sub.'

'We don't have any... no-one does... except the North Koreans. Dead or alive... can you tell?' asked Tracey.

While the sonar operator fiddled with his controls, Tracey turned to his intelligence officer, at six feet and six inches, and eighteen stone, not an ideal fit for a submarine. 'What thoughts, Grayson?'

'Could be coming from the array,' he suggested, leaning across the chart table and pointing to the promontory on Île d'Iroise where France had an automated communications complex of spidery aerials and white satellite domes sealed off from the rest of the island by a high razor-wire fence.

'Chief, how deep were we when you picked up the signal?' asked Tracey.

'I would say deeper than a hundred feet – no good for microwave but ultrasound, maybe.'

For two-way communication with Norfolk, standard procedure was for *Halifax* either to unfold its radio antenna at periscope depth or surface. When submerged, ultrasound was for short-range communications, five miles at most.

'We're within range,' Grayson advised. The rocky coastline was no more than a mile off the submarine's port side.

'Perhaps I'm old school,' said Tracey, 'but I can't differentiate between this ping and what we get bouncing off a wreck on the sea bottom.'

Tracey knew ultrasound bandwidth was very narrow and for the signal to be converted into an audio contact the receiver would need to be in the right place at the right time. While the *Halifax* had an ultrasound receiver, it was one hell of a coincidence to arrive exactly at the right spot to receive a transmission.

'The Valley of Death... that's what U-boat captains called these waters in the Second World War,' said Tracey. 'There are dozens of wrecks down here... U-boats bombed by the RAF when they made a run for the North Atlantic.'

'It could be coming from one of those, I suppose,' agreed Grayson, 'but after seventy years!'

The pinging stopped quite suddenly. 'Perhaps we've moved out of bandwidth,' whispered Grayson. 'Have we, Chief?'

'No, sir... either shut down automatically or someone's turned it off.' Stretching his legs and removing his headphones the chief sat back. 'Not ultrasound... old-fashioned sonar, sir, I'm sure. It found us... it's alive.'

'Periscope depth,' ordered Tracey. Île d'Iroise was hidden by a cotton-wool curtain except for a small stream tipping into the sea through a cleft high up the grey-green cliff. The horizon was buried in a thick belt of fog about a nautical mile off the starboard side. 'Let's try for a closer look,' said Tracey ordering ballast tanks blown, *Halifax* surfacing on to a leaden sea. Tracey and a lookout were quickly on the bridge. 'Not good,' Tracey muttered. Any nearer the coast and *Halifax* might fetch up on a submerged pinnacle of rock the charts indicated existed without showing precisely where.

Suddenly, the commander's shout 'Dive, dive' propelled both men down the conning tower, the lookout trampling on his skipper's fingers in his haste. Tracey had seen bow waves breaking from the fog right in front of them. The submarine's vents opened and the klaxon sounded 'Crash dive'. In seconds *Halifax*'s bow was down twenty degrees, the sudden tilt dumping Tracey on his backside, the crew white with apprehension, holding on tightly. A roar shook the boat, followed by a severe jar as she buried her nose in the shallow muddy bottom.

'Foremost planes locked,' the dive officer cried out.

'Adjust trim and slow blow,' ordered Tracey. Slowly *Halifax* lifted off the bottom, Tracey snatching the periscope for the briefest glimpse of a large trawler disappearing back into the fog after slicing through the water feet above their conning tower. 'Must have seen us,' he growled.

'You mean run us down... surely not,' Grayson muttered angrily.

Tracey saved his reply for COMSUBLANT. 'She neither attempted to stop or turn,' was all he said, but he also knew how close the *Halifax* came to the trawler's razor-sharp bow. If the submarine's reactor was breached they'd be looking for 'France', not a 'ping-ping', he thought.

After reporting to Norfolk, Tracey waited. An hour later *Halifax* exited French territorial waters in a hurry, heading home. COMSUBLANT advised the Director of the CIA at Langley, Virginia, that the 'ping-ping' was, as far as could be ascertained, shore-based and no longer the navy's problem.

Chapter 22

THE FERRY CROSSING to Île d'Iroise might well have been a reunion. Lebrun was there, determined to find those responsible for his niece's death. Then there was Mathias from MI5, suave and urbane in a sharp dark-blue double-breasted suit with loud stripes, and the CIA's red-necked muscular American, Donovan, bursting out of jacket and slacks. Flynt acknowledged their skirmish at Paddington Green Police Station with a sharp nod when they eyeballed each other across the crowded saloon.

'I bet you never thought you'd see me again,' someone whispered in his ear. The powder-blue jacket was unmistakeable – Dando from the *Chronicle*, one of a dozen hacks and several TV crews sent to cover the anticipated confrontation between the French constitution and islanders. 'I'm now the office expert on The Breton Problem,' said Dando. 'The feature went down well. I see you brought your very own interpreter. Perhaps Monique could help me out… I'll pay.'

Monique smiled at what would once have been a very different proposition.

'This business with the Bretons… true they've declared UDI?' asked Dando.

Flynt despaired at how the situation on the ground got lost in translation. 'Not quite a unilateral declaration of independence. The islanders refuse to speak French, only Breton.'

'And walked out of the inquest on your wife, according to our News Desk. Christ, what's that all about?' After Flynt explained in simple terms what had happened, Dando exclaimed, 'So they think you pushed her?'

'That was the general idea but no longer. I have more or less cleared that up without the Bretons having to corroborate.'

Dando was taking a note. 'Why are you doing that,' Flynt complained. 'I'm not the story. They are.' He waved his hand at the crowd around the saloon bar, adding, 'Your round… go get some drinks.'

The ship's saloon was steaming with bodies, the Investigating Magistrate Rouselle and his lady clerk in one corner in serious conversation with a tall, straight-sided, straight-haired individual with a solemn mouth.

'The Teacher,' declared Lebrun. 'They've sent The Teacher to remind the Bretons that French is the language of the constitution.'

The Teacher was a mean-looking individual – one of a panel of teachers the French Government had recruited to teach recalcitrant immigrants to read and write proper French. The panel's reputation was formidable. It was said it took no prisoners – that those who failed to co-operate got deported. Flynt guessed this particular teacher was a thrasher, kids writhing under his gaze as he forced French down their little throats. His movements were jerky, puppet-like when he headed for the bar where a dozen men jostling for drinks and wearing T-shirts proclaiming '*La France Française*' parted for him like the Red Sea.

'Who are they?' asked Flynt.

'Storm-troopers from Académie française,' replied Lebrun. *Le weekend* and other Anglo-Saxon intruders are anathema to the Académie, the custodians of proper French.'

'And who would you say they are?' Flynt indicated a middle-aged couple hiding in the corner. 'Don't tell me more bird-watchers!'

'You mean the Immortals.'

'What!'

'The high priest and priestess of Académie française – the Immortals – that's what members of the ruling council are called – elected for life, official authority on the language since the seventeenth century. For God's sake, Flynt, they publish the French dictionary! How would we survive without that?' said Lebrun with a wry smile.

Flynt pointed to three gendarmes drinking coffee at a table in the centre of the saloon, surrounded by enough baggage to settle permanently on Île d'Iroise. 'The gendarmes,' replied Lebrun, 'will ensure the Bretons don't argue with Académie française… that they end their *petit* rebellion against the constitution. The Ministère de l'Intérieur has commandeered a property on the harbour as the police station.'

'Is he another of the gang?' A priest in a black, ankle-length cassock sat alone, a man at peace with God if not the world.

'A priest is the last person Paris would send,' said Lebrun. 'Priests tend to side with the natives.' A tall but easygoing man, his close-set parochial eyes never shifted off The Teacher.

'Wasn't the church abandoned?' Flynt recalled the *Werwolf* graffiti on the door, the rotting fish inside the entrance. No chairs, no candles, only the musty stench of neglect.

Dando was back with their drinks, notebook flapping from a jacket pocket. 'What did you say, what did you say?' he hissed, fearing he'd missed something.

'Nothing to worry about,' said Flynt. 'We were only saying that they've brought reinforcements – the coppers.'

'They're expecting trouble then.' Dando's eyes lit up. Trouble he could handle – it was the analytical stuff the *Chronicle* wanted that threw him. 'Why are the French so bloody-minded,' he asked. 'We've let your lot speak their language… use it for everything, isn't that right, Jack?' adding for Lebrun's benefit, 'Jack's Welsh.'

'France is a rogue state… refuses to recognise minorities,' replied Flynt. 'The French talk a lot about human rights but it's only for others. Napoléon created one nation, one language and the French are expected to stick to it.'

Dando scribbled furiously. This was just what the *Chronicle* wanted, analytical.

'Not true!' Lebrun bristled at Flynt's take on the story. 'We've got bilingual street signs and education in Breton.'

'Road signs… mere tokenism!' declared Flynt. 'As for teaching Breton, only if you send your kid to private school. That's why Paris has sent The Teacher. Public schools don't offer Breton, you know that. Paris and your Académie française regard Breton as barbaric, unsuitable for an academic education. That means Breton kids don't get to go to university unless they speak French.'

'So that's it,' said Dando, 'we're here to watch a bunch of kids being forced to speak French.'

'More or less! Without the kids, Breton, just like Welsh, has no future, ceases to be the language of the hearth. End of story.'

'Do you speak Welsh, Jack?' asked Dando.

'No. That's my point. My school celebrated St George's Day not St David's. The majority of Breton speakers are old, in their eighties. The language will only survive if it's constitutionally recognised… and supported.' For someone who really didn't care, Flynt had plenty to say.

Lebrun agreed France should be more relaxed about diversity. 'The constitution is a weight around French shoulders,' Lebrun added, 'recognising only one language. But if we allow Breton into the constitution what next – Arabic? And the end of the Fifth Republic! That's why this lot are here – to make sure that never happens.'

'Very good,' muttered Dando closing his notebook. The

Chronicle man had his background. Now all he had to do was report what happened.

'And here comes more trouble,' observed Flynt. Mathias and Donovan were heading for their table. Lebrun looked surprised. 'I never expected to see them again... can't still be looking for wreckage from our fisheries patrol ship. We know what happened.'

'A Russian submarine?'

'Not at all,' said Lebrun, 'You sunk it, the British.'

Flynt said, 'And how did we manage that?'

Lebrun replied, 'It struck a naval mine. One of yours from the last war must have broken from its mooring on the seabed.'

'How do you know it's British?'

'From the explosive residues on the wreckage. RDX was a high explosive used by the British in naval mines.'

Without waiting to be asked, Mathias and Donovan took a seat. Flynt wasn't waiting either, diving in with what he did best, confrontation, rude and crude but effective when pussyfooting around failed.

'Welcome back!' Flynt's opening salvo was squeezed out of the corner of his mouth. 'So, what you looking for now, not more bird life, surely?' Bending down he pulled the Bakelite from the Carrefour bag at his feet and dumped it on the table. 'I've still got it... hasn't rung again... and the voice, a recording of my wife pleading for help. But I imagine you know that. So help me find Emilie... make yourselves useful.' Flynt directed his harangue at the Englishman hoping to rile Mathias into letting something slip. This happened when people were ruffled. They were more vulnerable to Flynt's tactics.

The MI5 agent smiled weakly, CIA looked irritated but neither said a word. Dando shifted uncomfortably, ready to beat a rapid retreat when Flynt suddenly pulled a small digital camera from his jacket pocket to take a shot. Mathias and

Donovan turned their backs instinctively. The reason they were returning to Île d'Iroise couldn't afford page one exposure.

'Come on, guys,' said Flynt, pushing the camera in their faces. 'Give me a picture for the *Washington Post*... your fifteen minutes of fame. Someone's bound to recognise you.'

Momentarily, Donovan squared up as if to flatten Flynt with one swing until Lebrun held out a hand and the American checked himself awkwardly. Sensing he'd parried a punch on the nose, Flynt sniffed the air and pressed on regardless.

'So what do you want? Never was birds, and now you've found the wreckage, not a Russian sub. Tell me what you're after. And you as well, Lebrun... and don't say bloody collaborators from the last war.'

Dando held up an arm. 'Christ, Jack! Leave him alone. He is only trying to help.'

At this Lebrun stood up, staring out to sea at the white-tipped waves racing past the bow of the ferry. With a weary shrug he turned to Mathias. 'I suggest you tell him before he blows it for us. He knows a lot already.'

'No,' snapped the American. 'The guy's a loose cannon. Listen to him! He'd sell his mother for a headline.'

Flynt leaned across the table, his face a few inches from the American, and sneered, 'I've already got enough on you, pal, to make page one of the *Washington Post*. Someone is sure to pick you out of a CIA line-up from the snap I took. Aren't you out of your fucking jurisdiction?'

Donovan was ready to explode, the veins in his neck like blood-red violin strings, his hands itching to grab hold of Flynt. Mathias moved further back in his seat, struggling to hide behind the disdain with which his class regarded upstarts. One more push and Flynt knew he'd have them.

All eyes were on the small, silver bullet-shaped mobile nestling in Flynt's palm as he dialled the number for the *Washington Post*.

That he hadn't a signal didn't really matter, so long as the spooks thought he was ringing in the story when he asked loudly for the 'City Desk.'

Lebrun capitulated first. 'There's no need for that,' he said, pulling at the hand holding the mobile. 'There's too much at stake.'

'Everything… do we need to tell this bugger everything?' asked the Englishman imperiously, directing the question at Lebrun. 'It's your jurisdiction… the island!'

Lebrun said, 'Can we trust you, Jack, off the record?'

'You'd better,' Flynt snapped. 'Just don't take me for an idiot. I know Mr CIA here thinks this is all way above my head but I'll get there in the end with or without your help. Trust me? Yes. If I'm guaranteed first crack at the story.' Flynt's half- smile didn't guarantee a thing.

'And me. We'll share, Jack,' said Dando hurriedly.

'We're searching for the source of a signal – a "ping-ping" – the sound a sub's sonar makes.' Mathias shuffled uneasily, embarrassed by having to talk to a hack. 'It's been heard a dozen times by fishing trawlers, but not reported until the patrol boat blew up.'

'That's why,' Lebrun interrupted, 'the media speculated the boat was sunk by a torpedo. It didn't take a huge leap of imagination to make that a Russian torpedo from a Russian submarine.'

'The sonar reports came from Spanish trawlers fishing off Île d'Iroise,' continued Mathias, 'but there was nothing from the local fleet.'

'Perhaps they had other things to think about.' Monique, who'd sat quietly listening to the exchanges, pointed a pretty finger at the Académie française's storm troopers and gendarmes. 'Why do they terrorise these poor people? I'm Breton. Why shouldn't I be free to speak my own language?

But in Paris I'm afraid to. They look at me like I'm some kind of barbarian.'

Mathias was momentarily knocked off course by Monique's honesty. Flynt found himself agreeing. The supression of the Breton language by the French Government was self-serving and predictable.

'We've checked the obvious source of the sonar,' said Mathias, picking up his thread. 'The French are reluctant naturally to give details of submarine movements but have assured NATO the mystery ping is not theirs.'

Flynt beamed at Monique. Her little intervention had bought him time to remember – to remember a detail that had lodged in his mind for eight years. But that's what trawling for news every minute of every day did to a man's mind. It created corners where bits and pieces of no immediate relevance could stick until they found a home. The ping-ping had probably stuck fast because of the occasion – the few days he and Emilie spent on Île d'Iroise after they were married. They'd taken a walk along the cliff, the wind tugging at their coats fading quite suddenly to a murmur and, in the stillness, a ping-ping before it was blown away. He mistook it for a ringing telephone, but that couldn't be on Île d'Iroise. Emilie heard it too, seemed uncomfortable and insisted on turning back to Port Maria.

Flynt had saved the ping for when he needed a lever.

The atmosphere was still tense when Île d'Iroise appeared out of the mist. Donovan seemed intent on making it more fraught. Leaning forward, he whispered to Flynt, 'If you're not using your hooker tonight, I'd like to borrow her.' Flynt lunged across the table, the big American swatting him aside like a fly before taking a full-blooded whack from an unexpected quarter. Monique had slammed her elbow into the American's face, a trick picked up the hard way. Donovan reeled backwards, dabbing a finger at blood trickling from a nostril, the murderous look in his eyes promising he'd come again. Dando turned and hurried away.

'Leave it alone,' said Lebrun, raising a hand between them. 'It's the Bezen Perrot we should fight, not each other.'

Flynt snarled, 'For Christ's sake Lebrun, give over... rabbiting on about the bloody Bezen Perrot.'

'Don't you imagine I've tried to move on after all these years? It would have been best if I never knew how my father died – and now Elise! Oh, my God, could they both have been killed by the Bezen Perrot?'

Mathias threw him a stony stare. Donovan stopped dabbing the blood streaming from his nose and growled, 'Stow it, Lebrun.'

When so-called friends fall out it is generally an opportunity to kick them in the balls.

'And how about you Donovan, how come the US is involved?' Flynt's timing was always good. 'You've found the wreckage and the bodies, stuck your nose into Emilie's death, and now you're pinging around the island!'

No-one answered. An uneasy truce descended until Mathias broke the stand-off.

'I enjoyed your article – not signed but I take it you wrote "The Lost Tribe of Europe". I believe we touched on the subject when we last met.' Mathias meant Paddington Green Station.

'The majority of islanders don't exist in French Civil Registration records... isn't that what you told me?' said Flynt. 'But I thought completing a census form was compulsory; it is in Britain. They can stick you in jail if you don't.'

'Same in France,' said Mathias, 'but no problem for the Brevilets... sticklers for form-filling... in French... always show respect for the constitution... have an ID card to run the ferry, sell their fish on the mainland.' Mathias paused, leaving Flynt to figure the rest for himself. The MI5 man was suggesting that the cultural stand the Brevilets took at the Investigating Magistrate's hearing – Lan refusing to testify in French – was bogus.

'The language, the French language is only a problem when the Brevilets are back among the natives,' continued Mathias.

'You're saying they're play-acting – that they couldn't care a toss for the language… that they're not really pals at all?'

'Let's say the relationship between Clan Brevilet and the others is not a happy one, at the very least strained,' said Mathias.

Flynt said, 'Crabby!'

Lebrun stood up slowly, breathing heavily, but not with difficulty as might be expected if he was having a seizure. His short, sharp breaths were more angry than terminal. 'Show him, show him… the photographs,' he gasped. 'Now you'll believe me, Flynt.'

Donovan shrugged, resigned to the inevitable, or so it seemed. Taking his shrug as a yes, Mathias scanned for the images on his mobile phone, his finger stopping at a picture of a large slab, a headstone or commemorative plaque sunk flat into the ground. 'What do you make of this?' he asked Flynt:

Paul Radenac
Bezen Perrot
1915–2007

Flynt straightened up. 'So you've found Radenac's grave… so what… so he lived the life of Riley on Île d'Iroise before kicking his clogs… good age. So who cares?'

Lebrun smiled triumphantly, vindicated. The Bezen Perrot hadn't died with the end of the war.

Dando's ears were swinging like satellite dishes – 'I find traitor's hide-out' firmly in the *Chronicle*'s sights, the follow-up more promising than the original tale.

'Tell me more,' said Dando whipping out his notebook, his head across the table, close enough to give Mathias a great big smacker.

'Leave it! And put your bloody book away, Dando. These guys should be helping me find Emilie, not sweeping up after the Second World War.'

Dando was twitchy, Flynt sensing that the *Chronicle* hack would blow everything if he could get to a phone. But Dando couldn't move the story off the island without access to Flynt's satellite phone. The landline from the hotel to the mainland was almost certainly 'out of action'. It always was.

The tension around the table eased sufficiently for Mathias to pick up his account of the post-war search for Radenac, or rather the reason it took seventy years to find him.

'Our resources were stretched sorting out the mess left behind after the German surrender,' Mathias said. 'There wasn't the manpower to chase shadows. After five years the Allies gave up looking for Radenac.'

'Since then,' continued Mathias, 'reports have surfaced suggesting the existence of an organisation with all the characteristics of being a truly long-term undertaking which survived by merging with protest groups in post-war Europe. But nothing has been found to prove the existence of *Werwolf*, its disposition, or modus operandi, only that it was rumoured to be a series of unconnected groups, supposedly waiting for the call.'

Lebrun added indignantly, 'The Allies stopped short of a thorough victory over the Nazis, allowing the most fanatical to escape... to prepare the ground for a Fourth Reich.'

Flynt said, 'Now you've found Radenac, perhaps you'll find my wife.'

The ferry was approaching the breakwater at the entrance to the harbour at Tourmant. Dando hadn't finished. 'Can I have a copy of that picture... where Radenac's buried?' he asked Mathias.

'He's not buried there.'

Flynt who was exiting the saloon for disembarkation, turned and waited for Mathias to flick through more images. He stopped at a photograph of a farmhouse, the door and windows boarded, the cement covered roof sagging in the middle. The next was of a derelict barn across a muddy farmyard.

'The Jalenes' farmhouse!' exclaimed Flynt. He recalled how he and Emilie had sheltered in their barn from the storm eight years ago.

'And this,' said Mathias, 'inside the barn.'

Flynt bent forward for a closer look at the picture of the Second World War open-top German army staff car, no longer pristine but a pile of rusting metal – and on the rear seat a grinning skeleton wearing the remains of a Waffen-SS uniform with twin lightning flashes on the collar and Bezen Perrot cotton patches stitched to the chest.

'Paul Radenac was old man Jalene,' said Mathias. 'He never escaped to South America but made it to Île d'Iroise. Lived here for sixty years… buried with his car!'

The visiting hacks and TV crews led the charge ashore once the gangway was raised. A small, round-faced individual, with a Gucci man-bag slung around his neck, drew Flynt aside as he disembarked. 'I'm Emilie's brother.'

'And I'm her husband. What brings you to Île d'Iroise?'

'The same as you – to find Emilie.' Quatrevents was a fashion photographer from Paris and the women at Hôtel du Port on his earlier visit models on an advertising shoot. From their brief conversation Flynt gathered that lingerie looked particularly sexy stretched across an ancient brass bedstead in a beat-up hotel.

Chapter 23

THE GREY, CHEERLESS women were waiting on the quay in muted protest, mouths covered with strips of grey binding tape. Dando led the media charge the moment the ferry berthed, clicking his mobile while cursing the News Desk for not sending a snapper. Flynt held back. The protesters were dug in for the day. He'd file later by satellite phone, leaving the other hacks to discover their nearest mobile signal was on the mainland.

Lebrun searched the horizon beyond the harbour, his face bleaker than usual. 'Storm forecast,' he announced. 'We could be stuck here for a week. It happens.' The weather was closing in and still no sign of the French coastguard cutter *Tapageuse*.

The sand drifting against Hôtel du Port was deeper after the autumn gales, the hotel less inviting, shutters bolted and no sign of life as Flynt and Monique rattled on the door ahead of the media pack.

'Closed for the winter,' a hack shouted after finding the rear entrance also locked.

'What kind of hotel is this?' someone asked.

'Very strange... but they'll open up... eventually,' said Flynt. 'Be patient! Visitors not welcome, don't you see the sign!'

'Kick the door down, Mr Piggy,' another yelled. 'That's why the *Chronicle* pays you.' Dando bristled at the taunt, itching to wade into the pack after his tormentor.

When the door did open the old crone hadn't even changed her greasy apron. Flynt got the room with the gravelly sheets,

Monique chuckling at the sign hanging on the wall in large black capitals: '*NE PAS CRACHER PAR TERRE OÚ PARLER BRETON*'.

'You know what it means?' she asked.

Flynt took a stab at it. 'No spitting on the floor or speaking Breton,' he suggested.

'*Bon!*' said Monique. 'Once it was hung on the wall of every school in Brittany.'

Hôtel du Port served dinner that evening beneath the familiar grey foam ceiling tiles.

'I'd expected French,' said Dando waving the menu. 'I take it this is Breton.'

'*Pesk* is fish,' explained Monique. 'You'll find lots of *pesk*.'

Flynt pointed to a paragraph at the top of the menu. 'What's that say?'

'*Dieub ha par en o dellezegezh hag o gwirioù eo ganet an holl dud. Poell ha skiant zo dezho ha dleout a reont bevañ an eil gant eg en ur spered a genvreudeuriezh.*'

'Here,' said Dando, pushing notebook and pen across the table to Monique. 'Translate for me.'

'All human beings are born free and equal in dignity and rights. They are endowed with reason and conscience and should act towards one another in a spirit of brotherhood.'

'Article 1 of the Declaration of Human Rights,' said Flynt.

'I'll use it.' Dando slipped the translation into a pocket, and ordered *legestr* (lobster).

The attention necessary to crack open a lobster silenced Dando but not for long. 'Tell me more about the Bezen Perrot,' he asked between mouthfuls of white meat. Flynt yawned. 'Not again, Dando… haven't you been listening?'

'Collaborators,' said Lebrun seizing the opportunity, 'A Breton extremist group that fought alongside the Nazis… murdered my father.' Lebrun was ambivalent, one moment sympathetic towards the Bretons, the next wanting only revenge for what they'd visited upon his family. 'French is the language of the Republic. If we recognise another language, what happens to France?'

'You're running down the clock, aren't you?' interrupted Flynt. 'How many Breton speakers will there be in ten years... maybe a few thousand? The French have nothing to fear from the Bretons. It's the Muslims they're worried about.'

The man from the *Chronicle* was scribbling. At this rate he'd have the analysis in the bag before the news story. That's how the desk wanted it. 'Analysis is for an inside page,' he muttered, 'earlier deadline... breaking news later.'

'And don't forget your back-up... me!' Flynt delighted in reminding newspaper staffers how important agencies were if they miscued.

A siren sounded. In the darkness beyond the hotel, lights were moving across the harbour. The *Tapageuse* was arriving.

'Your status quo is safe,' Flynt told Lebrun. 'Your gunboat is here. Now the only chance the Bretons have is to poison the fucking lobster.'

Across the dining room Rouselle and The Teacher sent to beat the Breton language to death stood up and headed for the door followed by Monique and Flynt.

'Cold?' asked Flynt offering his jacket when they stepped outside for a closer look.

'Not really,' she said. 'It's this place... those women on the quay. Did you see their eyes? They seemed more frightened than angry.'

It was much the same the last time Flynt was on Île d'Iroise – the women gagged by a home-grown fear, not the arrival of more outsiders.

'The old woman at the hotel – is she stupid? When I complained about sand in the bed she didn't seem to understand

I wanted the sheets changed. I tried in Breton and French but nothing, not even an apology.'

That night Monique slept fitfully, the slightest sound jerking her awake, her dreams filled with sinking trawlers and cries for help in an angry sea until Flynt, ignoring the 'no country for old men' sign, slipped an arm around her waist. Without resisting his clumsy advances, Monique rolled over murmuring, '*Allons-y, allons-y*'. If this was foreplay, the bubble burst when they slipped off the mattress in a flurry of arms and legs.

Just before dawn strange voices woke Monique again. Crossing to the window she saw three figures disappearing in the darkness.

'Jack,' she said, kneeing Flynt's side of the bed to wake him. He looked up and smiled, stretching his hands behind his head. 'Can't sleep… want to try again?' Monique stood there in red knickers, her breasts white and firm.

By the time she climbed between the sheets Flynt was tempted. 'I think I could last longer now I've had some practice,' he whispered. Monique settled in his arms, the sea washing against the harbour wall, the lights from the trawlers flickering on the ceiling above their heads.

Monique broke the spell. 'Do they speak German on the island? I heard voices beneath our window… men whispering in German!'

Flynt pulled away. 'Why should they? You must be mistaken.'

Monique said, 'I'm not stupid. They were speaking German, certainly not Breton or French. Don't you think I'd know the difference? How many languages do you speak, Jack?'

'OK! You've made your point. I'll ask Lebrun… knows everything about this bloody place. Get some sleep… tomorrow won't be easy.'

Monique drew the sheets around bare shoulders. The older

hands working Paris Gare du Nord were wrong. Selling sex didn't mean she'd lost her right to love.

The next morning, after dipping their croissants in muddy coffee, they were joined by Lebrun for a spin around the block. The wind had picked up, the TV people already out and about taking location shots. But where were the islanders? The doors of the white, austere cottages around the harbour were bolted, windows shuttered, no sign of life.

'Mass... they'll be at mass,' said Lebrun heading for the church.

'Not if it's the way it was,' said Flynt, 'vandalised.'

'I don't think so. The priest was on the ferry.'

The skateboarders were nowhere to be seen, the smell of incense greeting Flynt at the entrance to the church. In the darkness candles flickered. The font was full of holy water, the rubbish swept away. 'The priest has celebrated mass already,' observed Lebrun

Having removed his cassock and tucked his grey clerical shirt tightly into his waistband, Father Joseph was up a ladder scrubbing graffiti off the church wall.

'Good morning, Father... I see the church is back in business,' Lebrun called out cheerily.

Monique greeted the priest with a wide-open smile when finally he descended to terra firma. Flynt was disappointed. He was hoping for another look at the *Werwolf* graffiti scrawled on the church door but that too had vanished beneath a new coat of paint.

'I imagine you're here for the games!' said a fresh-faced Father Joseph, waving a hand in the direction of the harbour where Académie française members were already snooping around.

'To cover the games, not participate... and find my wife,' said Flynt. 'Emilie Quatrevents... did you know her?'

'I heard she fell from the cliffs at Port Maria.'

'No she didn't,' Flynt said, 'not fall… nor did I push her. Were you at the hearing?'

'No, only here for Sunday Mass.' Father Joseph smiled with relief. 'I never met your wife or my predecessor Father Oswaldo but he seemed to think she was very committed to the children, although there weren't many… about a dozen… that's all.'

'When did Father Oswaldo retire?' Lebrun asked.

The priest's smile dimmed. 'I'm afraid he didn't retire. Father Oswaldo was another accident… also fell from the cliffs at Port Maria… very sad.'

Behind the priest's hesitation was a reluctance to say more. But he did, explaining that since Father Oswaldo's accident two years ago Île d'Iroise had been without a priest until the islanders petitioned Rome.

'They went straight to the top you might say.' Father Joseph's parish was at Brest and he crossed from the mainland once a month to celebrate mass until repairs to the church were finished and a resident priest inducted to St Anne's.

'If they hadn't petitioned the Holy Father I doubt whether the diocese would have appointed anyone,' he said. 'The congregation has shrunk. Once there were a hundred or more for mass, now it's tiny, barely thirty. I've still not met all the islanders and their children. I'm told they're home-taught.'

Flynt said, 'How did Father Oswaldo fall?'

'He slipped.'

From the colour filling the priest's face Flynt suspected he was casting around for a more plausible explanation. 'The Church doesn't condone suicide,' he said. 'Suicide is a mortal sin.' Shaking his head the priest made to walk away, his expression pained and confused.

Then he stopped, turned and added, 'The isolation

and loneliness must have been a heavy burden for Father Oswaldo.'

Flynt asked, 'Why was that?'

'These people are consumed by their struggle to preserve their heritage, have been for centuries, before even Christianity arrived on Île d'Iroise. Devotion has always come second to their traditional beliefs.'

'I don't see why this should be a burden – for them perhaps, not your predecessor.'

'He was weighed down by despair for their plight – felt they were constantly retreating … and nowhere left to hide.'

Flynt got the picture, especially the running away bit. Some years earlier he'd taken a flight across the Amazon with a pair of anthropologists, a husband and wife team, who'd found a tribe that had never before had contact with Western civilisation. Their light aircraft swooped low over a clearing in the forest, smoke spiralling from a cluster of bamboo huts. Twenty minutes and fifty miles later, on their return to base, they crossed a ring of fire and smoke eating into the pristine forest as the loggers and ranchers advanced. 'Come back in six months,' said one of the anthropologists, 'and they'll be gone, moved on… or perished. From the air we've only counted thirty… not much more than an extended family but with their own language and customs.' Flynt wondered whether Île d'Iroise was a clearing in the forest.

'Come with me,' said Father Joseph, leading the way among the tombstones in the adjoining graveyard. Most had fallen over or been pushed by whoever had desecrated the church. But the priest had sprayed the weeds, cut the grass, while members of his congregation had placed fresh flowers on some graves. In front of these they'd also set a small china dish containing what seemed to Flynt like the remains of a meal after the birds had finished pecking.

Lebrun took one look and muttered, 'The Celtic Cult of the Dead!'

'What's that?' Flynt asked.

'The belief there's no distinction between the living and the dead – that all inhabit the same world, one visible and the other not.'

Father Joseph added, 'That's why they put food out – to feed the invisible. For them death is not so much a change of condition but a journey, a departure to another world. Unfortunately Father Oswaldo permitted an essentially pagan belief to attach itself to the Christian footprint. The Church didn't agree.'

Flynt had seen this before. Roman Catholicism usually travelled well, the Vatican sometimes having to bend to accommodate local traditions. But not on Île d'Iroise it seemed.

Lebrun got in first with the *Werwolf* question.

'Did Father Oswaldo's flock believe in the *Werwolf*? You saw the graffiti on the door.'

'I did,' said Father Joseph. 'I've been scrubbing more off the church wall.'

Flynt sighed. The Frenchman was sure to ask whether the Bezen Perrot had been seen hanging around the graveyard.

Father Joseph was uncomfortable with the direction of the conversation. 'No mention of *Werwolf* in Father Oswaldo's journal,' he said quickly.

'He kept a journal!' Flynt exclaimed, eyes shining at the prospect.

'There was one but the Bishop confiscated it after the Father's death.'

'Have you seen it? Any mention of Emilie?'

'Only that Father Oswaldo was concerned about her… that she worried about the shrinking numbers in the school; that

Herve Brevilet was telling her what to teach. Have you met him... the leader?'

'So Brevilet gets a mention, too!'

'Mostly uncomplimentary... that he never attended mass or confession... that he was manipulative and interfered with Father Oswaldo's ministry... that nothing much happened without Brevilet's say-so... that he was an evil influence.'

'I still can't see how jumping would save Father Oswaldo's flock.'

'He believed he'd failed his congregation. These are simple people.'

Licking his lips Flynt asked, 'Could Father Oswaldo have been pushed... dead men don't talk!'

Father Joseph didn't argue, saying only, 'They never found the body... a fragment of black cassock, that's all.'

Having travelled that road already, Flynt was wary of taking another wrong turning. 'But you have to agree,' he told Lebrun as they walked back into Tourmant, 'a long black cassock at the ankles is not ideal for rambling along a treacherous cliff path. Too much like Emilie's red dress!'

Lebrun offered two words, the usual two, 'Bezen Perrot.'

Sundays in Tourmant were most probably always as silent as the grave. No kids disturbing the peace was good for Flynt who, logging on to his satellite signal, picked up a batch of service messages from Yates at INS in Paris. His 'Lost Tribe' had found a market, a dozen or more subscribers, some in Amish country, others in corners of the world with ethnic minority problems wanting 'specials'. By the time he'd tailored each to suit the subscriber's market, Flynt would be written out. Specials made good money for the agency but were a pain in the backside for a correspondent having to find a dozen different ways to say usually the same thing.

Curled up in a chair at the bedroom window with its view across the harbour, Monique waited impatiently for him to finish while providing a running commentary on events unfolding in her line of sight.

'The gendarmes,' she shouted to Flynt hammering at his laptop, 'are putting up their sign – *Hôtel de Police – Brittany Préfecture.* What do you think has happened to the people in the cottage? They can't just throw them out?'

Flynt sighed – interesting but not essential for what he was writing.

'Why don't you take a walk? I'll be finished in an hour.' He would be if Monique gave him space.

'Out there!' she exclaimed, tapping the window with her fingers. 'What about the *Werwolf*?'

Having spent an hour quizzing the priest about local superstitions, Flynt felt obliged to stop writing for five minutes to explain to Monique that the shape-changing creature only ever existed in the imagination of ignorant peasants. Monique wasn't so sure.

'Oh… oh, yes!' she whispered excitedly. 'The magistrate and that terrible man you call The Teacher… they're sitting on the harbour wall.'

Planning how to stuff French down the throats of the kids when school started on Monday, thought Flynt.

That evening the dining room at Hôtel du Port was topping up on lobster when, after a day foraging for 'pings', Mathias and Donovan dropped their backpacks inside the entrance and found a table close enough to eavesdrop. The dining room was no place for private conversation, Donovan showing an interest when Flynt asked Lebrun, 'German… do they speak German on the island?'

'I wouldn't have thought so,' said Lebrun, aiming a morsel

of white flesh at his mouth. 'The island was occupied by a small garrison of Germans during the last war because of its proximity to the U-boat pens at Lorient. It is said they were shot, executed before they could surrender.'

Flynt had seen the abandoned concrete pillboxes along the coast – and the photograph of Radenac buried in the back of his German army staff car. 'Monique thought she heard someone speaking German outside the hotel,' he explained.

'Bezen Perrot!' exclaimed Lebrun, setting down his fork, eyes sparkling. His obsession was relentless. 'They always come again, the Germans… never settle for peace, instead use the space to prepare their next adventure!'

Flynt said, 'Give up, man… that was seventy years ago!'

Lebrun's cry was loud enough for everyone to hear. 'The French have good reason not to forget. Brittany was once a great reservoir of hope for the Republic, the mainstay of its navy, God-fearing, peaceful people. We can't forgive their treachery.'

'Only a handful collaborated, you told me so yourself that most fought with the Resistance… does that not absolve them?'

Donovan stood up and with a grin beckoned to Lebrun. 'I speak German… I'll ask,' he said wagging a finger at the woman in the greasy apron hovering near the door. '*Ich kann bitte eine Flasche Weißwein haben?*' he said. More startled than confused, she paused before leaving the dining room to return minutes later with bottle of white wine.

Donovan uncorked a large booming laugh. 'I don't imagine she learned that from passing German tourists. You're right Lebrun – the Germans have walked over Europe twice and could try again.' Mathias and Donovan were sounding more *Starsky & Hutch* than *Smiley's People*.

Flynt was growing weary of his companions, especially Lebrun blathering on about a bunch of 1940s terrorists. Slipping from sympathetic grin into sneering mode he snapped at the

Frenchman, 'I'm not looking down any more holes for you. I want answers. Don't we, Dando?' The man from the *Chronicle* was slumped at the table, asleep, his lobster thermidor cold and unloved. Dando had given the bottle in his room a hammering.

Lebrun replied, 'The security business is not unlike the media. Both have an agenda and because only we see the end, our motives are almost always suspected by those whose interests we're protecting.'

Riddles again, thought Flynt. Did they have to talk like John le Carré wrote!

'Sometimes,' continued Lebrun, 'it's necessary to aid an enemy to achieve a result.'

'I take it I'm the enemy, the media?'

'Unless you're managed properly. In fact some matters are better resolved publicly, by the weight of public exposure. That's where you come in.'

Flynt answered by ordering another bottle of Château Shit. There was no bar at the hotel. Drinking was done at the table. Digging into the bag at his feet, Mathias contributed a bottle of twelve-year-old scotch.

Flynt was getting drunk and frustrated. 'I don't think you give a shit about anything... just play your little games,' he declared to everyone within earshot. Monique's hand on his crotch beneath the table told him to shut up before he got thumped. 'And you,' he barked at Lebrun as Monique led him off to bed, 'find me a live Bezen Perrot and I'll write it.'

Chapter 24

A BAND WAS playing 'La Marseillaise'. Flynt's leg straddled Monique, her head resting on his shoulder, the gentle breeze blowing off the harbour rustling the bedroom curtains. The storm troopers of Académie française were lining up below the window, a CD player hung around the neck of their leader waving a very large Tricolor. The high priest and priestess of the Académie applauded the gendarmes arriving to accompany the demonstrators up the hill to the schoolhouse. Across the harbour, Donovan and Mathias were huddled over a satellite phone pressed hard to the CIA man's ear as he noted the co-ordinates of the sonar signal plotted by the *Halifax*.

'They're moving,' said Flynt, gently shaking Monique. No woman was more desirable, beautiful and trusting, black eyelashes curled delicately across pale cheeks. Monique blushed beneath his gaze.

Dressing quickly they caught the marchers climbing the cobbled street towards the schoolhouse, television cameras leading the way, Dando and the other newspaper hacks hurrying alongside taking notes.

'Have we missed anything?'

Dando shook his head. 'There's no-one around. Where are the people? You can't have a demo without someone to demonstrate against.'

The supporters of Académie française were unnerved by this, their leader adding to their sense of frustration by switching off his CD player. 'Vive La France' wouldn't sound too good on TF1 without an enemy.

'No Bretons,' Flynt whispered to Monique. 'No pictures… television needs pictures… otherwise no story.'

Disappointed hacks rattling on cottage doors to turf the recalcitrant Bretons from their dugouts at last found an elderly couple to prod into a comment.

'What they saying… what they saying?' Dando demanded, dragging Monique over to interpret.

'The old man says Breton is their identity and that if their children aren't taught the language they'll lose everything – that they have already lost their schoolteacher.'

'He mentioned Emilie!' Flynt was surprised.

'Only that their teacher had been taken from them.'

'Ask him if he knows where.' Flynt saw the Breton shake his head and turn away. The couple had become increasingly agitated after seeing Herve Brevilet hovering at the edge of the media scrum.

'Try again… ask what they intend doing.'

Monique listened to the wife. 'She says that since the French consider the Bretons barbaric, they will act like barbarians. Her husband disagrees. The Bretons of Île d'Iroise will always renounce violence, he says, whatever Paris does… are prepared to die for their culture, their language… that *Liberté, égalité, fraternité* was for French speakers only.'

Flynt squeezed her shoulder. 'You're doing well… no need to interpret every word for them,' he whispered, nodding at the hacks crowding around. 'Save the best for me… let them work it out themselves. I'm paying the bills, remember.'

As Herve Brevilet elbowed his way to the centre of the group to face the cameras, the elderly couple retreated quickly into their cottage as though not wanting to share a platform with the man.

'All we ask is to be left alone,' Brevilet said, speaking French. Cameras moved closer in anticipation, news reporters scribbled – then he walked away preferring not to lock horns.

Rather than take the opportunity to defend the islanders'

cultural position, say something about their human rights, he'd backed off. Public opinion still counted for something and Flynt was expecting Brevilet to plead the islanders' case before the cameras.

The diehard republicans from Académie française were being squeezed, the French nationalist point of view sidelined until the man with the flag butted in. 'The Breton language threatens the founding principles of the French Republic,' he insisted, delivering his message to the TV cameras. 'They have their bilingual signs, what more do they want?'

'To hell with the French,' growled Flynt.

Lebrun said, 'Hell must be crowded, considering the number of French sent there by the English.'

'Your lot are scared,' continued Flynt, 'Too scared of what migrants are doing to France to allow the Bretons an inch. The French don't like diversity – not part of your political DNA. First the Roma, then Muslims with headscarves, and now you're reducing these people to museum exhibits!'

The marchers were at the school door. The CD player struck up 'La Marseillaise' and The Teacher, escorted by gendarmes, stepped forward purposefully, a spring in his step, a swagger rocking his scrawny shoulders. Pushing open the door he backed away quickly. The schoolroom was empty. Hands on hips, he appealed to the high priest and priestess of the Académie, shrugging despairingly before stepping aside for the demonstrators to surge past, intent on leaving 'Vive la France' scrawled on walls and desks, and piling every Breton text and book in an untidy heap outside. Someone struck a match and Île d'Iroise's investment in its cultural heritage went up in flames.

'The Nazis burned books,' Flynt remarked.

'A big mistake,' Lebrun agreed, his ambivalence swinging back towards the Bretons. 'The children… what will they think? This is how terrorists are produced.'

Emilie had said the school had only a dozen children. 'I imagine they're hiding… taken out of harm's way,' said Flynt. 'If I had kids I wouldn't want them caught up in this kind of stunt.'

'What next?' Dando was at his shoulder asking for help.

'Back to the hotel and write… and await developments… and the ferry tonight with luck.'

Dando said, 'Not an easy piece… and I can't get a signal. You'll let me use your satellite, won't you, Jack?'

'Did you get a shot of the book-burning?' asked Flynt. Dando nodded. 'I'll take a copy – then you use the satellite but only after I file.' Agencies had always to be first, INS one of the fastest if not always the most reliable.

On the way to the hotel, Lebrun drew Flynt aside for a quiet word.

'I'll see you back at the hotel,' Flynt told Monique, detaching himself from the pack and accompanying Lebrun along the harbour wall until they found a stone bench.

'I thought Brevilet disappeared pretty quickly after his little speech,' said the Frenchman.

'I guess he didn't want to hang around,' said Flynt, 'for the magistrate to serve a warrant for obstructing his investigation. A man of very few words but in perfectly good French, wouldn't you agree?'

Lebrun replied. 'He sounded more Greta Garbo – "I want to be alone" – than a friend of the natives.'

'Yes… the old couple who gave us a quote didn't seem to like him. I thought they were afraid.'

Lebrun nodded. 'Very different type, I agree.'

'How?' asked Flynt.

'You heard the old man – they're prepared to die for what they believe. Brevilet doesn't get even close.'

'You still believe he's a fraud?'

Instead of answering Lebrun changed tack. 'I meant to ask about your wife,' he said. 'Dubret tells me it's her voice on the phone.'

'Not dead,' said Flynt. 'She's here somewhere.' He waved a hand towards the heath behind their backs. 'I should be looking now, not chasing a bloody story about Breton human rights. But not me… the news junky… it's-all-about-the-story man… I don't do ordinary, like finding my wife.'

Lebrun seemed to understand. 'What you're doing is important. This is big… on every front page in France.'

'In France maybe,' said Flynt. 'I guarantee the rest of the world doesn't care a shit no matter how hard I hype it. There'll be something else tomorrow and the next day. News moves on. Nothing gets resolved. Minorities must learn to swim with the tide or drown.'

'The intelligence business isn't very different,' said Lebrun. 'I was off on my next assignment before the dust settled on the last. My life was one long misunderstanding… my misunderstanding until my wife came along and gave it purpose. You need to find Emilie, someone, before you overdose on news.'

Flynt asked, 'And where do I start looking?'

Lebrun replied, 'With Mathias and Donovan.' A seagull swooped and shat on Flynt. A bad omen! 'They know something,' continued Lebrun.

'You mean the fucking seagulls!' said Flynt. 'This stuff is concentrated acid,' he muttered, brushing at the white blob burning a hole in his jacket.

Lebrun wasn't listening. 'Why would Mathias show you the photographs unless he thought you might have something to trade?'

Flynt had clean forgotten the lever in his tool bag – the location of the ping made by a hammer striking a metal plate, the sound he'd heard while walking.

'Here he comes, ask him,' said Lebrun.

Mathias, in mottled-green fatigues, was making his way along the harbour wall.

'Any luck,' Flynt called out, 'found any pings?'

Pulling up in front of them, Mathias said, 'I take it you'll be leaving on the ferry tonight?'

Flynt swivelled sideways on the stone bench to face the ferry moored at the quay. 'Only if I find Emilie, then I'll leave.'

Mathias bent down, found a flattish stone and sent it skimming across the surface of the water. 'Quite possible,' he said, adjusting his metal-framed glasses, 'if we find the pinging, you'll find your wife.'

Flynt was waiting for this opportunity. 'I have heard something,' he said.

Mathias replied with that long penetrating look perfected by people who spend their lives asking questions. 'When was that?'

'Eight years ago, like the sound of a hammer, or a phone ringing. But it couldn't be a phone, not on this bloody rock.'

'Where was that exactly?'

'If I've got this right the locals call it Ar Poull-nevial Du – Black Pool in English, a narrow inlet really between high cliffs.'

'We've been there – nothing, only cliffs,' said Mathias. 'We'll look again... couple of other places to check first.' He didn't seem confident.

'But if it's still pinging away after eight years it's not likely to be a hammer. Wouldn't you agree?' suggested Flynt. 'Surely with all your gear you've got the co-ordinates?'

'We do – your Black Pool but, as I said, nothing except cliffs.' Mathias tugged at the creases in his mottled-green trousers. A tidy man from a tidy background, he was always careful about his appearance. 'It's all very curious. We wouldn't have been looking if the Spanish report about unidentified sonar in Biscay hadn't coincided with the sinking of the fisheries patrol boat by a rogue mine.'

'A freak sound, the ocean must be full of them,' Flynt suggested. 'Did you not see the film *On the Beach?*' Mathias had. 'The Coke bottle, you mean… northern hemisphere wiped out by radiation after a nuclear war and a submarine is sent from Australia to investigate a mysterious Morse signal coming from San Diego. When the sub arrives the crew find, not a human operator, but the neck of an empty Coke bottle vibrating in the breeze against a Morse-code key. I can't imagine it's anything like that. The Spanish trawlers heard sonar. So did a US sub. The ping-ping is land based.'

Flynt said, 'What do the locals say?'

Mathias laughed. 'Blank… don't seem to want to communicate in any language.'

Flynt suggested, 'Or afraid to. Have you asked Brevilet?'

'He's gone fishing, again. Every time we get close he goes fishing, although he doesn't have a boat.'

'Why didn't you nab him when you had the chance outside the schoolhouse?'

'Disappeared before we could,' said Mathias.

'And you missed Radenac for sixty, seventy years, by which time he was dead. Why hadn't the other islanders blown the whistle on their nefarious neighbour?'

Mathias nodded. Flynt caught his eyes boring back at him. 'You've made a very valid point,' the MI5 man said eventually.

Flynt looked along the harbour to where the same fishermen were repairing nets. They were always mending nets in the shadow of that wreck rotting on the slipway. 'Are they simple or simply stupid?' he wondered aloud. 'What price their culture? They don't have television for Christ's sake!'

'Zealots,' Lebrun suggested. 'You can push them just so far… unpredictable.'

Mathias turned and headed back along the quay to where Donovan was waiting.

Lebrun wasn't moving, instead dipping into his jacket pocket for a photocopy of a page taken from the accounts of La Société Commerciale. 'What do you make of it' he asked Flynt. The page was headed '*Les passagers à pied*' and the number using the ferry crossing in October: 168.

'I mentioned Île d'Iroise's healthy tourist traffic.'

Lebrun said, 'Yes, but you assumed these were return tickets. Not so!'

'I'm well able to read a trading account,' Flynt snapped.

'I'm sure you are… and you're right. The tickets are entered as return fares in the accounts. But they're not. They're all one way – from Île d'Iroise to the mainland – forty-two a week through October – and every week – according to the passenger manifests filed with customs at Brest.'

Flynt had always suspected a fiddle.

Lebrun explained that a second ferry operated during summer months, and a third provided a summer service to three smaller islands in Biscay after calling at Île d'Iroise – that there was an arrangement allowing passengers to use any of the services for the return journey.

'Customs assume discrepancies in the numbers are explained by passengers island-hopping or staying over, using one ferry for the outward journey, another to return. Passenger manifests are more or less a formality for boats operating on French inland waters and that includes our territorial waters. That's fine, until September 30, when two of the companies suspend their service for the winter, leaving only La Société Commerciale's once-weekly service.'

Flynt said, 'Who are these passengers?'

Lebrun pulled himself to his feet with greater difficulty than usual. 'I shouldn't sit for so long.' They'd walked only a dozen steps towards the hotel before he replied, 'That is the reason the French Government sent *Tapageuse*… not to beat these poor people into line. They can't escape… nowhere to go.'

Chapter 25

AFTER CHECKING THROUGH his copy and hitting the send button, Flynt leaned back and patted his jacket pockets looking for a cigarette. There wasn't one. He'd given up smoking but Dando had plenty. Flynt inhaled deeply, cupped his hands behind his head thinking about where to start looking for Emilie.

Monique watched quietly, Dando impatient to use the satellite.

'Yates would go spare if he knew I'd loaned it to the competition.'

'But we're not,' insisted Dando. 'The *Chronicle* subscribes to INS.'

'In which case tell your desk to run my copy.'

Dando shook his head. 'And put myself out of a job. But I'll take a look at your story… give it a bit of spin…'

'No you don't… write your own stuff. Let's see what the *Chronicle* prefers, yours or mine.' Dando could never compete with agency hacks knocking out stories in minutes, not the hour or more it took him to pull the facts together.

'I must start at Port Maria,' Flynt decided. Monique knew it was coming.

Dando was in mid-sentence on the satellite when the Bakelite rang again. 'What's that… what's that?' he said, his attention fixed on the Carrefour bag on the table. 'No phones, you said there were no phones here.'

Without answering, Flynt took the Bakelite from the plastic bag, opened the bedroom window and threw it hard on the cobbles, the phone exploding into a dozen pieces.

'Doctor's orders,' Monique said. 'That's what Monchette told me to tell you… get rid of it.'

Flynt's anxiety had hardened into furrowed brows, his mood as dark as the island's granite cliffs.

'I'll be back,' he said.

'It'll soon be dark,' exclaimed Monique, 'The ferry leaves at nine.' They'd seen the ship's freezers being packed with smelly crates of fish.

'That means nothing,' said Flynt. 'It'll sail when Herve Brevilet says… where is he?'

Dando said, 'Lying low. The TV people want him for a piece to camera.'

The setting sun was hidden by a thick grey blanket, the hill behind Tourmant cut off at the waist by the leaden sky. On other days it could be so very different, the sun against a golden sky touching the sea with turquoise.

'I'm coming,' Monique announced.

'No need! I'll not take long… an hour at most.' Monique's flashing determination held a peculiar charm for Flynt even with his focus on finding Emilie.

'I'm coming,' she repeated.

The island had two tracks, one north-south and the other east-west. The small thatched shelter for the only public telephone on Île d'Iroise stood at the crossroads. On an island small enough to shout, phones were hardly necessary.

On a good day Port Maria was a comfortable walk but, as dusk turned to night, the stony track glided through pools of water draining off the heath and passed stunted thorn bushes offering little protection from Atlantic gales. The wind was picking up, blowing away the cloud cover, the moon rising into the night sky, casting deep shadows across their path.

Flynt felt Monique's hand slip quickly into his, then checked his stride, stopped and looked over his shoulder. 'I think we're being followed.' Picking up a stone, he flung it hard back down the track at a shadowy figure, head poking momentarily above the bank before ducking out of sight behind a patch of ragged gorse.

Quickening their step, they turned off the track and on to a narrow path running down to a rocky inlet, Port Maria a brooding silhouette in the moonlight tucked into the hill at its back. 'Five minutes and we'll be there.'

Monique was too cold to answer, too afraid to look when eventually they arrived at Port Maria's large dark oak-panelled door at the top of a flight of slippery stone steps. Under pressure from Flynt's right shoulder, the door creaked open, releasing a musty, disagreeable smell. In the half-light a broad staircase was framed by a stained-glass window at the end of a long, dim hallway.

'Come on.' Flynt's voice disappeared into the darkness, his hand steadying himself against the hall table just inside the door.

'I'm here.' Monique hung on tightly, the shadows running ahead of Flynt's flashlight – and the smell in the air calling for an open window.

Cautiously they entered the dining room. Flynt saw the dirty plates and empty wine glasses scattered on the table. Monique felt his hand tighten on hers in anticipation. 'You ate here?' she asked.

'With Emilie… the night she disappeared.'

Bare walls, an ugly mantelpiece and empty grate stared back at them, shadows flitting noiselessly to their right and left. Monique shivered, imagining something at her back, watching, wrapped in darkness.

And there were sounds, not loud, but real enough. 'Creaks, cracks, you always get them in old houses, especially near the sea… the wind,' said Flynt reassuringly. But in the Stygian gloom he imagined other sounds, the blood singing in his veins – and something padding around the bedroom above their heads.

Flynt could barely make out Monique in the darkness. If he could he'd have seen an extraordinary transformation taking place, her face a spreading mask, wrinkled and lined, no longer young but old. Terror did that to a person. Drawing her close, the mask dropped away. Something was working on their subconscious, no longer the ringing Bakelite, something stranger.

'I'm cold. There's something upstairs, isn't there?' whispered Monique with a false chuckle. 'I can't go up.' Reluctantly, she followed him down a narrow passageway into the kitchen, a large room with a lofty beamed ceiling, and several doors, some opening into tall cupboards, cold and empty. No sign of food, not a scrap, only black beetles scurrying across the kitchen floor.

'Now the stairs,' Flynt said. They were only halfway up when the front door opened then closed. 'The wind,' he said, holding Monique tightly. Her face was livid. The hair on the back of Flynt's neck rose at right angles as someone crept along the passage towards the foot of the stairs. 'Who's that?' Flynt pointed his flashlight until the beam settled on the round smiling face of George Quatrevents... Emilie's brother.

'Christ, you frightened the life out of us! Were you the person I tossed a stone at down the track?'

Quatrevents nodded. 'Why didn't you invite me to the wedding?'

The banality of the question astonished Flynt. 'You mean eight years ago! Emilie never said she had a brother. OK, now I know... help us look around, the bedrooms first. Do you know Port Maria?'

'It feels as if I do. Emilie mentioned the house often in her letters.'

Flynt said, 'I only ever got the one letter… an invite to visit… kiss and make-up, I thought.'

'You mean she never told you?'

'Told me what…? We weren't in touch… not until the week she disappeared.'

'About Nonn, your daughter?'

Dismay tightened on Flynt's throat. 'Why wasn't I told?' he stammered, 'Why wasn't I told?' Monique held his hand.

Quatrevents couldn't say, only that Emilie wanted Nonn raised on the island, speaking Breton.

'Where is she, my daughter?'

Quatrevents didn't know that, either. 'She adored Nonn, wrote about little else. I'm sure we'll find them together.'

'Nonn… that's my…' Flynt hesitated. 'Daughter' wasn't a word he expected to need. Monique felt his hand slide away.

'She never said anything to me… about our daughter…' Even in the darkness Flynt's astonishment felt visible, his agonising frown, voice struggling to make sense of what he'd been told. 'What else did Emilie say? Was she happy?'

'She never really said, only that I got the impression from her letters she was afraid for herself and Nonn.'

'That fits.' Flynt snapped back into gear. 'You said it, Monique. This is a fucking awful place, the island, not because of their bloody language… they're trapped.' Flynt had seen this in the accounts of the ferry company listed under '*remboursements*'. No mention of what the fishermen were paid for their lobster. 'Nothing… they get nothing. Brevilet must take the lot… runs the ferry… even organises the groceries!'

Quatrevents said, 'I sent Emilie a thousand euros a month or so ago… no reply.'

Taking Monique's hand, Flynt led the way into the first bedroom on the landing. Something sprang at him as he pushed the door open. Monique screamed, rooted to the spot, fighting to catch her breath. Flynt felt an icy chill run down his spine. 'Christ, what was that... did you see it?'

Monique hadn't but knew they'd found the source of the nauseating smell. She was aching to escape, to feel the wind blowing off the sea.

The bedroom was a dungeon, Flynt's flashlight picking out a decrepit bedstead covered with a duvet, a dirty cane chair, a chest of drawers, and a cracked mirror on the wall. Monique saw nothing, eyes tightly shut, both hands locked round Flynt's wrist.

'Smells like a cat. The poor bugger must have starved to death,' said Flynt stepping back. 'Give it a moment to clear...'

It didn't. The wretched smell persisted until, turning to Monique, he said, 'I'd better take a look.' With a hand over his mouth Flynt edged across the room. Port Maria was bleak and uninviting even on a bright summer's day, the bedroom windows like arrow slits high up on the wall offering little respite from the funereal feel. With no lights or heating, it was an ice box, the cold carrying the putrid stomach-churning stench into every corner. Why Emilie was attached to the place Flynt never did understand, unless it was that cultural bug again.

The floor was covered with cat shit, the cat not dead but purring happily, eyes like diamonds in the darkness. Sweeping the room with his torch, the beam settled on the bedstead. Gesturing to the others to stand back, he gently lifted a corner of the duvet. An arm flopped out, gnawed to the bone. The hand collapsing on the floor had a wedding ring on the second finger. The other clutched an envelope.

'Stay there,' he shouted over his shoulder to Monique. 'It's Emilie. Oh, my God the cat's been eating her.'

Flynt stepped back quickly, bumping into Monique in his anxiety. 'Get out,' he ordered, snatching up the envelope. 'No wonder the fucking thing looks healthy,' he growled, lashing out with his boot at the furry little monster rubbing against his trouser leg. With a squeal the cat dived between the bannister rails, plunging head-first onto the quarry tiles in the hall and lying motionless.

After the battlefields of Iraq, Flynt thought he was bulletproof. Bodies were disposed of before decomposition set in, not left for cats and dogs to nibble on. The partly-eaten corpse looking at him from beneath the duvet was an unimaginable horror. Bizarrely, not a hair on Emilie's head was touched, neat and tidy, but her nightdress was torn to shreds by the cat foraging for tasty morsels.

'Quiet!' Emilie's brother held up a restraining arm. The putt-putt of an outboard-motor was followed by the grounding of a boat on the ribbon of shingle at the head of the inlet. Not long afterwards moonlight spilled through the front door. Without a sound, three men entered, gliding along the hall before stopping, shoulders bent forward, listening. Flynt's tongue stuck like leather in his mouth when the craggy features of Brevilet's younger brother Lan were caught in a burst of moonlight. Eyes fixed on Emilie's bedroom, Lan Brevilet missed the three figures hiding in the shadows. Moments later there was a quivering shriek followed by retching, the Bretons heading for the front door, Brevilet shouting, '*Aussteigen! Aussteigen!*'

'You heard that, saw what they were wearing?' whispered Quatrevents. 'Waffen-SS tunics!'

Without another word, Flynt dragged Monique out of the house, stopped and tore open the envelope. Just one page, the single sentence snatching at his throat: 'They have our daughter Nonn.' Flynt flinched. Emilie had known he'd come looking.

The Bretons were on the beach pulling their boat across the shingle towards the sea. 'Damn it! They've seen us... they're coming back,' said Flynt dousing his flashlight and heading for the path climbing up the cliff from the inlet. Quatrevents took off in the opposite direction.

Port Maria was an inky blackness against the bracken-covered heath when they stopped to catch their breath and check if they were being followed. On the night he'd chased after Elise Lebrun believing it was Emilie, the house lit up like a roman candle when the security lights switched on. Emilie must have hidden behind Port Maria before scrambling up the bank and across the heath to reach the phonebox at the crossroads. 'Help! He's trying to kill me,' she'd screamed believing it was Flynt who answered. Instead her call was intercepted by Brevilet and recorded by the KGB bug.

'She went back to Port Maria… to hide,' he panted through clenched teeth.

Flynt sank to his knees, breathless, the wind tugging at his jacket, his only thought that he'd abandoned his wife to save his skin. 'I saw no food in the house, did you?' Flynt groaned, 'Just empty tins… and that fucking cat.'

The beams from the flashlights spilling across the beach stopped at the foot of the cliff before zigzagging up the path towards them.

Flynt snatched Monique's arm. 'Faster, faster…!'

The path was getting narrower, a long rocky outcrop pushing it closer to the edge. Flynt pulled Monique into a niche in the rock wall and pressed a finger against his lips as heavy breathing approached. His boot sent one of their pursuers hurtling off the cliff, his screams cut short by the jagged rocks below.

The heavy breathing of a second man drew close. Monique screamed a warning but too late. Flynt crashed to the ground, his assailant launching himself from the rocky overhang. In the darkness he saw Lan Brevilet's thick features and savage eyes, the younger, stronger brother forcing Flynt closer to the edge and the jagged necklace of rocks swimming in the surf. Flynt was spitting blood, Brevilet poised to finish him with a large lump of granite when suddenly he crumpled, blood spilling from a hole in his head. Rolling clear, Flynt stared up into the smiling face of the square-necked CIA agent, revolver in one hand, Mathias at his side.

'I was finished!' Donovan pulled Flynt roughly to his feet. 'A few more seconds and I was done for… couldn't hold him much longer.'

Donovan kicked the dead Breton off the cliff. He didn't want thanks – just what Flynt knew about that sonar ping. 'I told Mathias… it was not far from here… just above the Black Pool. Emilie heard it too. We turned back.'

'We've been there.'

'Well, you'd better look again. How far did you get? Emilie said there was a track leading down to a tidal cave beneath the cliff.'

Donovan and Mathias set off at speed, Flynt and Monique struggling to keep up.

'Better if you went back… you'll be safer in the village.' Donovan waved an arm towards Tourmant.

'I don't think so,' said Flynt, breathing hard. 'We'll stick with you. I don't want to bump into Herve Brevilet now you've shot his brother.'

Donovan offered Flynt an automatic pistol. 'No, no… not for me… I'm strictly a biro man. I'll write it up afterwards.'

Turning off the path, they ploughed through stubbly heather towards a headland with the dark grey outline of a Second World War concrete lookout post rising from the cliff edge. The wind was beating itself to death against Île d'Iroise when Donovan stopped and pointed to a light out at sea. A vessel was heading towards the entrance to the Black Pool.

Then they heard it – the ping-ping of a submarine's sonar beneath their feet.

After a whispered conversation with Mathias, the American hurried ahead. By the time Flynt and Monique reached the lookout post, an elderly Breton lay dead, Donovan standing over him with a knife. Monique turned away, her shoulders dropped, hands hanging at her sides, paralysed with horror. Flynt bent over, shielding her from the bloody sight.

'Are you allowed to do this kind of thing?' Flynt meant to ask, but Donovan, after committing the body to the sea, was off again, searching the dense undergrowth.

'Down there,' he said, pointing to some roughly-hewn stone steps cut into the rock, slippery and steep, open to the sea on one side, the other hugging the cliff face, dark green and flaky, veins of pink and white mica glistening in the moonlight.

'Stay with the girl,' said Mathias, 'we might run into trouble.' Flynt again opted to stick with the experts rather than wait for trouble to arrive.

Donovan led the way, stopping every so often to listen to the unmistakable sound of sonar pinging before it was drowned by the thunder of Atlantic rollers dashing against the ramparts of Île d'Iroise.

The steps ended at a narrow cleft in the cliff face opening into a cave left high and dry when an ancient sea receded.

The source of the sonar was close, the ping-ping hurled from side to side like a football in the darkness.

'What's this?' exclaimed Mathias. The walls of the cave were worn smooth, glistening like glass under the MI5 man's flashlight, the beam settling on a bronze head with piercing blue eyes and a jaunty seafarer's cap on a stone plinth flanked by flags. Flynt remembered a smaller version in a niche on the landing of Herve Brevilet's farmhouse. According to a polished plaque the bronze commemorated:

'Kapitan Karl Scheer
Walter U-1405, Commandant

Geboren März 1922-Gestorben Oktober 2007'

'Meet pa,' Donovan announced, 'father to Herve and Lan Brevilet.'

Scheer and Radenac never made it to the pampas. Instead, the last survivors of the Third Reich and Bezen Perrot settled with their descendants on a miserable bit of moorland in the Bay of Biscay seized from a poor, defenceless bunch of cultural fanatics.

Moving closer to the shrine, Flynt heard Mathias say, 'The flag is the *Werwolf* pennant, the other the black cross of Bezen Perrot.'

Donovan called out, 'Take a look at this.' He'd torn the top off a wooden crate standing against one wall. The crate was filled with rusting Second World War weapons.

'A Beretta,' he said pulling out a sub-machine gun, 'and Karabiner infantry rifles and Browning pistols. Standard Waffen-SS issue.'

Mathias had opened a second crate. '*Einstossflammenwerfer*,' he said, 'flamethrowers issued to *Werwolf* cells.' They'd finally found one.

On a wooden lectern next to the Scheer bronze was an open book, the entries all in German.

'A book of remembrance,' said Donovan, turning to the cover page. The book listed the names of Germans who died in the battle for Île d'Iroise. Instead of being defeated, as was supposed, and their bodies thrown into the sea, the Germans were the victors. 'The Second World War didn't end on 6 May 1945, not here,' exclaimed Donovan.

'Shush!' whispered Monique. Quickly they ducked out of sight into the mouth of a dark passage leading off the cave and waited as the clatter of boots on steps got nearer and agitated voices grew louder. Herve Brevilet and his followers all wore the grey-green tunic of the Waffen-SS, double lightning flashes on the points of their collars and Bezen Perrot cotton badges on their chests.

Brevilet and his *Werwolf* stopped before the Scheer monument, heads bowed, muttering in German. Flynt cursed himself for not listening when Monique said she heard German being spoken. Brevilet's next move, however, was vintage Breton as he replenished the food in the small earthenware dish placed before his father's shrine. Every belief, Flynt knew, no matter how morally repugnant, had its icons and rituals.

The ritual over, Herve Brevilet flicked a switch before exiting the cave with his clan onto a narrow concrete balcony clinging to the side of a floodlit tidal cavern, the roof soaring above their heads like a colossal railway arch, at their feet the sea creaming and foaming at the cavern's mouth before falling back with a groan and mass of spray.

Brevilet led the *Werwolf* down an iron ladder onto a rocky ledge raised above the floor of the cavern now awash from the incoming tide.

Stepping out onto the concrete balcony, Donovan stopped, beckoning to the others to follow. The sonar had cut out – the source a vintage German U-boat moored against a blood-red sandstone wall.

'What is that!' exclaimed Mathias.

Donovan added, 'And what's it for?'

Flynt replied, 'I'd say the *Walter U-1405*. The prototype for a new submarine Hitler believed could win the war.'

'But didn't the British sink it?' asked Donovan.

'We thought we had,' said Flynt.

'It can't be operational,' whispered Mathias.

'I'm not so sure. Not a spot of rust,' said Flynt, pointing to a mountain of barnacles and limpets strewn with scraps of seaweed rotting in a corner of the cavern. 'They've had the cleaners in!' He recalled the Nazi staff car hidden in the

Jalenes' barn, in pristine condition until Radenac took it for a hearse.

'Not this time,' Donovan muttered. 'It won't escape again.' Dropping to his knees and unzipping his backpack, he was fitting together a Heckler & Koch sub-machine gun.

Flynt was astonished. 'You're not intending to use that… but why?'

Donovan and Mathias didn't answer.

'Will they surrender?' Mathias asked.

Donovan replied, 'I don't think so. Not even if we ask nicely. They're armed!'

The only weapons Flynt had seen were rusting in a seventy-year-old packing case, and no reason to re-open the conflict. The whispered conversation between Mathias and Donovan about taking on the *Werwolf*/Bezen Perrot cell in the final act of the Second World War sounded to him surreal, even comic.

Mathias said, 'We could wait… call in the military.'

'Can't… no satellite signal… not down here,' said Donovan.

'Up there we'll get a signal.' Mathias pointed to the roof of the cavern. 'The sub's not going anywhere.'

'Christ, hold your fucking horses.' Flynt choked on his protestations. 'What have they done? I've no time for Brevilet's lot but what have they done to start a war?'

'Old man Lebrun would say plenty,' replied Donovan.

The decision was taken from them when a motor launch Donovan saw heading for Ar Poull-nevial Du entered the cavern on the crest of a wave and moored alongside the U-boat, Brevilet barking orders from the bridge.

'Wait,' said Flynt, 'this could be our answer.'

Most of the women disembarking from the motor launch wore hijabs and carried Pierre Cardin and Gucci luggage – not desperate Syrian refugees but wealthy Arabs buying a new life in France.

No sooner were they ashore and the Arab women were searching through their designer bags for more fashionable coats and jackets for the next stage of the journey.

'People smugglers,' said Mathias. 'The U-boat uses its sonar to guide them in.'

Flynt said, 'First-class people traffickers.' This was Orient-Express-style travel with guaranteed delivery to Euro-land. At Brest, they'd walk ashore from the ferry and disappear. Flynt had found the phantom passengers in the accounts of La Société Commerciale. The name of the company's new game was 'Import-Export', the rocky quay at the back of the tidal cavern lined with packing cases recently arrived or awaiting shipment.

'We're going down.' Donovan and Mathias had decided.

'I'm coming, too,' said Flynt breaking his golden rule never to get involved. But this had got very personal. 'Stay here,' he told Monique. She wasn't going anywhere, frozen to the spot by fear.

'Watch your step... don't fall in,' said Donovan, slowly descending the rusting iron ladder. Flynt had no worries about that. Swimming was the only thing he did really well as a kid.

Donovan announced their arrival on the rocky quay with a burst of automatic fire into the roof, a shower of empty shells ricocheting off the walls. From the bridge of the U-boat, Brevilet was waving his people back aboard, leaving the terrified migrants hiding amongst their designer luggage and a tank with 'HTP' stencilled on its side.

A moment later a large wave burst through the mouth of the cave, dumping on the U-boat before spilling across the quay. Flynt couldn't see a thing until he surfaced between a Gucci suitcase and the 'HTP' tank, his only thought how the Walter boat's hydrogen peroxide propellant reacted in sea water. Then it was gone, the tank sucked through the mouth of the cave.

Donovan and Mathias hauled him out, all three on their knees coughing up the ocean.

'How many have we lost?' Flynt gasped.

'How many were there?' replied Donovan.

'I'd say forty-two. There are always forty-two,' said Flynt.

Mathias was counting. 'None missing, I'd say.'

'That's because of this,' said Donovan, pointing to a fishermen's net stretching through the water just below the lip of the stone quay. 'It must have happened before... a rogue wave.'

The sea was only doing what it had for millennia – cutting ever deeper into the softer underbelly of the cliff to carve an even more monumental cavern. Once the tide rose above the ragged reef guarding the entrance to the Black Pool, there was little to prevent the Atlantic breakers from dashing against the U-boat's hideout.

Flynt jumped to his feet. Without a word, he raised his arms above his head, bent forward slightly and dived beneath a wave crossing the cavern floor. Mathias and Donovan saw him surface twenty yards away, his arms biting at the water, racing to reach a dark head bobbing amongst the debris floating at the cavern mouth. A small girl was being dragged towards the open water of the Black Pool. Turning on his back Flynt paddled faster with his arms, riding the retreating white foam like a canoe. But by the time he got there she'd disappeared. Diving, he saw nothing in the inky darkness. On his second attempt a small hand brushed his face, Flynt shooting to the surface, one arm holding the girl tightly to his chest. His energy was almost spent, every stroke an agony, his clinging clothes threatening to drag him and the child under when another large wave burst through the entrance and drove them against the quay.

'Take her,' he gasped, holding the child above his head for Donovan to grab. Helped from the water, Flynt lay face down until he breathed more easily, his heart throbbing and jumping in his throat.

'I've not done that for thirty years... in fact never done it,' Flynt panted. He was on his knees throwing up the ocean for the second time. 'No more drinking... or smoking... I promise God!'

'I think you're right, Mathias. We'll call in the Marines,' said Donovan. One of the packing cases had splintered against the wall of the cave. 'They're running guns,' he said pointing to the shiny automatics in foam sleeves spilling across the quay.

Flynt rolled on one side. The submarine's bilge pumps were working overtime discharging the green sea that poured down an open hatch when the big wave broke. The propellers were churning the water.

'They're moving it,' Donovan muttered in disbelief. 'They got it in but won't get it out... don't have the water... it'll rip its belly on the rocks at the entrance... and the propellant... very unstable.'

Flynt had banged his head against the 'HTP' tank when he surfaced. 'It sounded empty.' Donovan and Mathias were reassured but it was time to get everyone out. 'If the sub hits the reef she'll take half the island,' said Donovan. Flynt was reminded of what the French Press Officer had said when showing him around the U-boat pens at Lorient: hydrogen peroxide exploded if it passed boiling point.

Unless he'd learned it at his father's knee, Brevilet wouldn't know how to skipper the *U-1405* inching its way towards the mouth of the cavern. Even if the submarine made it, a Force 8 gale was building in the Bay of Biscay.

Flynt recalled another submariners' ditty he'd picked up in Lorient – and would use it if ever he got to write the story:

Death for the Fatherland,
Glorious fate,

This is the end,
We, gladly await

Mathias was herding the migrants towards the steps leading to the surface. 'She won't get far,' he said, looking back, 'if she hits the bottom, duck!'

Accompanied by shouts and screams, they coaxed the Arabs up the rocky path, struggling against winds threatening to blow them on the rocks swimming in the surf.

Donovan called a halt. 'Fix this,' he bellowed to Mathias leading the climb. A lifeline was passed from hand to hand for Mathias to attach to the cliff face with a pair of pitons as a makeshift safety rail.

Monique was still afraid to move, clutching at the cold, bare rock. 'One step at a time,' Flynt whispered. 'I'm here, I won't let you fall.' A few paces below them a woman screamed. Flynt didn't see but thought he heard the thud as her body hit the rocks. Then he saw Donovan holding a child in his arms.

The climb seemed to last forever, the migrants on their knees thanking Allah for salvation after tumbling one by one onto the heather. Donovan was last up. The small girl didn't make a sound, her arms wrapped tightly around the big American's bull neck, eyes fixed in a wide open stare.

'The mother pushed the kid into my arms as she slipped… went over the edge,' Donovan panted. 'I couldn't reach her. Where's the kid's father?' No-one answered. Either the Arabs didn't know or were too busy praising Allah. The small girl hung on grimly, refusing to let go of Donovan. She was the one Flynt rescued from the sea an hour earlier.

Standing on the cliff edge they waited and listened. Donovan said, 'You don't think the sub made it… not again.'

His answer was that noiseless pulse of energy that precedes a clap of thunder and lightning. The catastrophic explosion that followed collapsed the tidal cavern, the concrete lookout post peeling off the promontory like an iceberg calving from a glacier. Flynt saw no sign of wreckage through the dust cloud rising from the Black Pool, only an angry sea swallowing a monumental slice of granite.

Flynt hung his head between his hands. Monique knew what he was thinking. 'I'm sure Nonn wasn't on the submarine, Jack.' Flynt wasn't convinced. If Brevilet was holding his daughter, Nonn might well have perished with him and his bunch of gangsters beneath a thousand tons of rock.

Rounding up the migrants, Mathias and Donovan were herding them along the cliff path towards Tourmant and the gendarmes when Flynt yelled, 'Don't push so hard... you'll kill us all at this rate.' Suddenly he stopped, unable to take another step. They'd reached the place where he almost died, where he thought Emilie had.

'This is it,' he muttered, eyes fixed not on the sea boiling against the foot of the cliff but on the gorse bush that broke his fall – and the fragment of red cloth caught in its branches. Flynt closed his eyes, gasping like an asthmatic. When at last he caught his breath and looked again, the fragment of cloth had vanished, either blown away or his imagination was playing tricks again.

'What's wrong, Jack? Are you OK?' Monique's worried look was reviving. Flynt had to be OK if only for her.

'Brevilet needed Emilie dead,' he said, the wind snatching at the words. Her call for help was finally making sense. 'Don't you see, she'd threatened to expose Brevilet's racketeering to me but couldn't because he'd taken Nonn. When Emilie disappeared Brevilet told the magistrate she'd fallen.' They both stared at the abyss beneath their feet.

Monique shuddered. 'Are you ready?' she asked. 'We'd better catch up.' The last of the migrants had disappeared around the rocky outcrop where Flynt almost came to grief.

'We don't have to follow, not immediately,' said Flynt. 'Wait a minute.' The pieces were coming together. Brevilet knew the torso recovered from the sea was Elise Lebrun but decided it was best if Lebrun's niece remained a missing person, rather than become the focus for a murder investigation. The clincher was the wedding ring he put on Elise's finger to persuade Flynt to identify her as Emilie.

'Mathias was right,' said Flynt. 'The walk out at the hearing was staged. Lan Brevilet wasn't making a cultural stand. He couldn't give his evidence in French because the only language he spoke besides Breton was German.'

The tide was creeping up the beach below Port Maria when Flynt and Monique caught up. A man Flynt recognised as Brevilet's bearded neighbour was waiting by the motor launch drawn up at the water's edge, waving to the column approaching across the sand.

Mathias shot him in the head.

Flynt gasped. The child, her arms still locked around Donovan's neck, sobbed quietly. 'But wasn't he surrendering…?' Flynt mumbled.

'Better if he didn't,' replied Mathias. 'We've found one *Werwolf* cell, there could be others – all bloody gangsters probably. We'll leave it to the Sûreté to tidy up. It was never an intelligence matter.'

Beneath the ashen clouds of a slate-grey dawn Flynt had not the stomach to face Port Maria a second time. 'But you must,' said Monique. 'There could be something there…' Flynt once read that conscience made cowards of everyone. His conscience was stuffed with regrets, most of all why he'd not bothered to save his marriage, why he'd never found the time to discover he had a daughter. He'd learn nothing from taking another look at Emilie's poor ravaged body but there might be something in the house for him to cherish.

Flynt waited on the landing while Mathias entered Emilie's bedroom. 'Not pleasant,' he said, emerging a few minutes later. 'I'd say your wife either starved or froze to death. No food in the house, just the dead cat in the hall.'

'She starved… why?'

'Perhaps she was afraid to leave the house to look for food.'

The next two rooms along the landing were empty, not a stick of furniture, just a thick layer of dust. The third was a revelation. Unlike the others there were no slit windows high up on the wall but a large bay window overlooking the inlet. The room was cheerfully painted, soft pastel colours not bright reds and yellows. Flynt knew the moment he saw the ragged doll on the pillow of the bed this was Nonn's room. And he sensed a presence as he had the previous night while groping through the darkness with Monique.

The child's plastic tea service set out on a small red plastic table with matching plastic chairs was a choker. But it was the framed photographs on his daughter's dressing table that crushed him. Flynt shook his head sadly. They were taken on their wedding day in Paris when Emilie first wore that red dress. Nonn knew about her father but how had Emilie explained his absence? Was he dead or alive in his daughter's memory?

Flynt's anger rose, then sadness swept his face when he saw his daughter's clothes neatly folded in a wardrobe, yet so threadbare they'd get rejected by a charity shop. He was angry with himself for not knowing about his family's struggle – for putting his bloody job before all else.

'Here,' said Mathias opening another drawer. 'These might interest you.' The MI5 man held up a bundle of pink writing paper held together by a rubber band. 'Letters…' Snatching them from his hand Flynt saw the childish scrawl, entirely Breton but each sheet headed, *Tad*. Flynt knew the word… it meant the same in Welsh. His mother had used it whenever he asked about his father! There were thirty, forty sheets. Nonn must have started writing to him soon after she knew how, pouring out her little secrets, which was probably why they were never sent. Emilie had his address, had written to him at the agency inviting him for that fatal weekend. Perhaps she was afraid their daughter would let something slip about Herve Brevilet.

'We'd better go,' said Mathias.

Flynt was reluctant to leave without a photograph of Nonn. The letters were a bond but how did his daughter look? 'She'd be eight or nine,' he said. 'Emilie must have had a photograph.'

'Come back... make another search when we've put this business to bed,' replied Mathias. The illegal migrants were waiting outside with Donovan who was impatient to hand them over to the French authorities, together with the small Arab girl once he could detach her from his neck.

The echo of boots on cobbles as the refugees from *Walter U-1405* entered Tourmant told Flynt something had changed. Instead of drawn curtains and bolted doors, the cottages were abandoned, open doors swinging gently in the wind. The Bretons had left their wooden trolleys in a disorderly pile-up on the quay where Lebrun was talking to the commander of the coastguard patrol cutter *Tapageuse* moored at their backs.

'Who are they?' asked Lebrun, suprised to see Donovan delivering a bunch of Arabs to Hôtel de Police – Brittany Préfecture.

Flynt replied, 'Didn't you hear the explosion? Loud enough to register on the Richter scale.' Lebrun nodded.

'You were right!' Flynt admitted. 'We found your Bezen Perrot... people smugglers and much more.' Lebrun glowed, savouring his vindication, Flynt adding with a smile, 'But you'll never find them... buried under a very large part of Île d'Iroise. That was the bang – the cliff collapsing on their hideout.' He didn't mention the U-boat. That would take time and the naval officer was impatient.

'They're getting ready to leave,' the French officer said. He meant the Bretons loading their baggage aboard a large trawler moored near the harbour mouth.

'Captain André Thiery-Reeves, commander of the *Tapageuse*.' Lebrun did the introduction.

Noting Flynt's surprise, Thiery-Reeves explained, 'Not all the British went home after the war. My grandfather settled in Lyons.'

'It happened,' replied Flynt, smiling at Monique.

The Breton trawler was casting off, standing room only on the deck amongst the piles of baggage and furniture. The village was decamping. 'Surely not everyone,' exclaimed Flynt.

Lebrun replied, 'Who's left! Most of the cottages are empty, abandoned, have been for years. Breton resistance had worn very thin. I advised Quai d'Orsay to leave them alone, that time wasn't on their side. No-one listened.'

Flynt had never seen more than fifteen or so adults, besides the grim-faced women on the quay collecting their groceries courtesy of the Bezen Perrot ferry. Then there were the children, ten or eleven at most, Emilie had said.

Turning to Mathias, Flynt said, 'In London, remember, at Paddington Green, you said that clan Brevilet numbered about thirty. The roof collapse must have got most.'

'Only an estimate,' replied Mathias.

Flynt said, 'Well, get after them.'

Lebrun shook his head. 'No-one said they were all collaborators. These are the victims, victims of Radenac and Scheer. They used the notion that Île d'Iroise is the last outpost of Breton culture as a cover. The islanders, the natives, faced what you call in English Hobson's Choice – submit wholly to France if they blew the whistle, or hang on to what they value most, their cultural identity, by ignoring Brevilet's little gang. Naïve and gullible, for sure, but these were simple people wanting only a simple life.'

'Where are they going now?' Flynt wasn't letting the story slip, nor would Monique let go of his arm. Having got this far, she would be there at the finish.

'Stop them… get the gendarmes to stop them,' Flynt insisted.

'Why?' said Thiery-Reeves, 'For what reason? They're fisherman, that's what they do. We'll follow. That's all I'm authorised to do – watch what happens.'

'It'll sink,' said Flynt, thinking only of his daughter. If she wasn't buried beneath thousands of tons of granite there was a good chance she'd be on the boat.

'The kids, where are they?' Flynt insisted.

'Already aboard, in the hold, I'd say.' Lebrun didn't sound as if he really knew. 'Wherever they're headed they'd not leave them behind. No children, no future… as simple as that.'

The commander of the *Tapageuse* was on the bridge. Very slowly, Lebrun was being helped up the gangway by a member of the crew.

'No you fucking don't,' screamed Flynt.

'We're coming,' Mathias agreed.

Monique already had a foot on the gangway. Lebrun was doubtful. 'I'll ask the captain.' Flynt didn't wait for an answer. He climbed aboard, followed by Mathias and Monique, up to the bridge where Lebrun persuaded the reluctant Thiery-Reeves to give them a ride.

A mile or so beyond the breakwater at Tourmant was an islet, more desolate than Île d'Iroise, a fraction of its size, not much larger than an uninhabited rock. Afterwards, nothing! Not until the eastern seaboard of North America more than three thousand miles away.

'They'll never make it.' Flynt remembered the Welsh had sailed even further to escape religious and cultural persecution to settle in Patagonia more than a century and a half earlier.

But the Bretons weren't making a dash for the New World. They'd chosen as their final refuge a barren rock, the last speck of land in the Bay of Biscay.

'Something's wrong,' said Thiery-Reeves. Up ahead the trawler trembled violently, then lurched to port when a large wave climbed over the bow. 'I think her engines have stopped.' The loud warning wail from the coastguard cutter's siren was swallowed by a fierce shriek of wind, conditions deteriorating rapidly as they often did off Île d'Iroise. Another wave crashed against the trawler, leaving those on deck clinging for their lives to iron stanchions.

Thiery-Reeves jabbed a finger at his chart. 'There, that's where she'll drift unless she gets her engines back.' He pointed to the reef around the rocky islet marked, 'Dangerous, cannot be approached with safety'.

'I'll pile the *Tapageuse* on those rocks if I get much closer,' he warned.

Another wave wrenched the trawler's only lifeboat from twisted davits and carried it overboard. Then, momentarily, the wind dropped, leaving the crippled ship hanging in a vortex, the sea piled high on either side poised to strike again. Flynt saw a man clinging to the wrecked lifeboat raise his arm and wave, not for help, but *adieu* before he disappeared.

Flynt's only thought was for Nonn, whether she was among those clinging to the deck, fearing the next wave would be their last.

'They're jettisoning the cargo,' said Lebrun. The furniture the Bretons had taken aboard for their new life went first, then their bags.

'Lightening the load,' said Thiery-Reeves, 'Get more

buoyancy to outrun the storm before she founders. Without engines she can't take much more or this. The captain will have to beach her... their only hope.'

Staring through the misty spray blowing off the crests of the waves, Flynt saw the rocky shoals ahead pounded by huge breakers. The only way the trawler would make it across the reef was as wreckage washed up on the shingle beach.

In the lull before the next wave broke, Thiery-Reeves took the naval cutter closer – close enough for Monique to see an elderly couple standing at the stern of the trawler, holding hands, the others singing.

'*Ar Barado*... that's what they're singing... a hymn, about paradise,' she said. Then, '*Mon Dieu*... what are they doing?' she cried in disbelief. A safety rail was removed from the stern and the couple stepped into the gap. After a last embrace they dropped into the sea. In the instant before they disappeared Flynt saw their faces – the elderly pair from the previous day's confrontation with Académie française. Zealots, Lebrun had said. Either they'd just been pushed too far, or sacrificed themselves to lighten the load in a last desperate attempt to save others.

The trawler was settling deeper in the water, edging closer to the reef, the desperate shouts from those aboard drowned by the wind. 'Every culture needs martyrs' – the words popped into Flynt's head, a line for the story if ever he got to write it.

The *Tapageuse* slowed then turned away to port. 'Christ, you can't leave them,' he screamed at Thiery-Reeves. He meant his daughter.

'I won't put my ship and crew at further risk.'

Flynt snatched the commander's arm, his face black with rage. 'Launch your fucking lifeboat. You must try.'

Each time the trawler rolled, cataracts of water washed against the bulwarks before shooting high into the air like waves slamming into a harbour wall. It was a miracle she stayed afloat.

'I'll need volunteers.' Thiery-Reeves was having second thoughts, not wanting to be remembered as the man who left a boatload of Bretons to drown.

'I'll go,' said Flynt. Mathias and one of the cutter's crew backed him.

'Go ahead, lower the boat,' Thiery-Reeves called out, his voice thick, choking on the words.

Mathias fired up the outboard. Flynt didn't know how but had shown he was a strong swimmer.

In a few minutes the lifeboat was bumping alongside the trawler – those on board reaching out their arms for help thrown back by the swell as both boats lurched heavily from side to side.

'A lifeline, we need to get a line aboard,' Mathias shouted. The lifeboat should have carried one for emergencies but didn't! The trawler did, one end hanging off its stern, trailing in the sea.

'I'll get it,' said Flynt, tearing off his jacket and dropping into the water. Before he could strike out, a wave caught him, Flynt tangled in the trawler's lifeline when he surfaced. Dragging himself aboard the striken vessel, he caught a thump in the guts and bang on the head as he fell heavily amongst a crowd of frightened faces. 'Take the end,' he gasped. 'Throw it to the lifeboat!' Someone understood. The crewman from the *Tapageuse* snatched the line out of the air, hauled it taut and made it fast.

One by one the Bretons crawled across the deck along the line and dropped over the side into the lifeboat. Five, six journeys later Flynt and the trawler's captain were the last to leave. 'The hold, what's in the hold,' he shouted at the captain. Without waiting for an answer Flynt tore open the hatch. A woman's body floated towards him amongst the flotsam and jetsam of

Breton life. Others might have drowned, trapped in the flooded darkness. Flynt couldn't see.

'The children… where are they?' he shouted. The captain understood, replying, '*An iliz*', whatever that meant in English.

No sooner was Flynt back aboard the *Tapageuse* and the trawler struck the reef, torn to pieces by a sea of boiling white foam.

'*An iliz.*' He fired the words at Monique. 'What's it mean? That's where the children are.'

Monique whispered, 'They're in the church.'

The hour it took the *Tapageuse* to return to Tourmant was one of painful foreboding for Flynt. One arm holding Monique's waist, the other hooked around a safety rail, he saw only the church, kids skateboarding in the square or sheltering inside. The bump he'd taken on the head had stoked his fears. Flynt had nothing to say, ignoring the commander's congratulations. Christ, he'd only volunteered because he thought his daughter was on board. Christ, that kind of stunt was for other people. Flynt's mantra was not to get involved, just count the bodies. But twice he'd stuck his neck out – twice on the same day.

Monique saw the bell tower of the church from the bridge of the *Tapageuse* as the coastguard cutter entered the harbour at Tourmant. Flynt stood at the rail waiting impatiently for it to be removed and the gangway slid into place. He would take it easy, walk not run, desperate to find the children safe inside the church, at the same time afraid to know.

The church was barely a mile from the harbour but for Flynt it was a marathon, every muscle bursting with mind-numbing apprehension.

Climbing the steps to St Anne's, Flynt froze, nudging Monique through the entrance, her voice emerging from the darkness heavy with relief. 'They're here.' That's all she said but it was not the answer Flynt wanted. Beyond the flickering candles Father Joseph in his long black cassock had his small flock gathered at his feet.

Urgently, Flynt scanned the frightened faces. The skinny little girl he'd seen begging in the market at the harbour a month ago raised her small dark head and asked, '*Ma tad?*' He knelt and, holding the child's head between his hands, appealed to Monique standing at his shoulder.

'She's asking if you're her father – she says her name is Nonn.'

Flynt swallowed hard and hugged the daughter he never knew he had. His next thought was the story, the biggest in his life – and he held its beating heart.

Ends

Other books by the author:

*Man from the Alamo: Why the Welsh
Chartist Uprising of 1839 Ended in a Massacre*

Gringo Revolutionary

Freedom Fighters: Wales's Forgotten War

Spying for Hitler: The Welsh double-cross

*Search for the Nile's Source: the ruined reputation
of John Petherick 19th century Welsh explorer*

Also from Y Lolfa:

ROB
GITTINS

INVESTIGATING
MR WAKEFIELD

'A superb, unsettling book, both culturally
significant and beautifully written.'

Jeni Williams

y Lolfa

£8.99 (paperback)
£19.99 (hardback)

THE LAST HOUSE OFFICER

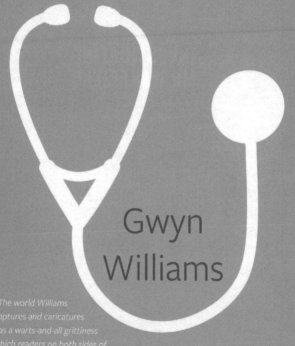

Gwyn
Williams

y Lolfa

£8.99

Last Rites is just one of a whole range of publications from Y Lolfa. For a full list of books currently in print, send now for your free copy of our new full-colour catalogue. Or simply surf into our website

www.ylolfa.com

for secure on-line ordering.

TALYBONT CEREDIGION CYMRU SY24 5HE
e-mail ylolfa@ylolfa.com
website www.ylolfa.com
phone (01970) 832 304
fax 832 782

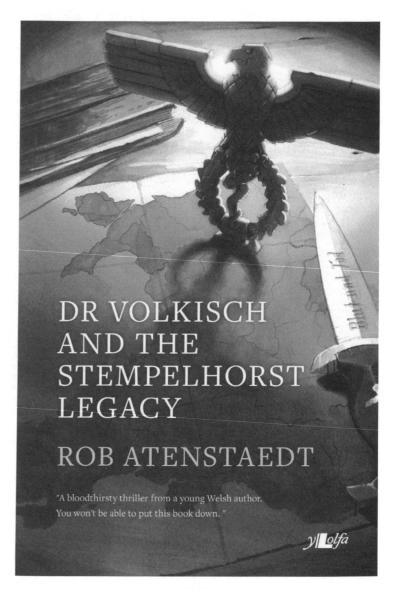

DR VOLKISCH
AND THE
STEMPELHORST
LEGACY

ROB ATENSTAEDT

"A bloodthirsty thriller from a young Welsh author.
You won't be able to put this book down."

£7.95